THE
QUANTUM
DOOR

THE QUANTUM DOOR

Jonathan Ballagh

Edited by David Gatewood
www.lonetrout.com

Cover design and internal illustrations by Ben J. Adams
www.benjadams.com

Formatting by Polgarus Studio
www.polgarusstudio.com

for Dylan, Connor, and Reese

Part One

> Chapter 1: Remote Control

THE AFTERNOON SUN reflected off the sign and shined into the boy's eyes. He took a step closer and held a cupped hand against his forehead to filter out the light. The metal plate's bold red letters stood in sharp contrast to the glossy black finish coating the surface. Even with his eyes squinted, the message was clear.

No Trespassing.

Several other signs just like this one were hung every quarter mile or so along the tall chain link fence that ran the stretch of land next to his yard. The fence, like the signs, felt oddly out of place to the lanky boy standing beside them—an artificial border that separated him from the unknown wilderness on the other side.

Brady Banks turned away from the sign and looked up at his younger brother, Felix, hanging on the fence beside him. The tips of his sneakers were crammed snugly through the metallic links high above the ground. Felix clambered up another few feet and came to rest near the top.

At fourteen, Brady was a little over two years older than his brother and almost a foot taller. It wasn't that Felix was short; rather, Brady was just exceptionally tall for his age. Next to his brother, he felt like stretched silly putty with a lighter complexion and closely cropped auburn hair. His early height gave him a very slender appearance; way too much so for his own liking.

Felix shook the fence as if to test its soundness, and it rattled violently in protest. He nodded with satisfaction as Brady rolled his eyes and turned his attention back toward the strange woods on the other side.

The two boys stood quiet for a few moments, taking in the dark sea of evergreens in front of them. In the distance, waves of branches rose and fell as gentle eddies of wind twisted through the trees. The restless forest was beckoning them forward, waving them in.

Try as he might, Brady couldn't help worrying about what they were about to get into. It was his nature to overthink everything. By contrast, such matters never concerned Felix, who seemed completely at home in even the most precarious situations.

Brady wiped the sweat from his forehead and thought about how they had ended up here in the first place.

10100110

For the longest time, the land across the fence had belonged to the Willoughbys, an older couple with no children—much to the boys' dismay. Brady and Felix would occasionally catch Mr. and Mrs. Willoughby driving their old Wrangler through town. The vehicle was a piece of art in its own right: it was adorned with colorful bumper stickers that left little of the original paint job exposed. The boys would always stop to watch as it passed by.

But the Willoughbys seldom socialized and never lingered. While Mrs. Willoughby was pleasant enough, Mr. Willoughby appeared not to be particularly fond of either of them. Either that or he had a twisted sense of humor. When they were much younger, he would arch an eyebrow steeply and curl the corner of his mouth downward into a threatening snarl whenever they approached—and then would chuckle deeply as the brothers ran away, fearing for their lives. At six foot four with a wild mane of silver hair, he was imposing enough without the need for added intimidation.

Their mother had long ago explained to them that the Willoughbys' property covered miles of the mountain hillside. Exactly how far she couldn't say for sure, but somewhere in the far recesses of the woods was a small cottage the couple called home. Because they were private and didn't appreciate visitors, their mother had told them they were best to mind their manners and stay far away.

This, of course, was an invitation for trouble.

Unsurprisingly, their mother's warning went unheeded. One time, long before the fence went up, the brothers had ventured deep into the woods in search of the cottage. After nearly getting lost, they'd heard the crack of a gunshot somewhere nearby. They took off running and never looked back. When they arrived home, Brady managed to convince Felix that Mr. Willoughby was out hunting *them*, and that it was best if they never set foot on the property again.

When they got a little older, Felix decided to try to find the cabin using his phone. With Brady by his side, he punched his address into a maps app and watched as pictures taken by a satellite stitched seamlessly together into a bird's-eye view of their house. Felix zoomed and scrolled around the imagery, but he couldn't find what he was looking for. There was too much land to cover, and the dense trees made it difficult to see much of anything. The issue of finding the cabin remained unsettled and was eventually forgotten.

The last time the boys saw Mr. Willoughby, it was a month after his wife passed away. His white hair and beard had grown long, and his sunken eyes had become hollowed pools of grief. He had come by the house to tell their mother that he was putting the land up for sale and moving to California—somewhere warmer, near the coast, he said. Their Mom hugged him tightly and wished him well. They exchanged their final goodbyes, and the boys watched the Willoughbys' Jeep, packed tightly with boxes and an overflowing carrier strapped to the roof, drive away for the last time.

After that, the property was left alone. At first the boys were excited about the prospect of a new, younger family moving in next door, but no one ever did, and the boys gradually lost interest as time went by and the land remained up for sale.

That all changed a few months ago.

One morning, out of the blue, they woke to find the fence, complete with ominous *No Trespassing* signs, standing near their back yard.

Their mom figured someone had purchased the property, but she wasn't sure who it was or if they had any children. She quickly shrugged off the question when Brady asked why someone would put up such a high fence, chalking it up to a matter of privacy, although both boys would later recall that she looked unsettled. Everyone agreed, however, that it was unlikely that a nice family with kids would attempt to seal off the perimeter of their yard with a chain-link fence.

And strangely, no one could recall ever seeing a car coming or going on the Willoughbys' old driveway.

But that wasn't all. There had been the bizarre power outages that began shortly after the fence went up. At first, lights in the house and around town would flicker briefly. Over time, the problem grew more severe. The power would go out for minutes at a time before being restored. Ms. Banks inquired into the problem, but unfortunately, not even the power company could put their finger on what was going on.

Several nights ago, Felix had stayed up late writing a mod for his favorite virtual reality game, Voxelverse. He was only a few lines away from completing his script when the power went out—taking the last unsaved hour of his life with it. In a fit of frustration, he'd pounded his fists on the desk; it was the third time in a week they had lost power. Minute after excruciating minute ticked by as he waited for the power to be restored so he could wrap up his code and get down to business.

An hour later, he was still waiting.

Finally, feeling the urge to stretch his legs, he went into the back yard for some fresh air. It was only seconds later that he was back inside, searching desperately for his brother. He swore up and down to Brady that he had seen something strange in the neighbors' woods, some kind of blue light.

Brady dismissed his story offhand, calling him crazy, but Felix vowed to get to the bottom of whatever was going on across the fence, once and for all. And he would do so with or without his brother's help.

So that morning, over a breakfast of cheddar eggs, orange juice, and buttered toast, he hatched an idea. He even managed to convince Brady that they should investigate together. After all, it was a fool-proof plan—just like every other one of Felix's ideas.

They waited until late afternoon, and then Felix, with a backpack full of high-tech wizardry, set out on a journey to the fence with his older brother in tow.

11001110

Still hanging on the fence, Felix called down to Brady, "I know this is going to work. It should have plenty of juice to make the trip. You ready?"

"I can't believe I let you talk me into this, Felix. Am I the only one who can read? Can't you see all the No Trespassing signs? If we get caught—"

"Like I told you before, *we're* not actually going over there," Felix replied.

"I think you're missing the point. They put the fence there to keep people like us out. This is a terrible idea, Felix. Something will go wrong; it always does."

Felix shook his head and released his grip on the fence. His mop of sandy blond hair lifted into the air as he landed next to his brother with a thud, sending a cloud of dirt up around them. Felix dusted off his jeans and made his way over to his latest project, which waited for him next to his backpack.

It was the latest in hobby drone technology. Felix had built the quadcopter himself, piece by piece, with equipment he had ordered from a series of obscure websites. It was financed by over a year's worth of chores and odd jobs around the house.

He picked up his prize possession and turned it over in his hands. It was not much larger than his fist and had small carbon fiber blades in each of the four corners. Felix had drawn a shark face on the front with model paint, and the sharp, painted teeth stood out against the dark gray hull. Twin cameras protruded from the intimidating eyes and allowed the copter to perceive depth.

There was no denying that it was an impressive piece of work.

Felix held it out for his brother to admire. Brady waved his hands in front of him. "It's great, Felix. Really. Just be careful and try not to get us in trouble—again. You've already gotten us grounded twice this summer." He grew more anxious with each word.

"Relax," Felix replied, his hand fumbling around the bottom of the craft for the power switch. "This thing can pretty much fly itself."

"Sure it can," Brady said dryly. He realized his brother was probably telling the truth, but why not give him a hard time anyway?

Brady knew his brother was too smart for his own good, although he would never admit it. Felix had been just six years old when he'd managed to construct a ten-foot triceratops skeleton with a software-modeling program and a 3D printer a relative had lent them. The brothers had thoughtfully placed the dinosaur in the kitchen, right near the mud room door, for maximum shock value. Felix had superglued LED strobe lights deep within the eye sockets and installed a motion-activated alarm to turn them on when an unsuspecting victim entered the room.

An unsuspecting victim had arrived right on cue.

Their mother, arriving home from the grocery store one evening, screamed in fright when the monster welcomed her in a blaze of flashing lights, dry ice fog, and ferocious jaws. She dropped her bags to the floor, and food rolled across the dinosaur's feet in slow motion as the gas from the ice engulfed the groceries in a dense fog.

Felix was smart, yes, but he also had an uncanny penchant for ending up in hot water. Brady had lost track of how many times his brother had gotten him into trouble over the last twelve years. Nevertheless, Brady had to admit that Felix did manage to keep things interesting in a town with not much to do.

Brady enjoyed seeing the results of his brother's various projects, but he didn't usually involve himself in them. It wasn't that Brady shunned technology; it was just a question of priorities. School, sports, and the outdoors left him with little time for such hobbies. His brother, on the other hand, prioritized gadgetry—and trouble.

Click.

The hull lights flashed and the blades locked into alignment with a succession of soft clicks. The quad was alive.

Brady could swear he saw one of the shark's eyes glisten forebodingly as the aircraft powered up.

"I'm pretty sure this is against the law," Brady muttered to himself, half under his breath.

Ignoring his brother's protests, Felix extracted twin pairs of sleek glasses from his backpack. He passed Brady one set and kept the other for himself.

"You brought our Orbatures all the way out here?" Brady complained. "You know they'll get ruined."

"They'll be okay. Just trust me for once, Brady. You'll see in a minute."

Only slightly larger and heavier than normal sunglasses, Orbatures were the most popular virtual reality glasses around. Small screens were embedded inside the lenses, displaying stereoscopic video received wirelessly from a phone. Everything was in realistic 3D, and it made you feel like you were actually inside the game.

Felix slid the glasses over his head and motioned for Brady to do the same.

"I've got the video feed from the quad streaming to both our glasses."

"What?" Brady asked, perplexed.

"It's pretty simple. We get to see what the quadcopter sees. In full 3D, of course."

"Of course."

Felix pressed a few buttons on his phone, and the craft's four tiny blades spun up with a whoosh, scattering leaves and debris in all directions. The drone lifted a few feet off the ground and hovered in mid-air, waiting for further instruction. The breeze caused it to wobble unsteadily for a few seconds before the stabilization circuits kicked in.

Felix couldn't help but grin as his creation levitated in front of him. There was no turning back now.

Brady had expressed his objections, as he always did; but his curiosity got the better of him in the end—as it always did. He took a deep breath and pulled his glasses down over his eyes. The lenses crackled to life.

Brady was staring back at himself and Felix. It was like looking in a mirror. He raised a hand, and the other Brady raised the same hand. It took a second for him to realize that he was looking at the world through the drone's point of view. He was seeing what the quad's camera saw.

A speaker located near the back of his glasses amplified the quad's audio feed, but it was currently nothing more than the soft hum of the rotor blades whirling through the air.

Felix swiped his finger upward on his phone, and the drone climbed higher, mirroring his motions. It stopped just above the fence. Suddenly dizzy, Brady reached down and touched the dirt to convince himself that he was still safely on the ground.

"Okay. Here we go—*hold on*." Felix tilted his phone forward. The quadcopter mimicked the position of the phone, so that the front of the aircraft pitched down as well. The drone advanced forward, slowly at first, then picking up speed and taking off into the forest. Thanks to his Orbatures, Brady felt like he was flying as well.

As the woods grew denser, the quad's artificial vision systems allowed it to dodge trees at a breakneck pace. It took some getting used to. At first, Brady recoiled with each passing branch, fearing an impact.

"I told you this thing was awesome," bragged Felix as he pounded Brady's shoulder with his fist.

Brady wanted to push Felix back, but he was too busy fighting back the beginnings of motion sickness. The quad's camera was doing its job perfectly—so well in fact that it managed to capture all of the quad's jerky motions as it bobbed and weaved along its path.

"It might be awesome, but your flying is going to make me heave."

"I'm barely guiding it at this point. It's doing most of the work by itself. Hopefully things will smooth out at some point. There are a ton of trees back here."

"Why don't you just fly it over the treetops?"

"Oh, come on, this is way more fun. Just hold on, it'll get better in a minute or two."

The craft ventured deeper into the forest. The scenery remained mostly unchanged: long, passing smears of dark green mottled with somber browns. Everything blended together at high speed.

The repetition was finally interrupted when the quad flew over a narrow stream that twisted through the gently sloping hillside.

Felix quickly eased back on the throttle and the quad slowed down.

Brady was fighting back the urge to vomit, but he felt better when the craft lost speed.

"There's got to be something back here," Felix said, his voice barely audible over the speaker in the glasses. "At some point, we'll end up flying over the side of the mountain." He made an adjustment on his phone, and the quad banked sharply to the right and took off again. "We'll follow the stream to avoid the trees for a bit."

As the craft accelerated, a flash of light streaked across their view. It was so quick that they would have missed it had they blinked.

"Did you see that?" Brady yelled over to his brother. "There was something moving on the ground."

"Yeah, but I didn't get a good look at it. I'll fly us back around to get a better look."

The quad spun in place and zipped back in the direction from which it had come. But whatever Brady and Felix had seen, it now appeared to be gone. The drone came to rest a few feet above the stream and waited for additional commands.

"Now what?" Brady asked.

Felix checked the battery gauge on his phone and sighed. "I guess I'll have to bring it back before it runs out of charge," he lamented.

The craft started up again and was in the middle of a U-turn when another burst of light flashed by, this time larger and closer than before. It was there one second, gone the next. And then...

Crunch.

The view in the glasses spun at a vertigo-inducing pace as the quad spiraled to the ground. Moments later, Brady and Felix were left with a close-up view of dirt and pine needles. The camera lens was hazy from dust that had been kicked up from the crash, and it was difficult to see. Forgetting his sight was not his own, Brady attempted to wipe the virtual dirt off the lens, with no luck.

Suddenly the view of the ground vanished, leaving behind a flickering blizzard of white and gray snow.

The uplink was dead, the feed lost.

Game over.

> Chapter 2: Pursuit

"WHAT HAPPENED?" Brady asked, his voice rising as he turned toward his brother in a panic. The color had drained from his face.

"I don't know—I can't figure it out. I'm *positive* there wasn't anything in front of it when it crashed. It's supposed to be smart enough to avoid things like that, I swear. You saw it fly between the trees. It didn't touch a thing! Not even a branch! And there was that strange flash of light again right before it went down…"

Felix's voice trailed off and he lost himself in thought.

"Maybe there was something wrong with the video feed or controls, or maybe you forget to charge the battery last night," Brady offered, unhelpfully.

Felix frowned and continued mashing virtual buttons on his phone. Gauges, dials, and numbers zipped across the screen. He kept his eyes fixed on the display as he spoke. "No, I charged it up last night. The battery was only half empty when it went down. It had enough power to keep going for at least another fifteen minutes. And I don't think it hit anything. I think something hit *it*."

"Like what? An animal? We would have seen that."

"Not necessarily. We might have missed it if it was fast enough. Anyway, we're wasting time here. I need to go get my quad."

Brady couldn't believe what he was hearing.

"No way, Felix. We're not going over there. That was the point of all of this, remember? Your plan that was supposed to be foolproof? Remember the No Trespassing signs? They're pretty hard to miss."

"We'll be in more trouble if someone finds it before we do."

"We don't even know where it is!" Brady couldn't help but raise the objection, even though he knew his brother's mind was made up and nothing he said would make a difference.

"Leave that problem to me."

"Because that's turned out well for us so far today, hasn't it?"

"Brady, just look." Felix held up his phone so Brady could get a better view. It showed a map that was currently zoomed in on their back yard. The word "Searching..." was written across the center of the screen.

"So what?"

"So, I turned on the quad's GPS system right before it took off. It's a tiny microchip that uses a bunch of satellites to figure out where it is. It'll only take my phone a few minutes to lock on to the coordinates—and then we can go get it. Just make sure to keep your glasses on, all right?"

Felix made a few final gestures on the surface of his phone, and the screen went blank just as their glasses crackled back to life.

An orange beacon sprouted up near the corner of Brady's glasses. Glowing rings grew from the center of the dot and faded as they expanded. Then a translucent yellow arrow appeared in front of him and pointed at the beacon. As Brady looked around, the arrow spun away from him.

"Whoa. Where did those come from, and what are they?" Brady asked, dazzled by the show of holographic images.

"It's an augmented reality map. The orange dot marks the location of the quad, and the yellow arrow acts like a compass—it always points toward the beacon. If we walk in the direction of the arrow, it'll take us right there, I promise."

Felix reached down and drew a line on the phone. On Brady's

glasses, a ribbon grew from Felix's feet and extended off in the direction of the beacon. The number "5920" floated in mid-air on top of it. Felix waved his hand and the number disappeared.

"Five thousand nine hundred and twenty feet. Hmm... that's a little more than a mile away from here. We can grab it and be back here in no time."

Brady remained unconvinced. "I think we're better off leaving it where it is. It's not like it has your name on it, right? How would anyone trace it back to us? Besides, there's something weird going on back there. We still don't know what caused your quad to crash in the first place. Like you said, something hit *it*, not the other way around."

"That's what I want to find out," Felix argued. "Plus, I had to save up an entire year to buy all the pieces for this thing. Do you know how many times I had to mow the yard last year? And yes, my name *is* on it. I carved it on the bottom this morning. My mistake. You can wait here if you want, but I'm going."

Before Brady could grab him, his brother had scrambled up and over the fence and was busy catching his breath on the other side.

Brady pleaded. "Listen to me, Felix! We're going to get caught over there!"

Felix ignored him and started fiddling with his phone again. Another dot, this one blue, appeared on Brady's glasses, just above his brother.

Felix pointed above his head to where the dot lingered. "Just keep your eye on my geo-beacon. It shows you where I am—*if* you decide to follow along."

And with that, Felix charged cavalierly into the woods. His dot lunged after him as he vanished into the trees.

01001110

With a heavy sigh, Brady climbed over the fence and took off after his brother. They had gone without rain for weeks now, and the parched soil was cracked and hard. The forest was silent apart from the rhythmic sounds of crushing brush and the occasional twig snapping beneath his feet. He followed where the yellow arrow directed. Figuring he was on the right path, he let his mind wander.

10100110

There wasn't a lot to do during the summers in Vermont, and this was especially true up in the mountains. Brady's family had moved here from Boston when they were much younger, after their dad had taken a job as a park ranger. His parents had wanted to be closer to the outdoors—they felt it was important to distance their children from city life, to let them breathe the fresh air. Life in Vermont was good for a short time, but tragedy struck a year later when their father passed away unexpectedly. Felix was two and Brady was four when it happened.

Brady only had a few memories of his father, but over time they had begun to erode, leaving him with only vague recollections of their time together. He relied on pictures around the house and his mother's stories to fill in the gaps.

He did recall one weekend fishing trip that his family had taken together the summer before his father passed away. Brady, Felix, and their father were out on a boat with fishing rods in hand and their cork floats bobbing lazily in the ripples of the lake. They were waiting patiently for a bite when their father turned away suddenly, distracted by a tug on his line. Seizing the opportunity, Felix grabbed a full cup of crawlers, flung it into the water, and then quickly peered over the side to watch the fish take the bait. He moved his face closer to the water, trying to get a better look. It was too late when Felix realized he had lost his balance. He fell overboard, causing the boat to pitch so hard that his father fell out the other side. Fortunately, Felix had a life jacket tied securely around his waist and shoulders.

Brady looked over in shock as Felix floated serenely on his back, the fish enjoying a tasty snack around him.

Felix had always regarded their father with mystery and awe. To him, their dad was a superhero gone too soon. Trying to remember back was much harder for him than for his brother, since he was so young when it happened. To this day, Felix would pepper his mother with questions when the mood struck him, and she always managed to come up with great stories that served to reinforce the legend.

Luckily, their modest house had been paid off by what little insurance they had. There was plenty of room for the three of them and they were comfortable. But when Brady and Felix got old enough to care for themselves, their mother was forced to go back to work part-time as a paramedic. She had taken on more shifts recently to help pay the bills, leading to erratic hours and forcing Brady and Felix to fend for themselves.

They did get lonely from time to time, especially without neighbors or nearby friends. A lack of parental supervision wasn't necessarily a bad thing for two boys, but Brady couldn't help wondering from time to time how life could have been different.

01101110

The sound of a freight train horn echoing from far below jolted Brady out of his thoughts. He stopped to catch his breath and looked around. The tallest trees stood like crooked sentinels watching over the forest below. The sun was starting to set, and dappled rays of light filtered through the woodlands in a dusty haze. There was more of the same in every direction he turned. It was way too easy to lose yourself back here.

Based on the blue dot in front of him, Brady estimated that Felix was about halfway to the crash site. His brother might be a super-genius, but Brady was in better shape. He wasn't too far behind and would catch up to his brother in no time at all.

And then he heard something that made him stop cold.

A chilling howl echoed through the forest.

There was something unnatural about the sound; it made him uneasy. The pitch was slightly off, and it had a synthetic quality to it: an eerie imitation of the real thing. Plus the noise was loud enough to hurt his ears. The cry stuck in his head as he looked around.

There it is again.

Before Brady could react, he noticed the orange dot on his glasses, the quad, starting to move.

Someone—or something—was out here with them. It had the quad—and it was headed directly toward his brother.

Brady ran as fast as he could. The trees blurred as he chased the blue dot, trying to get to his brother before the creature did. Several times his foot caught on a root or a branch and he stumbled, but he quickly recovered and kept moving.

A minute later, he was at the stream.

According to the orange dot, the creature was there too.

Then he noticed movement. A silver and bronze form sped across the bank and disappeared from sight. Brady heard the rustling of leaves, and a moment later, he heard the splash of water somewhere downstream. But to his surprise, the orange dot stopped moving. The creature must have dropped the quad.

Brady slid behind a tree and waited, unsure of his next move. A full minute passed with no movement of the dot and no sign of the creature. Finally he built up the courage to peek out from behind the tree. Just as he peered around the trunk, he felt a stern tap on his shoulder.

"Get off of my property!" a voice growled from behind.

Brady shrieked and spun around.

He found himself face-to-face with his brother. Felix was red from exertion and breathing heavily, but grinning nevertheless.

"Felix, you scared me half to death! You're going to pay for that!"

He shoved his brother hard in the chest. "How did you find me anyway?" he asked, as Felix struggled to catch his breath.

"You have GPS in your glasses too," Felix huffed. "I can see where you are, just like you can see me."

Felix pointed nervously in the direction where Brady had seen the shadow moving a few minutes ago.

"There's something over there. I think it has my quad."

"Did you get a look at it?" Brady asked.

"Not really, it was moving too fast."

"Yeah—I didn't see it either. I heard it though, and it sounded awful. We need to get out of here quick. Whatever that thing is, I don't want it to find us."

"No kidding."

Together, they crept cautiously away from the tree and started for home. They moved slowly at first, trying not to make noise, but soon they picked up the pace, eager to leave the woods and its terrible inhabitant behind. By the time they arrived at the fence, they were both out of breath.

They were so tired, in fact, that they didn't notice the stranger who had followed them back, watching from the trees as they made their way home.

> Chapter 3: The Electric Flame

MOONLIGHT SPILLED IN with a breeze, forming pale phantoms that twisted lazily across the wood floor. The window was left open, the curtains partly drawn. Brady had tried in desperation to cool his room, but it was no use. The weather was warm and humid, and the air was unusually heavy, even for late summer.

He lay asleep in bed, one arm draped over the side and the other cradling his pillow. White sheets were tossed haphazardly into a pile on the floor—anything to escape the heat.

Earlier that night, Brady had stayed up late watching a movie with Felix. Their mom was working a shift at the station and wouldn't be home until early morning. Now that the boys were getting older, she felt a little less guilty about leaving them alone at night. Not that she had much of a choice. Sometimes the evening shifts were the only ones available, so she gladly took whatever was open.

The boys had found a sticky note on the microwave, providing instructions on how to reheat the dinner she had prepared. They ate half the meal before throwing the rest away, deciding to indulge in much healthier treats: a bag of microwave kettle corn, two pints of ice cream, and orange sodas. The binge went on well past midnight.

The sugar rush ended with the brothers passed out on the couch, unperturbed by the explosions that rocked the room as the movie played on. With the bass blaring, soda cans, spoons and bowls vibrated across the hickory coffee table where the dirty dishes had been carelessly stowed.

After the final credits rolled, the hiss of static was enough to raise Brady from his slumber. The room, bathed in the garish light of the TV, fell into shadows as Brady clicked off the remote, headed upstairs and stumbled into bed. Felix remained behind and quickly reclaimed the rest of the couch.

Tossing and turning from the heat, Brady replayed the events in the woods over in his head. There were lots of questions, but no answers. His brother had spent the better portion of three days mourning the loss of his favorite gadget; he'd tried to compensate by hatching crazy schemes to retrieve it. One involved building another quadcopter to send on a rescue mission. None of his ideas, however, stood up to thoughtful scrutiny, and Felix had grown increasingly frustrated by the situation.

On the other hand, Brady secretly hoped to never see the quad again. Its return would spell uncertain doom if their mom discovered they were recklessly invading other people's privacy. The thought of a neighbor, wild with fury, clutching the broken quad and pounding on his front door held little appeal.

And still, neither of them had any idea what had caused the drone to crash in the first place.

The memory of the strange howl stuck with him as Brady closed his eyes and drifted off to sleep again.

10010110

Boom.

The sound woke Brady from his short-lived sleep. He sat up in bed, startled, and looked over at the alarm clock resting on his nightstand.

The display was off.

The power was out again.

Brady knew he'd be a wreck the next day if he didn't get some rest, but he felt troubled. He strained to hear something over the sound of his brother's snores echoing from downstairs, some clue as to what had roused him. But apart from Felix, the house was quiet.

Brady swung his feet over the side of the bed and tried to gain his composure. In the low light, he saw nothing out of the ordinary. But just to be on the safe side, he knelt down, lifted the sheet off the floor, and nervously looked under his bed. There was nothing there except for an old aluminum bat from his Little League days. He decided to take it with him.

His closet caught his attention. He crept over to it, sheets tugging at his feet. He paused, and then couldn't help but laugh at himself. *You're fourteen!* He turned the doorknob with his free hand, the bat trembling in his other. To his relief, nothing wicked lurked behind the door.

Realizing that whatever had caused the commotion was elsewhere, Brady made his way over to the window. The old wooden floorboards creaked as he tiptoed across them.

He looked out.

The roofline blocked most of the view, revealing only a sliver of the side yard. There was nothing strange in what little he could see.

He decided to check his mom's room next. It would give him the best view of the back yard and surrounding grounds.

By reflex, Brady flipped the light switch as he crept down the hall into his mom's room. Nothing happened, so he tried it a few more times before remembering that the power had gone out.

From the shadowy corner of his eye, he glanced at the old photos hanging on the picture wall by the stairs. There was one in particular that always caught his eye: a family portrait taken when he was three and a half years old. In it, his mom was wearing a red dress and was holding his baby brother tightly in her arms. She was younger, her blond hair still long, well past her shoulders. Dad had one arm around her, his other hand resting squarely on Brady's shoulder, and stared proudly at the camera. Brady stood in between his parents wearing a baseball cap and a smile that stretched from ear to ear. His hair snuck out from the edge of the hat and curled closely around his ears.

Now that he was older, Brady was beginning to see the resemblances to his father that his mother mentioned almost daily. His father had the same red hair that he did. Dad had also been over six feet tall; that was still taller than Brady was, but he was catching up quickly.

A thousand thoughts raced through Brady's head. What would his father think about him protecting the house this way? Would he be proud or ashamed? And if he found someone, what was his plan exactly? To scare them off with a bat? Surely he could do better than that. He wished his father were here to help him out.

Snap out of it, Brady. It was probably just a raccoon.

He pulled himself together and continued down the dark hall and into his mom's room. The bed was still made up from the day before. Centered on the rear wall was a large window overlooking their back yard and the hillside beyond the fence. The view was always beautiful during the day and one of the reasons his mother loved the house so much.

Brady opened the window to get a better look. A blast of warm summer air struck his face as he poked his head out. The forest tree line at the end of his yard cut the sky evenly: jagged black below and the starry dark purple of night above.

He quickly scanned his yard for the source of the noise. Seeing nothing nearby, he raised his gaze into the woods. And that's when he noticed it—a brilliant flame, icy blue, burning deep in the pines. At this distance, it was no larger than the head of a matchstick; a tiny ball of frozen lightning.

He squeezed his eyes shut tight for a few seconds. Just to be sure he wasn't imagining it.

When he opened his eyes and looked back at the peculiar sight, it was barely there; he would surely have missed it if he hadn't looked at just the right time.

Brady left his mom's room and bounded down the steps to the family room. His brother was still sprawled out on the couch, sleeping soundly.

"Felix!" Brady shouted. "Felix. Wake up!"

The snoring persisted. It took about a minute of heavy shaking to wake his brother.

Felix lay in silence while the fog of sleep lifted from his head. Finally he sat up, flecks of popcorn falling from his shirt and settling deep in the crevices of the couch.

"Felix, you have to see this! Get up!"

"See what?" replied Felix, rubbing his eyes.

"There's something going on back in the woods. I saw a light from Mom's window. It looks like a fire—well—sort of like it—not exactly. You just need to see it."

"You mean, like what I saw the other night? When you tried to tell me I was crazy?"

"Sure, Felix. I believe you now. Whatever. It's there again!"

That was all it took. Felix bounced off the couch like a coiled spring coming to life. Together they raced up the stairs into their mom's room.

At the window, Brady searched the trees for the blue light, hoping it was still there. Sure enough, it was. "Look over there," he instructed, motioning in the direction of the flame.

Felix eagerly squeezed himself through the window so that half his body was suspended outside. He gripped the windowpane tightly with both hands to keep from barreling forward. "Where did you see it?"

"You're not looking in the right place." Brady forced a finger past

Felix. "I'm pointing right at it. Look!"

Felix's eyes grew wide as soon as he noticed it. "That's exactly what I saw the other night," he said. "I *told* you! We have to go check it out." He carefully lowered himself back inside.

Brady looked worried. "But remember that weird-sounding animal we heard when we were over there? I don't want to run into that thing again, whatever it is."

"Go ahead and stay here, then… *Big Brother*," Felix taunted with a sly smile.

"I'm not scared," Brady said. "I just think it's a bad idea for us to go wandering over there in the middle of the night. No, forget that—it's a bad time to go over there *any time*."

"Whatever you say. I'll just go alone then."

"No way, Felix. You'll get lost or something, and then Mom will end up blaming me. I'm going too."

Felix smiled. His baiting did the trick every time.

The boys grabbed flashlights on their way out and left through the garage.

By the time they got to the fence, they could just make out the speck of blue between the trees. Their flashlights moved up from the dewy grass and came to rest on the No Trespassing signs, which appeared far more sinister at night. Brady imagined the letters written in blood. He shivered.

"Hey, Felix, you'd better mark our spot. I want to make sure we can find our way back. It's pretty easy to get lost back there, especially when you can't see anything."

"No problem." Felix pulled out his phone and obliged with a sequence of quick taps. When he had finished, the screen turned green and flashed, signaling the all clear.

They slid their flashlights under the fence, climbed over and dropped down to the other side, then cautiously entered the woods.

Here, in the earliest hours of morning, the trees rose above them like dark spires. Shortly after entering the forest, they heard a rustling from above and felt the breeze of something passing overhead. When they looked up, they saw the shadow of a bird drifting gracefully across the face of the moon.

After a few minutes of walking, they could see the light more clearly. With it guiding them on, they continued on until they came upon a glade where the trees gave way to tall, gently swaying grass. In the middle of the clearing was the flame.

The boys stepped out from the forest's edge.

A bluish-white torch burned straight from the ground and reached into the sky. It was at least as wide as it was tall. Ribbons of blue energy undulated around the periphery of the flame like an electric aura. The boys could feel air moving out of the light, creating a strong breeze.

Brady stood motionless, mouth agape. Felix was more curious than anything, and took a few steps around the flame to get a better look.

When viewed from certain angles, the light seemed flat, like a projection of fire onto film. Felix expected to feel heat radiating from the torch, but there was none, just an unexpected coolness that chilled the night air.

"What do you think it is?" Brady asked.

"I have no idea. But I'm going closer to get a better look."

This time Brady was two steps ahead of him. He locked his hand around his brother's arm.

"We're close enough, Felix."

Surprised by the firmness in his brother's grip, Felix acquiesced. But neither he nor Brady was able to take their eyes off the light in front of them.

It was mesmerizing.

Finally Felix broke the silence. "I need to get a picture of this." Brady had let go of his arm by now, so he walked closer to the light and pulled out his phone.

"Felix, get back here!" his brother hissed.

But Felix ignored him; he was too busy trying to wake up his phone. After several failed attempts, he sighed in frustration and turned around to face Brady, his back aglow from the fire's radiance.

"My phone's not working. That light must be messing with the electronics."

As Felix attempted to stuff his phone back into his pocket, a shard of metal pierced the surface of the light. It hovered cautiously in mid-air—as if testing something on the other side.

"*Felix!*" Brady warned in a loud whisper. He stepped forward, grabbed Felix, and dragged him back under the cover of the trees. Together, they watched from the shadows.

A few seconds later, the rest of the shard continued through, revealing itself as a nose. The nose was attached to an angular head, which turned from side-to-side as it emerged from the flame.

The creature—for creature it clearly was—had tall pointed ears and a dark metallic snout. It reminded Brady of a Doberman, only much taller, more angular, and made of metal. Its jaw receded on the sides to reveal two rows of pointed teeth, honed razor sharp, ready to tear. Its eyes were narrow trapezoids that tapered toward its mouth; they glowed a bright orange, the color of fire.

From a distance, the boys watched in amazement as more of the creature followed. It emerged bit by bit, as if stepping through an unseen doorway. First a toe, then a paw; finally a leg. Its neck and large body came next.

The creature's torso was covered with burnished bronze plates; in the gaps between them, the boys could see an assemblage of wires, pistons, gears, and servos. Brilliant rays of blue and white light from the fiery portal danced on the surface of the "dog" as it stepped confidently away from the door. A skeletal tail of metallic fragments wagged behind it. Strapped to its back was a tall stack of crates, but the creature appeared to carry the burden with ease, even though the pile was at least five feet high—almost taller than the animal itself.

After clearing the flame, the canine turned around and waited.

A minute later, a girl stepped from the light, looking around cautiously. She was a few inches shy of Brady's height, and only slightly taller than the dog.

The girl turned back to face the blue light; she was silhouetted by flame. Her straight, long hair blew to the side. She raised one arm in front of her and did something with a device on her wrist.

As she finished, the light began to change. The edges ripped apart and folded in on themselves like crumpling paper. The light grew smaller until there was only a bright speck of it left burning, and then even that was extinguished, flaring into a bright starburst before disappearing altogether.

The vanishing of the light was accompanied by another boom, just like the one that had woken Brady earlier—only this one shook the boys with its ferocity. Their eardrums rang.

Brady and Felix were left in darkness. Their pupils dilated to let in the moonlight.

The mysterious stranger walked up to the robotic dog and patted its side. "Good job, boy," the girl said, her voice gentle and assured. The dog's head twisted up slowly and rubbed its snout against the girl's hand. Brady and Felix could almost see the pistons extending and contracting, making the articulation possible. The creature's face seemed to soften as it looked at her.

The girl rubbed the dog's head and then moved to examine the packs on the creature's back. She appeared to be counting them.

Snap.

Brady looked down in horror at the broken stick beneath Felix's foot. Felix's face was red from embarrassment.

"Sorry, I—"

Brady dropped to the ground and pulled his brother down with him. When they dared look up, the creature had turned its head in their direction. In the inky black darkness, its glowing eyes were all they could see.

Felix put a hand over his own mouth, afraid of what might slip out. The brothers lay on the ground together, as still as could be, praying the cover of shadows would keep them hidden.

The girl spoke again. "What are you looking at? Let's go home."

Finally, the creature turned its head back and the eyes darted away. Brady and Felix watched the two walk off together and vanish into the trees, their shadowy forms swallowed by the darkness.

> Chapter 4: Chaos at Dawn

THE BOYS LAY STILL on the forest ground, fearful of what would happen if they moved too soon. They expected to see the machine's ghostly eyes materialize from somewhere in the forest, for the dog to turn its unruly gaze back upon them. As their imaginations ran wild, they listened intently for the sound of footsteps, for something out of place, for anything that would signal the return of the strange girl and her canine companion.

Time ticked slowly by.

The moon was just beginning its descent behind the trees. In the remaining hours of night, they heard only the sounds of the forest around them. They saw nothing unordinary. The mysterious pair was gone, leaving the brothers alone once again.

Felix picked himself up and walked over to the spot where he had seen the flame. He flipped on his flashlight and scanned it back and forth across the ground. After a second, he found what he was looking for: a gray line of ash that scarred the forest floor. It was several feet long, less than an inch wide, and marked the spot where the door had stood earlier.

He crouched down and felt around the dirt. It was freezing to the touch, and Felix recoiled from the sensation. The cold ran so deep the tips of his fingers burned.

He called over to his brother in a loud whisper. "Come check this

33

out! Look—the place where that fire was—it's ice cold!"

Brady continued to lie on the ground, ignoring his brother. His unblinking eyes studied the trees where the strangers had vanished.

Felix picked up a stick from the ground and threw it at his brother. It bounced off his leg with a *thwack*. Brady jumped three feet off the ground with a yelp, and Felix held in his laugh.

Annoyed, Brady turned around to face his brother.

"Why'd you do that?"

"You'd have fallen asleep down there. I didn't want you spending the night under that plant."

"Whatever. I was keeping an eye out for them."

"I'm pretty sure they're gone."

"Well, how do you know they won't come back?"

"I don't," Felix said. "Actually, I was thinking we could try to follow them. They can't have gotten too far yet."

"Are you crazy? We're lucky they didn't see us," Brady whispered. "And your fidgeting certainly didn't help things a few minutes ago. That dog, or wolf, or whatever it is, I think it may have seen us when it looked back here. Anyway, I bet it could rip us to pieces. Did you see its teeth? They were the size of knives. Probably sharper, too. I think we should get out of here."

Felix remained unconvinced. "I don't think it's dangerous. If it wanted to hurt us, it could have done so the other day. You know, the last time we were over here? Remember that strange howl we heard?"

Of course he did, Brady thought. He would never be able to get that awful sound out of his head.

"You know…" Felix said, "when we were looking for my quad, I'll bet that dog knocked it right out of the sky with one of those massive paws. There was definitely something that moved across the camera before we saw it crash. We just didn't know what it was." A light bulb went off in Felix's head. "Plus, I think it's a machine.

Some kind of *robot*. I've seen videos online of real robots, but never anything like that. Never so lifelike—so alive!"

Brady shuddered at the thought. He had never seen anything that large and vicious-looking, and the eerie howl from the other day made the creature seem even more malevolent, if that were even possible. And the fact that the monster dog didn't spook Felix was really starting to annoy him.

"Exactly," he said. "Alive and evil!"

"I'm just saying I don't think it would hurt us," Felix said. "I guess I don't know for sure though. Where do you think they came from?"

"You're asking me? You're the one who's into that kind of weird stuff," Brady said, brushing the dirt off his shirt. He looked back in the direction of his house.

"It's got to be at least five in the morning," he said. "We need to get home. Mom will be back in an hour or so, and she'll freak out if we're not there. She may already be back from work, and if she is, she's probably already called the police. I'll bet they're out here looking for us already. We won't be allowed out of the house for the rest of the summer!"

"Brady, try and calm down. We haven't been gone for that long." Felix paused for a second and then smiled to himself. "You know, that fire and that robot dog... that was the coolest thing I've ever seen."

"Yeah, well, me too, but let's get out of here before they decide to come back," Brady said.

Brady turned away the clearing and started walking home; Felix reluctantly followed. Brady felt a sudden surge of adrenaline as he looked around the forest, unsure if the beast was lurking somewhere in the shadows before him.

"Do you think they live back there in the Willoughbys' cabin?" Felix asked.

"Probably. I don't think there are any other houses back here."

"Well, wherever they came from, I'm thinking they were getting something they needed. Something that was on the other side of the door. Like supplies. Did you see all those crates on the robot's back?"

Brady was suddenly distracted by something buzzing around his ear. "What was that?"

He spun around, but whatever had made the noise was gone.

"What was what?" Felix asked.

"Mmm, never mind," Brady said, shaking his head. But just when he had convinced himself he had imagined it, the buzzing was back again, coming from somewhere around his right ear. And this time he could feel it too: a faint wind blowing against his face. He spun around quickly, but like before, there was nothing. He found himself eye-to-eye with Felix, who stared back at him, confused.

"You heard that, right?" Brady asked as he took a few steps back.

"No…"

"I promise you I heard something. At least—I think I did."

"Sure you did, Brady," Felix teased.

A blur of fluttering metal lurched in front of the boys and stopped just short of Brady's face. A tiny hummingbird hovered effortlessly in the air.

"Hey—I think it likes you!" Felix joked.

Brady was eye-to-eye with the flying robot. A long steel beak protruded from the bird's head and looked ready to pierce a concrete wall. Its sapphire eyes cast a bluish tint on its stubby body, and beneath its torso was a tail of metal blades arranged like a paper fan.

For a creature no larger than Brady's fist, it was menacing.

Brady looked over at Felix, who returned his gaze. When he took a step to the side, the bird moved with him. He took another step, and the bird followed again. Regardless of where he went, the bird matched his movements.

At last, hoping the bird would lose interest and fly back to wherever it had come from, Brady stood completely still with his arms at his sides—his version of playing dead. Still the bird hovered in front of him.

"Um, Felix? This thing won't stop following me. Felix?"

Brady spotted his brother creeping up behind the bird, quiet as a mouse. Brady shook his head in protest. "Not a good idea—stay away from that thing! *Don't do it Fe—*"

It was too late. Felix lunged at the bird, his arms outstretched; the bird deftly dodged his assault, moving higher into the air, and Felix slid face-first into the ground.

As Brady looked on, stunned, a plate on the bird's chest slid back, and the bird started to spin around. Its beak split wide and it let loose a siren that could be heard for miles. Bright lights flashed from the opening on its torso, adding to the effect.

Brady dragged his brother up by his shirt and took off running as fast as he could. Felix didn't hesitate to follow along this time.

But as they ran, the bird followed closely behind, never relenting. The noise was overwhelming, and the bird's flashing light seemed to slow time to a crawl. Terrified, the boys kept going, their washed-out forms moving frantically among the trees.

And then it ended as abruptly as it has started. The flashes of light stopped and the bird's beak slammed shut. It floated by their side for a second more, and then it drifted away into the night and vanished.

01110110

Fortunately, the garage was still empty when the brothers arrived home. They made their way to the kitchen, remembering to turn off the lights in case their mom showed up unexpectedly. Brady opened the refrigerator door, eagerly retrieved a carton of milk, and filled two tall glasses. He kept one for himself and slid the other across the countertop to his brother. Felix tore into a fresh pack of Oreos he had taken from their pantry, and responded in kind by pushing a stack of cookies back to Brady.

"Do you think they came from another world?" Felix asked.

"Another world? You mean, you think they're aliens or something?"

"Sort of like aliens I guess. But not from outer space. I mean, maybe that light was a door to somewhere else…"

"Your guess is as good as mine."

Before tonight, Brady would never have believed something like this. But after what he had seen, anything was possible.

Their conversation was cut short by the loud hum of the garage door motor churning to life.

"Mom's home!" said Felix, gulping down the rest of his milk. Brady grabbed the empty glass from his brother and put it in the sink, but not before Felix fished out a soggy cookie and inhaled it.

They made it upstairs in record time.

10101110

Brady took off his shirt and dove into bed. A few minutes later he heard the sound of footsteps coming down the hall. The thin streak of light on the floor widened into a yellow wedge as his bedroom door creaked open, his mom's shadow looming tall.

He closed his eyes as she picked a white sheet off the floor, shook it so it snapped taut, and let it fall gently over him. She stood there for a few seconds, then left the room and closed his door with a soft click. Brady listened to his mom's footsteps making their way down the hall to Felix's room.

Brady forced his eyes shut, knowing full well that sleep was out of the question. He wondered if his brother was having more luck. He doubted it.

The minutes passed as he thought about the woods. The sky beyond his window had gone from black to blue, the first signs of morning. The sun would be up soon.

Figuring there was no way his brother was asleep either, he let himself out of his room and tiptoed quietly down the hallway. He could hear his mom's TV soothing her to sleep.

He crept into his brother's room—a marvel of modern technology. It looked like a computer had exploded on the floor. Circuits, wires, LED lights, batteries, and other electronic parts were scattered in every nook and cranny. Felix's prized possession, a framed vintage poster of the Millennium Falcon, hung on the wall. It had been their father's, and it had yellowed a bit over the years and was beginning to curl up slightly at the corners.

A collection of colored plastic spheres dangled from the ceiling—a model of the solar system. Replica Saturn struck Brady in the forehead as he made his way across the room.

Felix was sitting up in his bed with his phone. "Hey, Brady. Having trouble falling asleep?"

"Yeah. I thought I'd come see what you're up to."

"Just reading a bit," Felix replied, flicking through some text on his phone.

"I've been thinking about what you said earlier," Brady said. "You know, the thing about other worlds? Maybe we could look it up online."

"It's worth a try. Let me switch my phone over to the monitor so we can both look."

Felix walked over to his desk and sat down in a cheap office chair his mother had picked up at yard sale a few years ago. Brady stood behind him and looked over his shoulder. Felix waved his phone next to a monitor propped up on the desk. The screen came to life with a progress bar that quickly filled up. After a second, the connection was complete, and the monitor now displayed exactly what was on his phone. They were looking at Felix's home screen, which was overflowing with colorful icons.

Felix set his phone down on the desk and retrieved a keyboard and mouse stashed away in his desk drawer. He swiped through page after page of games before he came to his favorite search app. He launched it, and a sparse white screen with a text input field appeared. He started typing:

door to another world

He pressed enter, and the screen filled with pictures of imaginary doors opening into different places. Some were of exotic locations on Earth, with old wood-paneled doors suspended in midair, opening onto remote paradises. Others included illustrations of otherworldly places, stone gateways and arches that led into unexplored universes rendered from the deepest recesses of someone's imagination. They were beautiful, but they looked nothing like what the boys had seen earlier tonight.

Brady frowned in frustration as Felix scrolled through the search results. These were all fantasy. What they had seen tonight, or at least thought they had seen, was the real thing. Something no one else had ever experienced. He had no idea what he was looking for, but he realized that whatever it was, he probably wouldn't find it here.

"None of those look right. Try searching for multiple worlds."

Felix cleared the search box and typed in the new words. The page quickly repopulated. These results were far more interesting. There were pages talking about many-worlds, parallel universes, and something about quantum mechanics.

Felix clicked on the entry that discussed parallel universes. Together, they read through the first paragraph or two before Brady gave up. The stuff was way over his head.

"Make any sense to you?" he asked.

"Sort of," said Felix, still reading. "I'll copy some of these so we can ask Ms. Cooper about it the next time we're in town. She'll know this stuff inside and out."

Ms. Cooper ran the local bookstore and knew all things science. Brady and Felix would spend hours in the bookstore on rainy days picking her brain.

"Hey, Brady. Do you think, if there really are multiple universes, that Dad's around in one of them?"

Brady stared down at the screen. "Maybe. But if so, there's probably another you and I that need him there more than this you and I need him here."

They sat in silence, considering the possibility. Finally, Felix reached out and turned off the monitor. From the window, they could see the first light of sunrise spreading across the land.

"I'm exhausted, Felix. It's already morning. We should try to get some sleep. Mom will probably be up in a few hours and will need our help around the house. She's not going to be happy when she finds out we left a mess downstairs."

With that, Brady said goodnight and let himself out of Felix's room. He made his way back to his own bedroom and lay down on his bed, exhausted. He was out as soon as his head touched the pillow.

> Chapter 5: Gutenberg's

HOURS LATER, Brady's door cracked open a hair and a voice called gently, "It's one in the afternoon. I think it's time to get yourself out of bed."

Ms. Banks poked her head into the room. Her hair was pulled back in a bun, and she wore a black Pixies short-sleeved tee with a white long-sleeved shirt tucked beneath it. With an exaggerated groan, Brady rolled over and pulled the pillow over his head to drown out the noise.

His mom tried again, this time irritated. "Time to wake up, Brady. I'm not going to ask again."

"Yeah, sure, I'll get up in a…"

Brady's voice trailed off and he fell back asleep.

Brady's mom burst through the door, walked over to his window, and pulled back the curtains so that the afternoon light flooded into the room. She yanked the pillow off her son's head and sat down on the bed next to him.

Brady scowled and recoiled from the light quicker than a vampire.

Ms. Banks spoke as calmly as she could bear. "I don't know what you and Felix were up to last night, but you left quite a mess downstairs. The living room is a wreck. There's popcorn all over the couch, and I almost tripped over an empty carton of ice cream last night when I came home. My shoes have cookie dough on them now. I want you both to clean it up—and the kitchen, too. You also left dirty glasses in the sink. I've told you before that I don't want to live in a pigsty. I'm only going to ask you once."

Brady retreated into the corner of his bed and held a sheet up to defend himself. "I'll get it in a few minutes. I promise."

"Thank you," his mom said, standing up.

"How was work, Mom?"

Her tone grew softer. "Long and uneventful, which is both good and bad, I guess. We were pretty slow last night. The good news is that I have the next few days off. I need to run a few errands in town, if you'd like to come along. I feel like I haven't seen either of you in ages."

"I'm pretty tired. I figured I'd just stay home today."

"Tired? That's the understatement of the century. Come on, it won't be that bad. You and Felix can go say hi to Ms. Cooper at Gutenberg's, maybe check out the books. She says it always makes her day when she gets to see you."

"Sure, I, um—is Felix up yet?"

"No, he's still asleep. I'm going to wake him up next." Brady's mom glanced outside just as a tiny bird fluttered by the window. She shifted her gaze to follow it, but it was gone as quickly as it had come. She turned back to Brady. "What were you guys doing up so late anyway?"

"There were some good movies on TV last night," Brady said. "We ate too much sugar and couldn't fall asleep." He wasn't lying exactly. Stretching the truth, perhaps.

As he became more lucid, memories of the previous night flooded into his mind. For a moment he considered telling his mom everything, but then thought the better of it after realizing it might not end well for him.

"Anyway," his mom said, "take a shower and get ready to go into town. Maybe we can get lunch at the diner. Or in your case, breakfast.

01100110

An hour or so later, Brady was clean, dressed, and running the vacuum cleaner hose through the cushions on the family room couch. The loud roar of the fan reverberated through the house, drowning everything else out. He was simultaneously amazed and disgusted by how filthy the room was. It had been spotless when his mom had left for work the previous evening. No wonder she was so irritated.

"Turn it *off!* Turn it *off!*"

Brady heard the faint sound of someone yelling over the blaring of the vacuum cleaner. He looked up in time to see a ruffled-looking Felix leaning over the balcony waving his arms frantically. Brady stomped on the vacuum's foot pedal and the house fell into a deep hush.

In an instant, Felix calmed down—Dr. Jekyll returning to Mr. Hyde. "Thanks. I have a splitting headache."

"No problem. Mom wants us to get the mess down here cleaned up before we go into town." Brady smiled up at his brother, knowing what was in store for him. "*And...* I saved *all* of the dishes for you, Felix."

Felix scowled. "Great. Where is Mom anyway?"

"Outside, working in the garden. She said she'd be done by the time we finished cleaning."

Felix ambled lazily down the stairs and collapsed on the couch, wiping the sleep from his eyes. "I still feel like the whole thing was a dream."

"It wasn't, I promise." Brady picked a pillow off the couch and tossed it at his brother. "Can you please help me get this stuff cleaned up?"

Felix picked himself up and sauntered into the kitchen. Brady could hear the water from the faucet running and dishes clanking together as his mom opened the front door and set a basket of fresh vegetables down on the foyer tile.

"Are you guys done yet?" she said, dusting off her hands. "I'm ready to go once you finish up." Her eyes perked up when she heard the sound of dishes from the kitchen. "When did your brother wake up?"

"A few minutes ago."

Brady's mom wore her worry on her sleeves. "Is everything okay with you two? It's not like you guys to sleep in so much. Especially Felix."

"We're fine. Like I said, we just stayed up too—"

"Hey Mom!" Felix interrupted as he rounded the corner.

"Good morning—I mean afternoon, Felix. I left the car running outside. Ready to go?"

The boys nodded, and a few minutes later the three of them were in the self-driving Bronco.

"Drive us to Daniel's," Ms. Banks said.

"Drive to Daniel's?" came a computerized voice from the car's speakers.

"Yes." Daniel's was a cozy diner they frequented whenever they were in town.

"Confirmed. The trip is estimated to take about ten minutes. Starting navigation."

As the computer finished speaking, the car's engine silently engaged and the car slowly accelerated backward out of the garage. It then turned around and began to wind down the long driveway.

From the front seat, Brady watched the shrubs and trees pass by and listened to gravel crunching beneath the tires. Ms. Banks leaned to the side in her seat and turned around to face Felix, who was slumped down in the back, almost dozing.

"Hey, sleepyhead. Are you hungry?"

"Starving."

"I figured as much. You must have burned a ton of calories in bed, wasting the day away."

Brady laughed under his breath but stopped suddenly when he noticed Felix glaring at him. Eventually the angry veneer faded and Felix gave a slight grin.

"Yeah, we stayed up too late last night. Sorry."

"Your brother said you guys got caught up watching movies. What was on, anyway?"

Felix stole a sideways glance at Brady.

"It was a horror movie marathon. Some really old ones from the nineties: classics. I couldn't fall asleep afterwards."

Ms. Banks rolled her eyes. "You know I don't want you guys watching that trash all the time. I would hope you would tune in to something more educational—like that's ever going to happen."

11110110

After breakfast, Brady and Felix made their way to Gutenberg's. It was a slow day in town and there wasn't much traffic. The bell above the door rang as they entered the red brick shop.

Wooden beams spanned the full width of the ceiling. Warm hues of red, green, yellow, and blue light shined through the collection of Tiffany lamps scattered throughout the interior; they reflected off the worn wooden floors like a kaleidoscope. The walls were lined with stained wooden trim that had turned a warm golden yellow over the years. Persian rugs were thoughtfully placed throughout.

To Brady and Felix, it felt like stepping into another time.

An older woman with a short gray bob and black, thick-rimmed glasses sat behind a computer pecking away at the keyboard. A ball-point pen was tucked comfortably behind her left ear.

Felix stepped out from behind his brother as they walked inside. "Hi Ms. Cooper, how's it going?"

The clacking of the keys stopped abruptly as two ocean blue eyes peered over the top of the screen. Ms. Cooper smiled down at the boys. She had once worked as a scientist, but after funding for her research had dried up, she was forced to try something different. Thus she'd owned and operated Gutenberg's for the last ten years. Brady and Felix had a mutual respect for Ms. Cooper that they didn't have for most other adults. She spoke to them like they were grown ups rather than kids; she didn't patronize. Over the years they had grown to trust her. It was never her style to judge.

"It's going okay," Ms. Cooper said. "A little slow today. Are you here with your mum?"

Brady and Felix looked around the store. It was usually brimming with people of all ages, but right now, they were the only customers in sight.

"She's picking up some groceries," Brady offered.

Felix began randomly thumbing through some books that lined the shelves. "Ms. Cooper—do you believe that other worlds exist?"

"Absolutely," she said. "Our universe is a very, very big place. Sooner or later you're bound to run into another planet like Earth. Some scientists even think that if you could travel far enough, you'd find an exact copy of our world—and of yourself. Not that that would be a good thing in your case, Felix." She winked at Brady. "But any such world would be terribly far away, so you don't have to worry about giving yourself a high five any time soon."

Brady spoke up, realizing she didn't quite realize what they were asking. "Well—what about other dimensions? Like parallel universes?"

Ms. Cooper removed the pen from behind her ear and rapped it on the wooden desk. "Why do you two look so guilty?"

Brady and Felix shrugged in unison.

She narrowed her eyes. "Well… sure—I believe it's possible. In fact, there are theories in science that actually predict this."

She smiled as the boys' faces lit up with wonder.

Felix continued the questioning. "You mean science predicts different universes?"

"Well, it's sort of complicated—but yes, that's one theory. It's actually called the multiverse. The idea works something like this: every time you make a decision, your current world branches into many new ones. Try to think of it this way. This morning you decided to come to see me. That's one universe. In another universe, you decided to stay home. In another you did something entirely different—like homework, for a change. There are an infinite number of them, actually. One for each possible outcome, for which there are infinite permutations, really."

"That's cool," Felix said. "So... is there any way you could travel between these different universes?"

"Again, it's all theoretical—but yes, I suppose. There is an idea of a wormhole. Generally it's thought of as a way to allow people to fold space and time. But it also has been suggested that a wormhole could allow people to bridge different realities as well." She paused for effect. "No one has ever seen a wormhole, but mathematically... they should be possible. Even so, it would take the gravitational pull of stars to open one, and even then..." She trailed off. "Are you two boys thinking about traveling to another universe sometime soon?"

Brady looked at Felix with mutual realization. What they had seen in the woods was true magic.

At that moment, the lights in the bookstore began to flicker, and Ms. Cooper looked around in frustration. Felix couldn't help but think out loud. "I bet it's happening again."

Brady nudged him in the arm with his shoulder.

"Ouch!"

"You bet what's happening, Felix?" said Ms. Cooper, peering down over her desk. She had stopped rapping the pen.

Felix caught himself. "Um... another power outage, Ms. Cooper. They seem to be happening more often these days." Felix thought about telling her the story of the light in the woods, but figured she wouldn't believe them. Anyway, he didn't want it getting back to their mom that he and his brother were spending their free time lurking around his neighbors' yard when she had clearly instructed them not to.

"Ah, yes, well... I wish someone would figure out whatever is causing it and put an end to it once and for all. It's starting to hurt my business."

The boys looked around the bookstore and were suddenly disheartened by how empty it was.

"Sorry, Ms. Cooper."

She quickly changed the topic. "So, are you two ready for school? It starts in less than a month, right? Brady, you're going to be a sophomore this year, I believe; and Felix, this is your last year of middle school, if I remember correctly?"

The boys nodded.

Another flicker.

Ms. Cooper stepped out from behind her desk. "Well, before you go, let me get something for you to read." She guided the boys through a maze of bookshelves and began scanning through an aisle. Her finger ran across a row of book covers as she narrowed her search. A wooden sign on top of the shelves read "Physics" in engraved black letters.

"Found it," she said, removing two leather-bound tomes from the shelf. "One for each of you." She put the books into their arms with a thud. "You can borrow them as long as you bring them back when you're finished."

"Thanks, Ms. Cooper," they said at the same time.

The lights flashed another few times, and then went out for good. The wooden ceiling fans slowly ground to a halt. It was if the life had suddenly been sucked out of the room.

"Sorry about the lights, Ms. Cooper. I guess Felix and I should probably go find our mom."

"It was great to see you both. Please tell your mom I said hello."

"Will do. Bye."

Books in hand, Brady and Felix left the store, squinting as their eyes adjusted to the sunlight.

"I bet that girl opened the door again, Brady," Felix said excitedly as they walked down the street. "That's why the power is out."

Brady nodded. He had been thinking the same thing.

> Chapter 6: Blitz Realm

THE POWER WAS STILL OUT when the Bankses arrived home. Felix and Brady were exhausted from the night before, and despite their mom's protests, they managed to sleep the rest of the afternoon away. By the time they woke up, the power was back on and dinner was simmering on the stove with a handwritten note stuck to the counter.

Felix read it to himself and tossed it in the trash. "Mom forgot something and had to run back to the store. She said she'd be home in a bit with dessert, but to go ahead and help ourselves to the food."

"My pleasure. I'm starving," Brady said, and he eagerly ladled steaming chili into two bowls. They garnished the dish with cheese, sour cream, green onions, and some corn tortilla chips their mom had set out for them on the counter. They were digging hungrily into the meal within seconds.

Finally, Felix paused to come up for air.

"What do you think about what Ms. Cooper told us?" he asked Brady, who was busy inhaling his food.

"I don't know what to think," Brady replied, swallowing a mouthful of chili. "None of this makes any sense. Last night feels like a dream—I still can't believe the whole thing even happened. I mean, I sort of understand what she said about multiple universes and all, but come on. It seems like someone is pulling a prank on us."

"It's no prank. No one could pull off something like that. And

51

even if they could, what would be the point?"

They continued the rest of the meal in silence, too hungry to speak. When they were done, they moved to the living room and plunked themselves down on the couch.

"You up for some Voxelverse?" Felix asked.

"Always."

Voxelverse was a digital universe that consumed vast quantities of the boys' free time—and then some. It was a different type of game. Instead of following a fixed script, players were free to do whatever they liked, which for the most part, involved building things from blocks and just trying to stay alive. There were no winners or losers. There was a block for almost any material imaginable—dirt, water, stone, lava, wood, glass, and many, many others. Different combinations of blocks could be assembled to make things in the game. In fact, people had worked together to recreate entire cities. Wood blocks could be broken apart into sticks, which could then be combined with stone to make swords, shovels, and other things. What had started out as a cult phenomenon had quickly grown into an international bestseller and become the currency of young and old gamers alike. And just when it had appeared that interest was starting to wane, a group of software developers revived it with support for virtual reality, bringing it to the next level. Now it was more popular than ever. For Brady and Felix, as well as most kids their age, it was safe to call it an addiction. It enraptured them and set their imaginations free.

Brady and Felix scooped their Orbature virtual reality glasses off the floor. Using his shirt, Felix wiped off the lenses—they had gotten somewhat dirty during their excursion in the woods. Then they launched Voxelverse on their phones and quickly pulled the glasses down over their eyes.

The title screen appeared in front of them, prompting them to choose a server. There were thousands of addresses to pick from, thousands of entirely different worlds, each with its own inhabitants and rules.

"Which server do you want to connect to?" Felix asked.

"I don't know. How about Blitz Realm?"

"Sounds good to me. Finding the address... Okay, we're there."

The lenses faded to black, and a loading bar appeared, floating directly in front of them. The next thing they knew, the boys were standing in a grassy meadow overlooking a vast, pixelated landscape. A waterfall splashed down to their left, sending hundreds of tiny aquamarine cubes hurling out of the froth and high into the air. A bright square sun hung directly overhead as cubic clouds drifted lazily across the sky. The outline of a castle loomed on the horizon; it had taken the boys weeks of careful assembling to build it.

"What should we do first?" Felix asked as a blocky pig with a vacant expression meandered by.

Brady had already wandered off and was busy chopping down a tree so he could make wood planks for new construction. "We could try to find some villagers to trade with," he suggested. "Or we could spend some time working on the dungeon. I'd like to put in a library."

"A library? In a dungeon?" Felix asked.

"Of course," Brady responded, as though it was a perfectly normal thing to do.

"If you say so. Let's just get going toward the castle. We should try to get there before the sun sets."

Felix looked over at Brady, who was now switching between different kinds of armor. His character's head changed colors as he cycled between gold, diamond, and iron helmets.

"Come on, Brady."

"Wait," Brady said, and his avatar froze. "Do you see that?" His character waved a rectangular arm at a strange dot moving on the horizon. It started as a single pixel that grew larger as it approached.

Soon the jumble of pixels coalesced into a person.

In Voxelverse, every player's character had his or her name written above it, and no two players had the same name. This made it easier to tell exactly whom you were dealing with.

But there was *no* name above the visitor's head.

The boys watched curiously as the anonymous player approached. Like everything else in Voxelverse, the game's characters were constructed from blocks. As the stranger came nearer, the boys could see that it was dressed in all black. Its eyes and long hair were as dark as its clothes, and its face had only an expressionless rectangle for a mouth. It hovered rather than walked when it moved. None of the other players were coded this way.

The visitor stopped when it reached Brady and Felix.

The words *walk with me* scrolled in front of their world.

Felix and Brady both knew that characters couldn't talk to other players without their approval first. The game was designed so that friends could only talk to other friends. So either this was a computer player, or someone had found a vulnerability in the code.

Troubled, Brady took off his glasses. "I've had enough weird stuff happen in the past twenty-four hours to last me a lifetime. I think I'm done."

Felix, who was still wearing his glasses, replied, "It's just a game. Calm down. They probably just added some new AI algorithms in the most recent update. Although... I admit though, this is pretty weird."

Feeling silly, Brady reluctantly put his glasses back on. The mysterious player was still floating in front of them, waiting. After a few seconds, the message repeated itself once more. Then the player in black turned around and started walking toward the waterfall.

"Where is it going?" Brady asked. "There's nothing but water and rock over there. We've gone back there a million times—the server won't let you break those blocks."

The player glided across the stream, passed straight through the waterfall, and disappeared.

Felix and Brady turned their cubed heads to stare at each other.

"*No way...*"

It was a rare occasion when something actually surprised Felix in this game.

He pushed his thumb forward on the phone screen and his on-screen character chased after the player. Brady did the same. They could hear the crystal clear roar of the waterfall in their ears as they neared the stream.

They plunged into crystal blue water before quickly resurfacing. Together they swam across the stream and into the waterfall. Brady looked up to see hundreds of cascading bubble blocks pass through him.

They were almost to the other side of the waterfall when their lenses went black.

The words "REDIRECTING SERVER" appeared in the center of their screen.

"What the—"

The message disappeared almost as soon as they read it. Now they were standing in a dark cavern. Two rows of flickering torches led down the rocky passage to a wooden door at the end. The walls were ablaze with fiery-hued pixels that blinked around the flames.

Felix glanced back at where they had entered. Ruby lava poured over the mouth of the cave, sealing them in.

The door was their only way out.

The boys made their way forward. Felix reached for the door-knob.

"You sure you want to go through there?" Brady said. "I don't think we're on the Blitz Realm server anymore."

"Only one way to find out." Felix opened the door with a *click* and stepped through. Brady was right behind him.

What happened next was almost too strange to describe.

The boys looked around and realized they were standing in their own living room—only this wasn't real. Brady reached up to make sure he still had his glasses on. Every part of their house had been exquisitely recreated using blocks. A pixelated couch sat in the middle of the room, along with the coffee table, television, and everything else. Black and white rectangles danced randomly around the TV. Every detail was there. Even the wall colors were faithful. It was incredible.

Felix spun around, only to find the door they had just entered had vanished.

"I don't like this, Brady. Someone's hacked into the server. Someone who knows who we are."

"Turn it off," Brady said urgently.

Felix took his glasses off to power down the game. On his phone's display were more words.

Continue on, Felix.

Yeah, right, he thought.

He pressed a few buttons to try to close out the program, but his phone wasn't responding.

"Felix, you really need to see this."

Curious, Felix put his glasses back on and was instantly transported back to the virtual living room. On the TV, the rectangular static was gone. There were now instructions waiting for them.

Go outside.

Beneath the screen was an arrow pointing toward the garage.

The boys followed.

As their avatars walked through their kitchen, they were astonished at how meticulously their house had been recreated, block by block. It would have taken Brady and Felix months to produce something this sophisticated, and even then, it wouldn't be anywhere near as perfect.

On the kitchen table was an exact replica of Felix's quadcopter. The word "Unwelcome" was painted in pixels on the exterior.

"Felix, do you see this?"

"I see it. Come on."

The boys hurried past.

Outside, the player in black waited for them by the fence across their yard. Its rectangular arm extended outward, pointing at something near the fence. It was too hard to tell what it was from this distance.

As they walked across the back yard, the sky began to turn from a light blue to a dark crimson red. The sky grew darker with each step forward.

And then they saw what the dark player was pointing to.

Two other players were climbing the fence. The first was tall and skinny with red hair. The second player was shorter, with blond hair. The realization hit Brady and Felix like a ton of bricks.

They were watching themselves.

There was no question now who was behind this. The sky continued to darken as they stood and watched the virtual Brady and virtual Felix drop to the other side and run off into the blocky woods.

Brady looked back to the player in black, but she was gone. In her place was a sign.

It read: "*Stay Away.*"

They heard the sound of a door opening somewhere. They looked around but didn't see anything. It took a few seconds for them to realize the sound had come from the real world. Then they heard the sound of their mother's voice.

"I'm home! Can you guys help me unload the car please?"

"Sure Mom, just a second," Felix responded queasily.

When they looked back at the sign, the words had changed. It now said: *Tell no one about us.*

The game stopped and the lenses went blank.

11000110

Brady's mind filled with questions. Were they in danger now, he wondered? He wanted to tell his mom what had happened, but thought better of it. The stranger in black had warned him against that.

The sound of Felix's voice brought Brady back to reality.

"They were watching us the other day."

Brady looked down at his brother, who was sitting on the couch with his glasses dangling around his neck.

"Yeah, I know. It's freaking me out!"

Brady felt his stomach tighten up as he started to realize the implications of what was happening. The stranger who had walked through the door of light was probably the same person who had sent this. Perhaps even more unsettling was the realization that someone had followed them home without them even realizing it.

It didn't help that the girl had a sinister-looking mechanical hound as a pet. She had looked human, but the animal did not. And whatever it was, Brady knew he wanted nothing to do with it.

But they know who we are.

Right then and there, Brady decided he would spend the rest of the summer inside. Where it was safe—hopefully. He had seen things yesterday and tonight that he didn't think were possible. If anyone else had shared these events with him, he would have thought they were crazy.

"I guess we're probably in trouble now," said Felix with resignation.

"Maybe. But this is pretty disturbing. I mean, they could have just said something to us instead of following us around like that. Not only do we have terrifying evil aliens for neighbors—now we have terrifying evil aliens who are unhappy with us. I told you it was a stupid idea to go over there."

"I don't think they're aliens, Brady. And they're probably not evil."

"Whatever. I'm not going anywhere near there."

Felix nodded. For once, the brothers were in agreement.

> Chapter 7: Nocturnal SOS

WEEKS HAD PASSED since they had seen the strangers come through the door, and things were starting to get back to normal. Their mysterious neighbors had made their point very clear—they wanted to be left alone—and Brady and Felix were more than happy to oblige. It was the Friday night before school started, and Brady's anxiety about the neighbors had been replaced by the dread of homework. The boys were hunkered in their beds, asleep, while a heavy rain battered the windows.

Buzz... Buzz... Buzz...

Brady stirred, but the sound of the rain lulled him back to sleep. His eyes were just starting to close when he heard it again.

Buzz... Buzz... Buzz...

Yawning, he glanced over and saw his phone rattling across his nightstand. The alarm clock was off. He knew too well what that meant: the power had gone out again. He felt his stomach churn.

Buzz... Buzz... Buzz...

He grabbed his phone and held it at arm's length so his eyes could focus.

There was a new message waiting for him—from an anonymous sender. *That's strange.* The phone was supposed to filter out messages from people he didn't know. His mind went back to the player dressed in black from Voxelverse.

Brady shuddered and clicked on the message. A single word was waiting for him.

Window.

His mind raced and he looked expectantly across his room. Behind the curtains, the window flashed, followed by the sound of rolling thunder.

Brady placed the phone back on the nightstand and walked over to his window.

He slowly pulled the curtains back.

At first he saw nothing but the rain streaking down the glass pane. He took a deep breath. *See,* he thought, *nothing to worry about.*

But then, through the downpour, he spotted it. Two glowing eyes were staring back at him from the corner of his yard.

A chill ran down Brady's spine.

The mechanical creature was shrouded in silvery mist, making the fiery eyes appear to float above the ground like disembodied embers. They burned with a supernatural intensity.

The rush of terror nearly knocked him off his feet.

It had come here tonight.

It had come to his house.

For him.

Another bolt of lightning lit up the sky, and Brady could see the dark form of the massive creature—waiting.

Was it possible that the creature had sent him the message just now? Was the girl waiting for him as well? What did they want?

Brady's head was spinning. He grabbed the curtains, pulled them shut, and stepped to the side, pressing his back against the wall. His pulse quickened, as did his breathing. As he looked around the room, he almost expected to find the creature there waiting for him, ready to tear him apart.

Get ahold of yourself. Felix is right; if it had wanted to hurt us, it could have done so. Don't be a chicken.

He slapped his forehead. *It's just a dream*, he thought. *It has to be.*

Slowly he turned back to the window. His hands trembled this time as he slid the curtains back open, inch by slow inch.

The machine was still there.

Without knowing what to do, Brady stood frozen at the window. The dog's eyes stared up at the boy; they grew brighter the longer Brady focused on them.

Buzz...

His phone buzzed again. Brady hesitated a few seconds before walking over and reluctantly taking a look. Again, a single word waited for him.

Help.

Help? If the creature was actually speaking to him, it had a cryptic way of doing so.

Phone in hand, he walked back over to the window. He thought about it for a second, then held up the device so the dog could see it.

The canine slowly twisted its head in the direction of the fence, then back to face Brady. It was motioning for him to come outside, into the storm.

Brady considered the request for a second. It looked awful outside—both the rain and the dog. And he was nice and dry in here, not to mention safe. His mom and brother were sound asleep just a few doors down.

And just when he had started thinking he could put everything behind him, this dog had shown up in his back yard.

What is going on?

Brady quickly realized that going back to sleep wasn't an option. He knew the machine would wait for him. But at least it was outside. He would have to deal with it before his mom caught wind of what was happening.

He grabbed a crumpled t-shirt from the floor and pulled it over his head. Then he tiptoed down the hall and snuck into Felix's room. If he was going outside, there was no way he was going alone.

Felix was sound asleep and snoring loudly. Brady whispered loudly into his brother's ear, "Felix! Felix—get up! It's here."

"What the heck?" Felix groaned and pushed his brother away.

"Remember the robot dog?"

"That's great..." Felix muttered nonsensically, turning over in his bed.

Brady ripped the sheets off his brother. "Get up, Felix! The dog. It's *here*!"

"At our house? Are you sure you're not sleepwalking?" Felix grumbled.

"Of course I'm sure. It's right outside my window. It texted me."

"The *dog* sent you a text? Now I know you're dreaming. Get out of here!"

"It said something about needing help."

"Help?" Felix asked, finally waking up.

"That's what it said. I'm not sure what it means."

"Is the girl with it?"

"It's raining, so it's hard to see anything, but I don't think so. I think the dog needs us for something. Just get up. We're going outside."

10010110

The night air was heavy from the humidity, and the hard rain continued to fall. A thick layer of clouds covered the night sky like a gray blanket; there was no moon to light the way.

Brady looked back toward his mom's room, hoping they hadn't woken her on their way outside. Her light was still off, so she was probably still asleep.

The dog had not moved from its position. The glowing eyes turned their gaze to the two boys as they approached. The canine appeared even more threatening up close, with metallic ribs that formed a cage around its wide torso. Steam from the rain rose off the back of the machine.

"This thing is incredible," said Felix, walking around the creature to get a better look. He reached out a hand to touch it, but the dog quickly jumped back and growled.

"Way to go, Felix. I think you upset him."

Felix nodded and lowered his head. "Sorry, whatever your name is."

The growling ceased.

"Now what?" Brady asked the creature. He found it odd to be speaking to a dog, but it wasn't the strangest thing that had happened to him this summer.

Its eyes narrowed, and the dog turned and began walking toward the fence. It paused after a few paces and looked back expectantly at the boys.

"It wants us to follow it," said Felix.

Brady shuddered at the thought. "No way. We should have learned our lesson the first time. Something awful happens every time we go back there."

"You said it needed our help, right? We need to at least see what it wants. I think we owe it that much."

"Of course we do," Brady replied, sarcastically.

Felix turned to face the dog. "Before we go—what's your name?"

Brady shook his head. How was the creature supposed to answer?

As if in answer to his unspoken question, his phone buzzed in his pocket. He grabbed the device and held it up for Felix to see.

Achilles.

Felix called to the creature. "Okay, Achilles, we're ready to go."

The boys stepped forward, cautiously at first, but then raced to catch up as the canine quickened its pace. They were at the fence before they knew it.

"Where to now?" Brady wondered aloud when the beast stopped. Then, in one fluid motion, the dog crouched back on its hind legs and leapt high into the night sky, easily clearing the top of the fence. Mud sprayed in all directions as the creature slammed down on the other side.

Felix was starry-eyed as the metallic hound extracted its paws from the ground and stood tall. "That was incredible! Did you see that?"

"I'm standing right here. I just hope it's on our side."

"Would you quit with that? If it wanted to hurt us it could have done it along time ago. Come on. It's our turn to climb over now."

"Fine." Brady started climbing over the fence. "But this is asking for trouble," he muttered under his breath as his fingers curled around the next link up.

"What was that?" Felix asked.

"Nothing."

As the brothers climbed down the other side of the fence, Achilles started to walk briskly again. The boys sprinted to catch up.

And then they saw it. The brilliant door of flame burning in the distance. It had moved since the last time they had seen it, but its appearance hadn't changed.

Achilles continued straight to the blue portal and stopped just a few feet away from it. He then turned to look back at Felix and Brady, who were still a good distance behind him.

"I—I think Achilles actually wants us to go through," Brady said, nervously.

"I guess that's why he brought us here. There's something on the other side he wants us to see."

"That's what I'm afraid of. We have no idea what's on the other side of that door."

Felix and Brady continued forward. As soon as they reached Achilles, the dog looked at the door, then back at Felix.

Felix took a step closer and carefully touched the light. The tip of his finger disappeared as it passed through the gateway. "It feels kind of cold." He pulled his finger back—fortunately it was still whole. "I think it's safe. I'm going through."

Brady envisioned his brother diving through and falling into a bottomless pit, completely helpless without him on the other side. He grabbed his brother's arm to hold him back. "Wait a second. The three of us should go through together."

Felix nodded, and Achilles wagged his skeletal tail.

And with that, Brady, Felix, and Achilles stepped through the light and left their world behind.

> Chapter 8: Rescue

BRADY CLOSED HIS EYES, balled his fists tightly, and walked toward the portal. As he took his first step into the light, he expected to be whisked along a celestial tunnel through the stars. But he never left the ground. Instead, he felt a slight pressure that pushed ever slightly against his skin like an invisible membrane. And then the sensation was gone—the bubble had burst.

He took another step.

The rain stopped.

Brady opened his eyes and saw Achilles and Felix standing next to him. They were side by side inside a dark room, with only their flickering shadows, cast by the portal behind them, there to greet them.

The canine wasted no time and started toward an exit at the far end of the room. As the dog approached, a metal door slid back to reveal a tunnel that stretched into murky darkness.

Felix wrung the rain out of his shirt and the water splashed down on the grimy metal floor. "Now what? Where are we?"

Achilles took a few steps into the tunnel and angled his head downward. A plate slid back on his head, and a small scope protruded through the opening. Once in position, the scope unleashed dozens of micro-thin lasers that formed a red lattice across the tunnel walls. The rays of light scanned up and down several times before dissolving altogether.

Then a spotlight shot out from the scope, carving a bright path through the gloom. At least they could now see where they were going.

The boys exchanged a worried glance, then shrugged. *We've come this far...*

The door grinded shut behind them as they followed Achilles into the long passage. The walls were made of concrete, with iron arches buttressing the ceiling along the way. The moldy passage had no windows to provide relief from the claustrophobia that was setting in. The air felt sour, sickly.

Achilles took slow, cautious steps forward through the tunnel. The brothers followed closely behind, their own steps echoing down the corridor. The floor gradually sloped downward. As they walked, Felix took his phone out of his pocket and pressed the power button a few times. He was dismayed when the black screen stared back at him, empty.

"Something's messing with my phone here. It's completely dead."

Brady tried his phone as well, but it, too, failed to turn on.

"There goes our only way of talking to Achilles," Brady replied.

"I'm sure he'll figure out another way." Felix slid his phone back into his pocket.

They continued to follow Achilles until at last they saw an intersection up ahead. Suddenly Achilles stopped in his tracks. The dog's ears and tail stood straight up, and his eyes narrowed to slits. He was leaning forward and growling softly. Something was wrong.

Realizing something was up, the boys froze as well. Achilles extinguished the light from the scope, and they waited nervously in the pitch black. Seconds later they heard it: a low, guttural noise coming from somewhere far down the side tunnel. The sound was full of despair and reverberated like a lonely whale song from the coldest, darkest reaches of the sea. It started out faint, but gradually got louder, nearer.

Brady and Felix huddled close together behind Achilles, who continued to stand guard. As the noise grew closer, the boys could hear something else. Something unpleasant. It sounded like metal brushing against the ground, sliding and scraping.

Soon it seemed like the creature was so close that only a few feet of darkness separated them from the source of the terrible noise. Brady clutched one of Achilles' armor plates: it was all he could do to stop from screaming.

At last the scraping passed, and the noise receded. The creature, or whatever it was, had crossed the intersection and was now moving away from them on its path down the adjoining corridor.

After another minute, Achilles turned the light back on and moved forward slowly. For a creature his size, he was surprisingly quiet. Brady and Felix were now much more careful about keeping their own footsteps quiet as well.

They continued down another short stretch of tunnel until they reached an archway that opened into a larger room. Green beams ran back and forth across the opening.

Achilles stopped in front of the beams, then turned to face Brady and Felix. The canine shook his head slowly.

Felix looked confused. "What? We can't go any further? Well we can't just turn around!"

Achilles bent his head down to shine the light on his leg. Another plate folded back, this time revealing a small canister. The dog looked up at Brady, then back down at the canister.

"He wants you to take it, Brady."

Brady retrieved the canister from Achilles' leg. It was about the size and shape of a spray can.

Achilles turned back to face the room; he whined and scratched the floor with his paw.

"He wants us to go in there," Felix said.

"Yeah, I got that, thanks. But I'm not going through those green beams. It reminds me of a security system from the movies. We'll walk through it and alarms will start going off."

Achilles let out a loud cry, and his scratching grew more intense. It sounded like nails on a chalkboard, and it only got worse as the boys stood there deliberating. The canine was clearly anxious about something.

Finally, impulsively, Felix stood up and walked straight through the beams as if nothing could hurt him. Brady held his breath, waiting for sudden flashing lights or the sound of an alarm.

Nothing happened.

"See? It's safe."

Brady exhaled like a deflating balloon and reluctantly walked into the room after his brother.

He turned back to Achilles, who stood there with orange eyes glowing in the darkness of the tunnel. "Your turn, Achilles. Come on!"

Achilles whined louder, but at least the scratching had stopped.

"I don't think he can," Felix said. "Maybe that's why he needed our help. He can't get past those beams without setting the alarm off."

"Why not?"

"I have no idea."

Achilles stopped crying for a second and stared at the boys.

Felix and Brady turned and looked around the room. Unlike the tunnel, the room was dimly lit, and piles of crates were littered about haphazardly on the floor. The crates looked just like the ones strapped onto Achilles' back the first time the boys had seen him.

And then they saw *her*.

Standing in the far corner of the room was the girl from the woods. Her head was turned to the side, and her long black hair floated in space. Thin with dark skin, she looked to be a few years older than Brady. She wore a gray t-shirt and blue jeans. Her eyes were wide and her mouth open, like she was in the middle of saying something. She held one of the crates in front of her.

But she wasn't moving.

"It's the girl from the forest," Brady said, stunned.

"She's frozen," Felix added. "I—I think we're here to help her."

"How are we supposed to do that?"

"Well, we can't do anything from here," Felix retorted, and he started to cross the room. Brady followed.

As they came nearer, they noticed that something else was wrong. The air around the girl rippled and distorted, like hot air rising off pavement on a desert road. The closer they came, the blurrier she appeared.

And there was something else. Something was spinning around the girl, although it was moving too quickly for them to tell what it was. Brief flashes of light streaked by as the object circled.

"The canister," Felix said. "Use it."

"I don't know if it's safe." Brady lifted the canister in the air and turned back toward the entrance where Achilles waited.

"Are we supposed to use this now?" he shouted.

Achilles let out an approving bark that nearly shook the room.

"I guess that's settled, then," Felix said.

"Okay. Here goes nothing." Brady held his breath, pressed the button on the nozzle, and waved his arm wildly around the girl. A jet of silver particles that streamed from the canister was immediately pulled into orbit around her, like curling strands of thread wrapping an invisible spool. The particles quickly diffused into a glimmering mist that encircled the girl in a reflective globe. The cloud held its form for a minute, then faded.

"Nothing's happening," Brady said, and he turned toward Achilles with a look of disappointment on his face.

"Maybe you didn't spray enough, Brady. Try it again."

Brady held the canister out in front of him, but before he could push the nozzle again, he noticed something.

The flashes of light were lasting longer now. Brady could begin to make out thick rings of metal that spun around the girl like a gyroscope. There were three of them, rotating at different angles and speeds. And they were slowing down. Soon they had stopped altogether.

Brady watched in amazement as the rings began to change. The difference was subtle at first. The reflective surface of the rings faded to a tarnished dull gray. Then the metallic coating began to decompose and pull away, leaving a tarnished layer of rust underneath. Flakes of rotting metal started to peel and break off the rings, like an ancient scroll thrown into a ferocious wind. Within seconds, the powdered remains of the rings lay scattered on the floor.

The stranger was free.

> Chapter 9: The Neurogeists

THE GIRL SNAPPED TO LIFE, shouting, as if finishing a sentence she'd started earlier, "—some sort of trap, Achilles—run and get help!" The crate dropped from her hands and clanked loudly on the floor.

The girl jumped back in astonishment when she realized someone was standing next to her. Brady backed up a few feet to give her some space.

"It's you!" she gasped, recognition slowly creeping across her face. Worried, she turned toward Felix, who was now standing next to his brother. "You're *both* here... but why?"

"Your dog came and got us. He needed our help," Brady said.

"*You* needed our help," Felix added.

The girl looked confused. "Help? My dog? You mean Achilles? What are you talking about? Achilles, please tell me you didn't bring them here."

From the tunnel, the dog whined and lowered his head and tail in shame.

"It's not Achilles' fault. You were..." Felix thought for a second. "Well... you were frozen, like a statue. At least that's what it looked like. And there were these metal rings flying around you that made some kind of a bubble. Your dog, I mean, Achilles, gave us a spray can to help get you out. It ate right through the rings and brought you back. You'd still be trapped if we hadn't come. Who are you, anyway?"

"I'm Nova. I guess I should thank you both for saving me."

Brady stepped forward. "It's nice to meet you, Nova. My name is Brady, and this is my brother Felix." Felix waved. "And I guess this is yours." He held the spray can out to the girl.

"Nice to meet both of you—face-to-face this time," the girl replied with a smile. She took the canister and rolled it over in her hands. "It's called a Field Wrecker, in case you're wondering. It contains nano particles that eat through electromagnetic fields."

Brady shook his head. "I don't understand a word of what you just said."

Felix jumped in. "The wrecker ate through the rings and destroyed the field that Nova was trapped in."

"Exactly," Nova said. "I must have gotten caught in a Time Hugger trap."

"A Time Hugger?" Felix asked.

"A special type of field that stops time. Whoever enters the field becomes suspended in time. The rings create the field, and it lasts as long as they're spinning."

"Why couldn't Achilles free you from it? Why bring us here in the middle of the night?" Brady asked.

"See those green beams in the archway?" Nova pointed over toward the entrance to the tunnel. "They would deactivate him instantly if he tried to step through. It's part of a security system that looks for a specific electronic signature and destroys anything that doesn't match up perfectly. Sort of a high-tech bug zapper."

"Why didn't it hurt us then?"

"You're a human, so you don't have a digital signature. It doesn't even know you're here."

"But why would someone want to trap you in the first place?"

Nova looked pensively at Achilles, then turned back to Brady. She hesitated.

"Because we've been stealing from them."

"Stealing?" Brady felt his heart stop. Suddenly he didn't feel like such a hero. He wondered if he had made a big mistake freeing the girl. What was he doing exactly—helping a criminal? He'd be better off at home still asleep in bed.

Seeing the look on his face, Nova added, "It's a long story, and not what you think. We don't have time to talk about it right now though. It's too dangerous here. They'll come for me. And if they find us, we'll be trapped forever. We need to go."

They made their way through the archway and back into the tunnel where the canine waited for them. Achilles' eyes grew brighter as they approached, and his tail wagged effusively. Nova wrapped her arms around the dog and gave him a hug. "It's good to see you too. Thanks for bringing help."

Just as before, Achilles turned on the spotlight to guide them down the depths of the tunnel. Eager to leave, they moved at a brisk pace. Brady couldn't help but think about what Nova had said earlier. Was he helping out a thief?

Soon they were back at the intersection of tunnels where the strange creature had passed by them in the darkness. Achilles shined his light down both ends of the crossing tunnel, looking for something out of the ordinary. Nova peered around the corners too. There was nothing there.

"I think we're clear. Let's keep going," Nova said quietly.

A deep, anguished bellow called out from the shadows near the end of the tunnel. It was followed by silence, then the sound of scraping metal.

Achilles dimmed the light and looked up at Nova.

She put her index finger to her lips and whispered to the boys, "A Neurogeist. The trap I set off probably alerted it. The good news is it probably thinks I'm still in the storage room, trapped. The bad news is that it's blocking our way out. We'll have to wait for it to pass by."

The noise was growing louder; it was coming closer. "That's the awful noise we heard before," Brady said in a hush, his face half covered in shadow.

They slowly backed up to the intersection of the two tunnels. Nova ducked around the corner and motioned for everyone else to follow.

"Kill the light, Achilles."

The dog obeyed, and everything went dark.

They stood against the wall and waited.

The scraping grew louder.

In the still of the tunnel, there was something else with them—faint but unmistakable. It announced itself with the same horrid noise as the other creatures. A second Neurogeist—this one coming from behind.

Nova looked around anxiously.

"There's more than one—there's no place to hide from them both. We have no choice but to try to make it for the door. On the count of three, we'll go for it. One... two... Achilles, lights!"

Achilles dashed around the corner and switched on the heavy beam. The harsh light revealed their fear.

It was there, waiting for them.

The creature's wretched body drifted through the air, buoyed by steel tentacles that slithered noisily across the floor. Centered on its trapezoidal hull was a glass sphere, recessed into a hollowed socket—a haunted eye. A vaporous red light burned within the globe, and it jerked about with stiff, erratic motions.

The machine was alien and awful; a mechanical jellyfish carved into sharp, menacing angles.

And it was sliding toward them.

Brady, Felix, and Nova huddled together behind Achilles, who stood guard. His ears were straight and his metallic razor teeth seemed to grow several inches. He stepped forward, toward the creature, letting out a vicious growl.

The Neurogeist retreated at first, then held its ground, hovering in place. Its eye stopped moving and locked on to the dog. For a moment, the two otherworldly creatures stood facing one another.

It was the Neurogeist that moved first. Without warning, the creature flung a lethal tentacle toward the dog. The end of the tentacle crackled loudly as electrical current surged through the flailing appendage.

Achilles jumped to the side, the tendril missing him by inches. He sprang forward with razor-sharp nails extending from his paws and brought the creature down to the ground with a crunch. Sparks flew from the surprised bot as it struggled to pry itself from Achilles' mighty grip.

The creature was shrieking, and its dark glass eye spun around wildly, searching for a way out. Achilles shoved the creature against the wall and turned his head toward the end of the tunnel. He looked back at Nova and the boys and started barking frantically.

"This is our chance," Nova said.

"What about Achilles?" Felix asked.

"Did you see him? He'll be okay. Come on!" Brady replied.

The three of them slid around the dog while the strange creature continued to writhe in agony. Tentacles flailed around looking for something or someone to latch on to.

As they sprinted down the passage, Felix turned to look back over his shoulder. What he saw filled him with terror. A mob of Neurogeists streamed into the tunnel, quickly filling the space behind the dog.

Felix slid to a stop while Brady and Nova continued toward the door. "We have to help him!" he shouted. "There's too many of them!"

Brady shouted back at his brother. "Felix! You heard Nova—we need to keep going! Don't be stupid!"

Nova was already at the door. "They've locked it!" she cried, her voice echoing up the tunnel. "I'll try to override the software."

Felix and Brady looked back at the crowd of Neurogeists. There were more now, all of them now bearing down on Achilles.

With his paw still pinning the fallen machine, the dog turned to face the onslaught. He barked with such force that the tunnel shook from the impact.

The horde froze, a sea of gray tentacles undulating against the floor.

They waited, neither side moving.

Achilles was so focused on the standoff that he didn't see it coming.

The creature trapped beneath his paw stopped moving and its tentacles fell limply to the floor. The red eye grew brighter, spun faster—and then ejected, striking Achilles with a clank and quickly affixing itself to his torso. Barbed legs grew from the eye and began to drill through Achilles' metal armor.

Sparks of light flashed around Achilles' body; the eye was electrifying him. He crashed to the floor next to the now-lifeless machine and lay on his side. His legs were thrashing in all directions while hair-like threads of lightning arced across his body.

"Achilles!" Nova cried. She was still busy trying to override the door controls with her watch.

"Brady!" Felix called to his brother. "We have to help him!"

Brady stood paralyzed, glancing back and forth between the door and the dog.

Felix could bear the dog's pain no longer. He ran over to him and climbed on top of his body. Reaching down, he grabbed the eye tightly with his right hand and attempted to dislodge it from Achilles' torso. He used his left hand to keep himself from falling over. The eye's grip was solid and wouldn't budge.

Nova realized too late what was about to happen. "Let go, Felix!"

she shouted.

Felix's whole body was shaking from the electricity as he tried to pry the sphere off the dog. Undeterred, he let go of the dog and grabbed the dark eye with his other hand. He leaned back and tugged with all of his weight. He pulled harder and harder.

And then it happened. The eye dislodged from Achilles, sending Felix flying through the air—the eye clutched tightly in his hands. He landed on his back, unconscious, next to Achilles. Brady watched as the eye fell out of Felix's motionless hand and began rolling across the floor searching for its host.

"Felix!" Brady yelled. But just as he began to run toward Felix, the Neurogeists started their advance. He realized the monsters would reach his brother before he could.

Suddenly, Achilles picked himself up off the ground, bent down, and wrapped his teeth firmly around the eye. Then he snapped his jaws shut with a loud crunch. The eye shattered, sending shards of glass and wires flying in all directions.

Achilles turned with bright eyes to face the army of Neurogeists and growled. Immediately, they stopped and moved back a few steps.

The dog then moved over to Felix. He slid his muzzle under the boy, nudged his unmoving body onto his back, and lifted him into the air. In a fluid motion, Achilles' rib cage opened wide and swung upward so that each rib encircled the boy. Interlocking blades of metal unfolded and connected the ribs together, forming a protective cage around Felix.

And then the creatures were upon him, rushing forward as a single mass. One by one they ensnarled the dog with their tentacles until at last he was completely covered by the hideous bots.

Nova finally had the door open; she ran back to Brady, who was still standing there in shock, and grabbed him by the arm. "Brady!" she shouted

Brady didn't move; he just stared back at Felix.

"Brady! Listen to me, please! They're coming for us next!"

Even as she spoke, a swarm of Neurogeists began rising off of Achilles and floating toward Brady and Nova.

Only one word slipped out of Brady's mouth.

"Felix…"

Nova grabbed Brady by the arm and tried to pull him away. He didn't budge.

"Achilles will protect him," Nova pleaded. "But we need to get out of here. There's nothing we can do right now. There's just too many of them. I promise we'll come back for him, but we can't do it without some help."

The machines were so close now that Brady could see his reflection in one of the creature's ink-black eyes.

"This is our last chance," Nova said. "If they catch us, there will be no one left to save your brother. He'll be trapped forever."

Brady finally snapped out of it, just as a Neurogeist raised its tentacle to ensnare him. Together he and Nova sprinted back through the door and into the room where the flame portal still burned brightly. Brady barreled forward through the door of light.

11100110

Brady found himself back in the clearing in the woods, the warm rain striking his face. He felt like his heart would burst through his chest at any second. Quickly he turned around, just in time to see a shadow form on the surface of the gateway. An instant later, Nova burst through, mid-stride, and came to a stop.

She frantically typed at her watch, trying to shut the door before it was too late. Lightning lit the sky.

Brady watched in horror as a metallic tentacle poked through the gateway. "Something's coming! Close it, Nova!"

Nova continued tapping on her wristwatch, and the portal continued its bright, cold burn.

The rest of tentacle burst through. It thrashed wildly about, searching for a victim.

"Hurry!"

At last the portal collapsed with its familiar thunderclap, severing the tentacle from the creature on the other side. The writhing limb fell to the ground, where it continued to twist before going still.

They were safe here, for now.

But...

Brady knew they had to go back for Felix.

They had to go back for Achilles.

And they were going back tonight.

Part Two

> Chapter 10: Nyx's Way

DESPITE THE UNUSUALLY warm weather that night, Brady stood shivering in the forest. His tears mixed with the raindrops that ran down his face, and his hands trembled as thoughts of his brother raced through his head. He tried to fight back the fear that coursed through his veins like wicked venom, threatening to take over at any second. Brady had already lost his father. He wouldn't lose his brother too.

He looked at the detached tentacle still sparking on the ground. Frayed wires and fused metal spilled out from the charred opening where a thin ribbon of smoke curled up toward the sky. The air was filled with the smell of scorched electronics.

Seeing the severed appendage forced him to think about everything Felix had done that night. *Brave Felix*: saving Achilles from the scourge of the horrible eye. That dreadful red glow that would forever haunt him from this night forward. He remembered Felix lying on the ground in the tunnel, unconscious, and he tried to swallow the sour taste of guilt rising in his throat.

It was useless.

Felix had acted with courage while he had been immobilized by fear.

Like a coward.

He should have been the one the Neurogeists had taken away.

How could he have let this happen? He had failed his brother, his family. Brady was tempted to run home, to tell his mom everything, but he knew he would never be able to look her in the eye again unless he got Felix back home safe.

"Brady?" called a voice from behind him. He quickly tried to dry his swollen eyes with his shirtsleeves.

"Brady? Are you okay?"

He turned around and found Nova watching him closely. Nova, the stranger from next door who had managed to turn his entire life upside down.

This was all her doing.

She had convinced him to leave Felix back in the tunnel. And what was he supposed to do now? There was no one else he could turn to for help; there was nothing more he could do by himself. He needed her help.

Nova walked up to him and rested her hand on his shoulder.

"I'm sorry about your brother," she said softly. Her wet hair clung to the sides of her face.

He brushed her hand away, but she persisted.

"We'll get Felix back," she tried to reassure him.

"You don't know that."

"I give you my word that I'll do everything I can. Achilles won't let anything happen to him. He'll give his life to protect your brother after what he did today. Felix was incredibly brave. You should be proud of him!"

Brady tried, unsuccessfully, to suppress the sudden jealousy he felt. It mixed with the hundreds of other emotions that buzzed through his chaotic mind.

And then he snapped.

"Proud of him? I told him not to do it. That was the stupidest thing he's ever done! I saw them take him away, Nova! You and I are safe here while those monsters are carrying him off to who knows where. *This is all your fault!*"

Brady's voice swelled with anger, and he lashed out with the harshest words he could conjure.

"I can't believe we helped you *steal! You're a thief!*"

Brady turned away and stared angrily down at the ground, immediately regretting his choice of words. He didn't truly believe what he was saying, yet here he was, insulting the only person who could help him. He wouldn't blame her if she walked away right now and left him standing here, helpless.

"You're right, Brady. I *am* a thief; and this *is* my fault," Nova said slowly.

"No, I'm sorry, I didn't mean—"

"I made a terrible mistake, and I'm sorry. I never wanted you to get involved in the first place. In fact, I tried my best to scare you and your brother away. But then I miscalculated and got caught. Everything that happened tonight is because of me..."

Nova paused and took a deep breath.

"The truth is, you saved me—and I owe you. *Achilles* owes you. I hope you both can... forgive me."

Brady ran his hand through his short wet hair and thought about the Neurogeists that had swarmed Achilles and Felix like a colony of ants organizing around a morsel of discarded food.

"Right now I just want to figure out how to get my brother back home, if he's even still—" He stopped himself.

"I know he's alive, Brady. Look, believe it or not, Achilles is like a brother to me. I will do everything I can to get them both back safely. I know they're okay. They have to be."

Brady grimaced. "But it's just you and me, Nova. There were hundreds—maybe thousands—of them down there! You saw those things—we don't stand a chance! What *were* those creatures anyway, those things you called Neurogeists?"

Nova hesitated, appearing to consider his question for a minute.

"It's complicated," she finally replied.

"Tell me anyway."

"Okay then. This is going to sound pretty strange, but... In the world I come from, there's a different kind of punishment for those who do wrong. A punishment far worse than you can imagine. The Neurogeists... are a type of prison."

"A prison?"

"A mental prison," she explained. "The Neurogeists start out as nothing more than containers—empty shells that are then filled with the minds of the banished."

"The banished? You mean criminals?"

"That's right, criminals—or anyone else who dares to disagree with..." Her eyes narrowed. "Certain rules."

"But how can you fill a shell with a mind?"

"Not minds like yours and mine. *Digital* minds: the minds of the machines. Their neural nets—sorry, their brains—are forced into the Neurogeist bodies, where new programming overrides their own thoughts with... other directives."

"Directives?" Brady was struggling to keep up, but also afraid to admit it.

"Rules. Rules that strip away personality. Rules that force them to wander aimlessly beneath the earth like packs of rats roaming sewer tunnels. They have no other choice. This is their punishment."

"Beneath the earth? What for?"

"They collect spent mechanical waste, garbage, anything that can be recycled into new bodies, new zombies that can then harvest more and more salvage. They spend their time underground because their programming prevents them from ever seeing the light of day again."

"That sounds awful."

"That's the point. They were designed to be awful. Fortunately for us, they're not the brightest creatures: again, by design. When a mind is transferred into a new Neurogeist body, their neural patterns, their thoughts, are severely limited by the host's logic circuits. Just imagine your brain thinking in slow motion, like running through water. I imagine that's sort of what it's like to be one of them."

Brady turned to face Nova. "If Felix is still... you know... what will they do to him?"

"I'm not exactly sure, but it'll take them awhile to figure out who, or what, he is. Believe it or not, they've never seen a human before today. To them, he's like an alien. Just like they are to you."

"Never seen a human? Why not?"

"Because where I come from... there are none."

Brady couldn't hide the shocked look on his face.

"And there haven't been any for a long time now," Nova continued. "At least, not until recently. That's why it's important that we get to him first. They can't be allowed to figure out what's happened."

Brady looked at her, his face revealing a worry greater than he could handle. He wanted to speak, but the words wouldn't come.

Nova could feel the fear emanating from him. "But don't worry—we'll get him before they have a chance to figure it out."

"Felix must be scared out of his mind. I'm still shaking from what happened earlier, and I'm safe *here*!"

"As bad as it sounds, your brother was unconscious when we left, so he probably won't remember much about this anyway. That is, if we can get to him fast enough. As long as Achilles is alive, he will protect Felix. You saw what he did back there to the Neurogeist that tried to attack us, right? Achilles is not someone to mess with, and he holds a *terrible* grudge."

Brady managed a smile, but it quickly faded when he imagined a pack of the monsters dragging Achilles and his brother away. He shuddered at the thought.

"Where will they take them?" he asked.

"I'm not exactly sure."

"Great! Then how in the world are we supposed to find them?"

"There may be a way. Achilles is equipped with a transponder. If he's able to turn it on, it will send out a signal and we'll be able to see it."

"Okay, so then we just open another door and go back and get him, right?" Brady asked anxiously.

"Unfortunately, we can't travel back the way we came—they'll be expecting us there. We'll have to try something else. But we're wasting time just standing here—we need to get going."

"Where to?" Brady glanced around at the trees towering around him. There was nothing but miles of forest in every direction.

Nova gestured toward the woods. "We have a hangar near the back of the property, almost a mile away from here. There's an aircraft inside that can take us where we need to go—at least, most of the way."

"An aircraft? You've got to be kidding. You know how to fly a plane?"

"It's more like a helicopter, except it has four blades instead of one. You know, sort of like that *toy* you and your brother sent over here to spy on us. Only this one is the real thing."

Brady turned away before Nova could see him blush. He heard her laugh under her breath.

"Anyway, the copter is pretty easy to fly. Its autopilot software does most of the work. You just tell it where to go, and it does the rest. And speaking of flying…"

Nova pushed a few buttons on her watch. Within seconds, her request was answered. Brady heard a deep rhythmic thumping coming from far off in the sky—the flapping of great wings. The sound grew nearer.

Overhead, Brady saw the dark form of an eagle circling in the night air.

Nova waved, and the bird let out an ear-splitting screech. Twin rays of white light poured forth from its eyes and lit up the soggy ground below. They could see the way forward.

"I still sometimes have trouble finding my way in these woods," Nova said. "My friend here will get us to the hangar though. Come on, we need to move quickly."

With the eagle guiding the way, Brady and Nova chased after the light. They fought through tangles of branches and shrubs before reaching a path where the thick underbrush had been cut back. Their pace quickened, mud splashing everywhere as they hurried across the puddle-ridden ground.

The flight of the enormous bird was steady, always keeping the light shining a few feet ahead of them. Nova was moving so fast that Brady struggled to keep up. Unfamiliar with the terrain, his strides were uneven, and he often had to catch himself from tripping and landing face-first on the ground.

He was beginning to think they'd never get there when at last the bird touched down on a knotted bough. It swung its twin beams of light through a clearing of weeds and grass onto a looming structure just ahead.

It was at least two stories tall and just as wide. Steep lines met to form a gabled roof, and the old oak siding was a tarnished mix of faded red with gray where years of weather had stripped the paint away. Some of the boards had rotted, come loose, or were missing altogether.

Brady quickly realized he was looking at a run-down barn, not the "hangar" Nova had mentioned earlier. Any hope he had of finding Felix drained away, and he wondered how anything useful could be inside.

"We're here," Nova called back as she raced toward the entrance. When she reached the front doors, she stopped, looked up to the sky, and waved. The guiding light blinked out, and the bird lifted off the branch and flew into the night. The eagle said goodbye with a final shriek and was gone.

"Cool bird. Is it your pet?" Brady called out breathlessly as he arrived at the foot of the barn. He cradled his side where a cramp was forming.

"It's a she, and *her* name is Nyx," Nova said. "She lives in the forest and thinks for herself, just like Achilles does."

"Sorry. I thought you were controlling her with your watch. My mistake."

"No one controls her," Nova said, annoyed. "I was just asking for her help and telling her where we needed to go."

"Okay, got it." Brady stayed a few feet away to keep Nova from seeing his face turn red. If he hadn't been so worried about Felix, he would have crammed his foot down his throat.

To cover his embarrassment, he walked over to a spot on the side of the barn where a piece of siding had slid down and was dangling by a rusty nail. Squatting down, he peered through the gap.

He saw nothing inside the barn other than a floor of dirt, rocks, and scattered hay. The place was empty.

Nova had promised a hangar, but for some reason they were wasting time at this rotting barn.

"Hey, Nova," Brady said, still peering through the gap, "why are—"

He stopped when he noticed something wrong. Streaks of moonlight lit the floor, shining down from cracks in the ceiling. But tonight, the sky was covered by storm clouds. Brady looked up, then back into the barn. Without the moon, the inside of the barn should have been pitch black.

As Brady bent forward to get a closer look, he suddenly lost his balance. He reached out his hand and caught himself before he hit the ground. He shook his head, embarrassed by his own clumsiness.

Then he saw that his fingers weren't resting on the side of the barn; they were resting on the empty void left by the detached piece of siding. His fingers pressed against thin air.

Brady pushed harder against the invisible support, and the view through the gap distorted into a rainbow of colors that rippled from his fingertips. When he stopped, the colors dissolved away and the view of the floor returned, unaltered.

"Nova? What is this place?"

"I'll explain later," came Nova's voice. "Would you mind giving me a hand with the door?"

Brady picked himself up and walked over to the doors, where Nova was busy unhinging a rusty latch.

"Grab the handle," she instructed. Together they pulled on the latch.

After a minute of heavy straining, the latch jerked backward and the iron shrieked. The old wooden doors groaned as Nova and Brady pulled them apart. Nova propped them open with heavy stones that lay nearby.

Brady stared into the empty barn.

"There's nothing in here," he said.

"Nothing that you can see *yet*..." Nova raised her hand up and pressed it against the air as if she was pantomiming the presence of a pane of glass. A small access panel materialized from the nothingness.

"Our security system," she explained. "Hold on a second."

Nova placed her thumb on the surface of the panel. After a moment, the image of the empty barn vaporized into thin air, leaving two giant metal doors, which slid slowly apart.

Bright light poured out of the barn, forcing Brady to turn away from its intensity. When he finally looked back, Nova was already inside.

Brady stared in amazement at the sleek interior of the building, his mind trying to reconcile the high-tech interior before him with the empty barn he had seen earlier. He walked in and looked around, his brain soaking up the technical marvels like a sponge.

The floor and the walls were made of sleek aluminum with an intricate lattice of trusses and girders providing support. Rows of LEDs lined the cathedral ceiling and bathed the room in white light.

"Did you build all of this?" Brady asked.

"Well, the barn was already here when we moved in. We made a few changes. Like it?"

"Like it? It's incredible!" Brady replied.

Standing near the middle of the room was an aircraft unlike anything Brady had seen: a masterpiece of precision-crafted metal and glass. Four long arms protruded from the corners of the hull, and an individual blade was attached to each mast. The craft's spotless exterior was painted a glossy white, and Brady could see his distorted reflection staring back at him. Situated just above the nose was a wide tinted windshield that extended up and over the roof, allowing the passengers an unobstructed view in almost every direction. As Brady looked on in wonder, his one regret was that Felix was not here to see it with him.

He turned away from the aircraft and surveyed the rest of the room. The walls were peppered with screens that showed surveillance footage from various areas on the property. One screen in particular caught Brady's attention—a view from the camera posted high atop the fence that ran along the perimeter of his yard. He was used to seeing the fence from his back yard; now he realized that he was looking back at his yard from the other side.

From the corner of his eye, he noticed a second screen with an image that was moving quickly. It was a view from high above and appeared to be moving fast. Small rainbow-colored forms slid across the screen as he watched.

Nova noticed where Brady was looking and answered his question before he could ask it. "You're seeing the world through Nyx's eyes. Pretty neat, huh? She can show us what she's seeing—but only when she wants to, of course. Her eyes have thermal cameras that allow her to see at night. The colors you're seeing represent heat coming from the forest."

It was hard for Brady to tell what was what. The ebb and flow of the thermal images was hypnotic and reminded him of his mom's old lava lamp.

Finally he managed to tear his attention away from the screen. "Where did this all come from? I looked through a crack in the wall outside, and I didn't see any of this."

"Oh, that? That's just an illusion. The inside walls are covered with double-sided high-resolution screens. You can't see anything from the outside. On purpose."

"No way! Anyone could tell that this place isn't real," Brady fibbed.

"It fooled you, didn't it?" Nova shot back.

"I guess so," he acknowledged. "But why go through so much trouble?"

"Security. We aren't exactly safe here—especially given who my father—" Nova stopped suddenly. She realized she had said too much.

Brady nodded and let the matter drop. Clearly there was something there that she didn't want to talk about.

Nova stepped over to a tall pile of crates in the corner of the barn. They were the exact same crates he had seen twice before: first being carried on Achilles' back, and then in the storeroom on the other side of the portal.

"Can you come give me a hand with these?" Nova called out.

Brady walked over and they lifted the crate together. He tried not to buckle under the weight and wondered just how strong Achilles must be in order to carry an entire stack of these like it was nothing. He could barely handle half of one without falling over.

"What *is* this thing?" he asked, his voice straining under the pressure.

Nova let go with one hand and opened the rear hatch of the craft. Brady grunted as he struggled to take up the slack. Together they carefully slid the steel box into the back of the vehicle.

"It's an Evercell," Nova said.

"Ever-what?"

"Evercell. It's a type of battery," Nova replied, tying the crate down with some cables. She cinched a knot tightly and patted the top of the box.

"All done. Just one more thing and then we can get out of here."

She whistled loudly. A few seconds later, something sped in through the doors and buzzed around the hangar. Brady recognized the sound at once.

The hummingbird.

He thought back to the creature's alarm blaring at full pitch and the dizzying array of flashing lights. His head hurt just thinking about it.

"Oh no. Not this thing again." Brady shook his head and backed away from the vehicle. "*That. Bird. Is. Totally. Insane.*"

The creature began to circle around his head. He took another step back and tripped over a stray crate.

"Cool it—you're going to upset him, Brady!" Nova said sharply, while Brady picked himself up off the floor.

Then her pitch grew softer and sweeter. "It's okay, he won't hurt you." She spoke to the buzzing air in front of her. The creature dashed back and forth between Nova and Brady before stopping in front of Nova.

"So let's see. If I remember correctly, you guys have actually met once before." Nova smiled. "Thorn, meet Brady. Brady, Thorn."

"Nice to meet you, Thorn," Brady said with a slight wave of his hand. "I, um, I'm sorry about what I said earlier."

Thorn continued to bob up and down in front of Nova. She held her arm out, and the creature dropped into the palm of her hand and settled down to rest.

Nova stroked the bird's miniature head with her fingers. It made several soft chirps before its bright blue eyes extinguished, allowing the dark gems to show through. The wings gradually stopped fluttering and the tail folded inward.

The bird grew still.

"I'll wake you up if I need you. Sleep well, Thorn."

Nova carefully placed Thorn in the back of the rotorcraft and closed the hatch.

"Okay, Brady, time for us to go." She moved around to the driver's side of the craft. The gull-wing door swung up and she disappeared inside. "You can ride shotgun."

The passenger side door whooshed open, and Brady climbed apprehensively into the empty bucket seat. Once inside, the doors glided automatically into place, locking with a tight seal.

The interior of the cabin was lit only by the soft amber glow of the dashboard. Nova was already busy setting various controls on the wide panel of glass in front of her. It was calm and quiet inside, apart from the faint hum of the instrumentation.

"You *have* flown this thing before—right?" Brady frowned as he searched for the nearest escape exit.

"Maybe once or twice…" She smiled. "We had to get it here somehow, right? I know what I'm doing. Try to relax."

All of this was cold comfort for Brady.

"So, how are you going to get us to Felix anyway? You said they'll be waiting for us."

"And they will be. That's why we're going in a different way. The Neurogeists mostly stick to the underground tunnels—so we'll just have to go over them." Nova continued to adjust the controls. "We'll avoid them as long as we can, although I suspect we'll eventually have to go underground." The headlights flashed on with a push of a button. "Ready?" Nova asked.

"Sure…" Brady tried to play off his anxiety. He felt his seat begin to vibrate softly as the four rotors spun up. The craft lifted gently off the ground and came to rest in the air.

"Nova?"

"Yes."

"Before we go… I—"

"What is it?"

Brady paused. He couldn't let it go.

"I—well… I was thinking about what you said when we were back in the tunnel. About how they, I mean the Neurogeists, would, you know, be upset because you were stealing from them. Why are you stealing?"

He paused.

"I need to know."

Nova looked at him for a second, then turned away and looked out the window. "Like I said before, it's not what you think. I'm only taking what—what my family needs to survive. I promise you. That's all I can say about it. Are you okay with that?"

Brady decided it was best not to push harder, for now at least.

"I guess," he replied, unsurely.

"Great. Now let's get out of here."

Nova guided the craft slowly forward through the hangar doors and out into the stormy night. Wipers kicked in automatically as rain sloshed across the windshield. Brady looked back and saw the twin metal doors slide together, and then the ghostly mirage of the empty barn reappeared in their place.

The aircraft glided to a stop in the clearing by the barn. The long blades of grass were forced to the ground by the gusts of air from the rotors. Dense evergreens blocked the way forward.

"How are we going to get back to the blue door?" Brady asked. "There's no way we can fly this thing through the trees."

"No, we can't go through the forest," Nova replied. "But lucky for us we don't need to. It's a good thing the barn is where it is. There are only a few ways into the place where we're headed. One of them is actually pretty close to here."

"That happened by chance?" Brady asked.

"Not really by chance..." Nova smiled. "Besides, the other door was too small. We'll just open a new portal big enough for us to travel through. It's going to take more power, though. A lot more."

"Ah, that's why we brought the Evercell along!" Brady said.

"Exactly. There's a quantum amplifier in the back as well. We can tie them together to create a door large enough for us to go through. Hopefully we'll have enough energy to keep the tunnel open until we make it back. I suppose we'll find out soon enough."

Nova opened the door and jumped out. At the back of the rotorcraft, she opened the hatch, retrieved the amplifier, and set it on the ground. Then she slid the Evercell all the way out until it fell to the ground with a thud.

"Everything okay back there?" Brady called out as he stared out the rear hatch. The heavy rain sluiced over the glass door.

"Yes. I'm going to connect my watch to the amplifier. By itself, it has enough energy to open the portal we traveled through earlier. It won't be enough now though, so we need something much stronger."

As Nova typed a sequence into her watch, the amplifier began to glow—softly at first, then brighter. When she was finished, she connected a wire to the battery lodged in the mud. She then braced herself against the back of the vehicle.

"I started the countdown—you might want to cover your ears for this. In five, four..."

Brady covered his ears with his hands.

"Three... two... one..."

A shockwave rocked the aircraft, knocking Brady out of his seat and onto the floor. He watched through the windshield as the blinding light tore through the rippling air. The door quickly grew until it was more than wide enough for them to pass through safely.

"Thanks for the heads-up!" Brady shouted, picking himself up and climbing back into the passenger seat.

Nova shut the hatch and climbed back into the driver's seat.

"Like I said, I'm not sure how long the battery can hold this open, so we shouldn't waste any time. Are you ready?"

The craft moved forward toward the portal.

They were on their way back.

> Chapter 11: Unwilling Passengers

SOMEWHERE ON THE OTHER SIDE of the portal, deep underground, the boy opened his eyes to a haze of shiny bronze just inches in front of his face. *I must be dreaming*, he thought. For a brief moment, the boy smiled to himself. His mind was still in a far-off place, a dream world decorated with the familiar trappings of his own room. He imagined hearing his brother and his mom talking downstairs in the kitchen, the smell of pancakes wafting up through the rafters and into his room.

Then the vision evaporated and the voices slipped away. His eyes came into focus, and he could see the scratches, dents, and seams in the metal that wrapped him like a cocoon.

Felix was lying on his side with his legs bunched up to his chest. He tried to stretch out, to roll over, but found no room to spare. He was stuck here for the time being.

Where am I?

Memories rushed into his mind. Brady, Nova, the portal. The Neurogeists, and...

Achilles. Where is Achilles?

Somehow Felix was still alive. He wasn't sure about everyone else though. He wondered if he had been captured. It certainly seemed like it.

The steel cage shook suddenly, and he was jolted against its side.

His head pounded as he lay there, disoriented. After several tries, he just managed to squeeze his hand around to the back of his head. *Ouch!* He felt a large welt, tender to the touch.

He looked around the metal coffin and started to breathe faster. Then Felix did something he had never done before. He began to panic.

There was a rhythmic motion below him. The cage that held him would move for a second, stop, and then move again. An unseen force was pulling him forward. From outside he heard the whooshing sound of air around him and the low haunting whale-like bellows of the electric zombies.

The Neurogeists are nearby.

Where were they taking him?

As the seconds passed, he felt his head begin to swell. The throbbing pain was becoming unbearable. His vision began to blur until the seams in the cocoon disappeared, leaving him floating in a foggy gray sky.

He was losing consciousness again, grasping desperately for something to anchor to, but it was useless. The last thing he remembered was sliding down to the end of the cage as he was pulled upward on an incline, higher and higher. Felix closed his eyes and drifted slowly into peaceful unconsciousness.

10000110

Achilles lay on his side, his legs bound together by ghastly tendrils. He slid across the floor inch by inch as the Neurogeists dragged him onward through the pitch-black tunnel. The dog remained aware, but barely. He had diverted most of his power to protecting Felix. Any energy that remained was used to keep his backup systems active. Achilles even dimmed his eyes in order to maintain power reserves in case of an emergency.

A small group of Neurogeists drifted about languidly in front of

Achilles, pulling the beast and boy slowly across the tunnel terrain. Achilles had lost the fight. There had been too many of them. At first he had been able to swat them back as they advanced, but more and more Neurogeists had joined in, and they had managed to wear him down until, finally, he fell.

Afterward, most of the crowd had dissipated back into the recesses of the tunnel, leaving only a few behind to tend to their fallen prey. The machines were cautious at first, poking and prodding the listless dog with the end of their tentacles. Pent-up electrostatic energy caused firecracker-like pops to ring out as the tentacles discharged on contact. Finally convinced of their victory, the creatures slithered around the animal and prepared him for the journey to come. Now they moved with slow-witted determination toward an area far underground where few dared to venture.

A lumbering train roared into the station where hundreds of Neurogeists were gathering, carrying their scrap and salvage behind them like trophies. Its arrival was announced with a deep, low, foghorn-like sound that reverberated for miles through the tunnels. It groaned to a stop, then sat waiting for the frothing horde of undead machines and their prized collections to come aboard.

Over time, the locomotive's exterior had developed a patina of rust and grime, a terrifying tapestry of orange, brown, gray, and green textures. Pieces of scrap had been welded to the sides where holes had rusted through the exterior frame. The front was flat with no lights and no windows to lend it character except for a double-sided plow of sheet metal that formed a sharp V. Instead of snow, the train pushed scrap to the side as it traveled. The engine stood between two gigantic parallel rails that disappeared down the length of the dark tunnel.

Suddenly the ghastly machines began to part to make room for something. A group of new Neurogeists had entered through an antechamber off to the side of the room, and the new arrivals were pulling something different behind them—something that demanded respect from the others.

A large metal hound.

The terrible melody of the Neurogeists echoed off the metal walls as they spoke to one another and floated up to the side of the train with their victims in tow. When the doors on the rail cars grinded open and ramps extended down to the tunnel floor, the scavengers floated up and onto the train. The ramps rescinded back into the train and the doors closed. Then this freighter of anguish lurched forward, continuing on its journey deeper into the underworld.

> Chapter 12: Mesh Brain

THE ROTOCRAFT DRIFTED quietly through the portal on powerful torrents of air. Nova and Brady found themselves inside a large, dimly lit room with tall concrete dividers that stretched lengthwise like towering aisles in an oversized warehouse. Stacks of Evercells covered the shelves and reached high into the shadows that canvased the ceiling.

Brady craned his neck around his seat and peered out at the portal through the rear windshield. Behind the door of cold fire, the concrete aisles receded into the distance. He struggled to comprehend the number of cells stored here. Like the stars, they were far too numerous to count.

As the rotorcraft hovered in place, Brady broke the silence, his face still poking over the top of the passenger's seat.

"There must be enough batteries in here to last you a lifetime. For, um, whatever you need them for."

"Unfortunately, they're all empty," Nova replied softly, more to herself than to Brady.

"So, where are we?" Brady asked, taking in the sights around him. Through the aisles he could see mechanical arms pivoting and swinging in synchronized motions. They were grabbing the cells and loading them onto conveyer belts that disappeared into gaps in the far walls. Attached to the shelves were steel rails that allowed the arms to slide forward and backward through the rows.

"We're in an old storage room that connects to the rest of the energy farm."

"That's what this place is? An energy farm?"

"Yes. One of hundreds, actually."

"Hundreds? Seriously? What could possibly require that much power?"

Nova paused. "Machines."

Brady's eyebrows perked up and he turned back around in his chair. Nova had his attention now.

"Some of the machines, computers here, if you want to call them that, are highly evolved; they operate on an entirely different plane of existence. Take the fastest supercomputers in your world, and imagine them about a million times more powerful. It takes an enormous amount of energy just to keep them alive. My father told me once that all the fossil fuels in your Earth would run out in a week at the rate energy is used up here."

"Keep them... alive? What kind of energy do they use?" Brady mumbled, watching the conveyer belts carry cell after cell out of the room.

"Fusion and solar power. There's a fusion reactor not too far from here. Think of it as a small sun burning inside a box. And this place is surrounded by fields of solar cells that capture energy from the sun with near perfect efficiency. Nothing is wasted."

"But generating the energy is only half the problem. The computers needed a place to store it, so a new type of battery was created that could hold enough energy to power an entire city for a month: the Evercell."

Nova gestured around the room with a wave of her hand. "All of these are just sitting here waiting to be charged up."

Brady's thought went to Felix and Achilles. "Are we safe in here? What about the Neurogeists? They'll be looking for us now."

"I don't think so. Remember, they spend most of their time moving about in the tunnels beneath us. We opened the portal higher up this time. We're still pretty close to the spot where I was captured earlier tonight." Nova glanced down through the transparent floor of the vehicle. "Actually, we're right on top of it."

Just the thought of the awful creatures stirring beneath him caused more terrible memories to flood into Brady's mind, and he curled up in his seat.

"But why bring us back to this place at all?" he asked. "Why not bring up the portal so that it takes us somewhere outside? It seems like it would be a lot easier."

"Sure, until something discovers the portal floating out in the open and sends thousands of machines streaming back into your world. I needed an area large enough to hide the gateway while it's open. This room is fully automated, and I don't think anything ever comes in here, so the portal should be safe while we're here. At least for a little while."

"Okay, that makes sense, I guess. But why do you have to keep it open? Why not just close down the portal and reopen it when we're ready to go home?"

"It's not that simple. When a door opens, it leaves a quantum signature behind on the side where it was created. Sort of like a trail of breadcrumbs between universes. The people in your world aren't advanced enough to pick it up—yet—but it's a different story here. They would find it, and then…"

Brady put the pieces together. "You're saying if we open a new portal here, the bots would see the signature. They'd be able to figure out where we came from and follow us home."

"Exactly. We might as well just leave them a map."

"So no one here knows about our world? Then how did *you* find us?"

"It took my father years. He visited world after world until he found one that was suitable. There were equations that helped, but still…"

"Your father sounds like a genius."

Nova suddenly grew tense. "Yes, you could say that. Anyway, we should get going."

The headlights on the rotorcraft shined down the dark aisles. The paths between the shelves were narrow, not nearly wide enough for the aircraft to fit through.

"How are we going to get out of here?" Brady asked. "It doesn't look like there's room to go anywhere."

Nova dragged a wireframe map around the control panel and pressed a dot on the screen. The spot lit up as her finger made contact. "Don't worry; this thing has a few tricks up its sleeves. Hold on tight though, this is going to feel pretty snug."

Two belts extended down from the roof of the vehicle, crossed over Brady's chest, and clicked in place near his waist. He had to suck in his stomach to avoid them pressing too hard into his skin.

"Okay, that should help. Hold on. This will feel a little weird."

The left rotors spun faster and faster until that side of the craft began to lift up. When they were completely sideways, the left blades stopped moving, leaving the right rotors supporting the full weight of the vessel.

The craft moved vertically along the aisles. Fortunately, the belts held Brady into his seat as gravity tried desperately to pull him out. He watched through the glass roof as they passed stack after stack of Evercells. It felt as though the craft might tip over at any time.

At last the craft cleared the aisles and came to rest in front of two towering steel doors. The left rotors reengaged, and the craft returned to its normal orientation. Brady glanced back; the portal had vanished somewhere in the lattice of aisles behind them.

"Let's just hope we don't have to do that again in a hurry," Nova joked, shifting her focus back to the controls. Her fingers moved nimbly across the virtual buttons.

"Before I open the doors..." she said.

"Yes?"

"Just so you don't get freaked out... We won't be alone anymore when they open."

Brady was offended by the accusation. "Freaked out? I don't—I mean—I won't get freaked out!" His voice grew softer. "But... what exactly do you mean by *we won't be alone?*"

"Well, there are the Rariis, for one."

"Rariis? They sound like some type of car."

"Actually, they are. Sort of, if cars could fly, I guess. The Rariis are cargo bots. They're wired to do the heavy lifting for everyone else in this world. They operate in colonies, sort of like worker bees. It's strange, they even sort of look like bees. You'll never see one by itself. Anyway, Rariis kind of have two minds. Sometimes they think for themselves, and other times they share their minds with each other, like when they need to problem solve. Bad things happen if they get too far away from one another."

"Bad things? Seriously? Like what?"

"I don't know. I've never seen it happen."

"But why are they here?"

"They're here to pick up their cargo so they can move on to their next job. Normally they'll leave other bots alone, but they can get pretty nasty if they feel threatened. Have you ever thrown a rock at a hornet's nest?"

Brady imagined being engulfed by a buzzing swarm of bees. It was not a thought that appealed to him in the slightest. "That, um—sounds pretty awful actually. So, where are these things?"

"Right on the other side of the door."

Brady's eyes locked on to the doors, and he tried to remain calm. "How are we supposed to get around them if they're sitting right there? From what I can tell, there's only one way out of here, and it's *right* through that door!"

"We're not going to go around them."

"Huh?"

"We're going to travel *with* them. These doors open into a hall-way that will take us straight to the atrium. From there we go up and out. Then we can try to lock onto Achilles' signal."

"That sounds like a terrible plan. I can't imagine we look anything like these Rariis. They'll spot us as soon as the doors open."

"Fortunately for us, looks don't matter. At least, they won't for a while. The Rariis rely on sound to echolocate, and they communicate using a wireless peer-to-peer protocol."

Nova saw the confusion on Brady's face.

"Sorry. What I mean is, Rariis that are nearby each other send signals over the air to tell each other what they're thinking. They know how to work together to figure out who goes where and when. That way they can figure out the best route for everyone. It's actually kind of cool when you see them together."

"If you say so. But how does that help us?"

"The Rariis use a pretty simple protocol to communicate with each other. It's basic enough that the AI unit on this craft can figure it out and mimic it. We'll fit right in with their flight pattern, so we shouldn't draw too much attention to ourselves. The only problem is that they're constantly evolving their protocols—so the AI will only be able to keep up with it for a few minutes. Let's just hope this trick works long enough for us to get out of the building. Are you ready?"

Brady nodded. "Sounds pretty complicated, but what other choice do we have?"

"I'm going to shut off the lights in case any of the Rariis have their visual sensors enabled. It shouldn't be a problem, but it never hurts to be on the safe side. Same thing goes with the acoustic sen-sors, which are pin-drop sensitive. Fortunately the craft has sound cancelers—but still, try to keep quiet. Okay, here we go—cross your fingers."

Nova pushed a final button and the headlights slowly extinguished. The room went completely dark except for the faint glow of the controls.

"Opening the doors," Nova whispered.

A few seconds later, the doors began to grind open, revealing a dimly lit hallway beyond. A continuous stream of floating machines zipped through the passageway.

For the most part, the Rariis looked similar to one another, although there were subtle variances in size and shape. They were charcoal gray with a smooth concave underside that had a long fin protruding downward toward the rear. The tops of the chassis were flat like a tray, and most of the Rariis had several Evercells stacked on top. A single rectangular light glided back and forth around the perimeter of each creature, and they had large, claw-like arms on opposing sides.

Brady couldn't help but cringe each time one of the Rariis passed by. As far as he was concerned, their indifference to the craft made them all the more intimidating.

The stream of bots gradually slowed and stopped, holding in place on the other side of the doors. The Rariis left a wide gap in which Brady and Nova could take their proper place in the line.

Slowly the craft moved into the hallway, did a ninety-degree turn, and sandwiched itself in the gap between the bots. There was a Rariis only a few feet in front of them and one immediately behind them. Brady looked out the side window just in time to see the doors closing on the storage room they had come from. He knew there was no turning back now.

It scared him to be so close to the machines. The shiny metal claws glistened in the low light of the tunnel. Brady almost jumped out of his seat when one of the claws twitched slightly.

Nova saw his movement and smiled. "It's normal, Brady—just a fasciculation in its neural net. Nothing to worry about."

Easier said than done, Brady thought as he held his breath. They were sitting ducks. If something happened now, they were trapped.

The seconds passed slowly while the rotorcraft hovered in place. Brady's anxiety grew. He wondered why they weren't moving. Had they been detected? Nova was watching something scroll by on the controls. She looked up at him and made an okay sign with her fingers.

After what seemed like an eternity, the stream of bots finally resumed their advance like cars on a roller coaster. The rotorcraft propelled itself down the long, narrow tunnel, moving slowly at first, but gradually accelerating in order to keep pace with the Rariis.

Brady turned and looked out of the rear window. There were hundreds of bots lined up behind them now, all heading toward the same destination. He felt the walls closing in on him.

They continued on for a minute, passing countless doors on either side, no doubt concealing more storage rooms like the one they had come from. There was one door, however, that was considerably larger than the others.

"That's the way to the fusion reactor," Nova said.

Soon the tunnel opened onto a dome-shaped atrium. It was enormous—easily the largest room Brady had ever seen. A spiral of lights twisted their way around the ceiling toward a broad hole in the center that opened to the night sky. Thousands of Rariis flowed in and out of the opening, weaving tightly between each other.

More bots poured in through other doorways along the circular wall, then funneled into streams that led to the center.

"This is unbelievable," Brady whispered, watching the swarm of Rariis entering and leaving. The bots that were leaving were carrying cells, while the ones entering had empty cargo beds. "Are they all talking to each other?"

Nova nodded. "They're built with short-range transmitters, so they can only talk to other Rariis that are nearby. Those Rariis will then relay the message to the next Rariis, and so on. That way they can create a mesh brain that can span great distances."

"But why share a mind?"

"For lots of reasons. You see how all of them are flying around without crashing into one another?"

Brady nodded.

"Their movement is coordinated. All of their thoughts are shared with everyone else. Imagine if you could be in hundreds of different places at the same time. That's probably what it would be like."

Brady had a hard time wrapping his head around that one.

The line continued moving toward the center of the room. When the rotorcraft was directly under the opening, they began their ascent.

But it was a rocky climb to the top. The craft twisted, turned, rose and fell, its flight system doing overtime trying to match the flight patterns of the other Rariis. They were getting close to the exit when Nova began to look nervous.

"Everything okay?"

Nova pointed down.

Brady looked down through his window. The tributaries of bots had broken formation and spread across the floor. When he looked back up, he saw that the bots ahead of them had reversed course— they were now flying back toward their craft. Soon they were enshrouded in a fog of buzzing machines.

"They've found an intruder," Nova said. "There's no use pretending anymore. Hold on—this is going to be close."

Nova increased the throttle, and the craft rocketed upward so quickly Brady was forced into his seat. He could no longer see the ground through the swarm. The bots were filling the atrium and coming straight for them.

"You have a backup plan, right?" Brady asked. A Rariis struck the roof like a colossal ball of hail. The glass held.

"Sort of. The Rariis have to be close together in order for them to communicate with each other. If we can outrun most of them, anyone left should turn around when they lose contact with the others."

Suddenly the craft shook hard; something had crashed into it from the side. The impact forced the craft to sway, and Brady steadied himself against the side door. He clenched his jaw and held on for dear life.

The exit was getting closer. Most of the bots were loaded down by their cargo and couldn't match the craft's speed. But those that were able to keep up continued to swarm angrily around them. Every second or so one would hurl itself at the craft, but the craft was able to dodge most of their attempts.

After a few more seconds they were out. They continued to climb, higher and higher into the night sky. The Rariis drifted about like golden fireflies, and for a second, there was calm.

It was mesmerizing.

When Brady looked down again he was amazed by what he saw. The building they had just left stretched for miles in every direction. The lights of the Rariis below came and went at various locations near the base of the building. There were fields of solar panels that blanketed the ground beyond the complex.

The craft continued to rise until it pierced through a thin layer of clouds. There were only a handful of Rariis flying this high, although more and more continued to burst through the fluffy white blanket in pursuit of them.

Nova slid her fingers on the control panel, and the craft jerked forward in response, speeding off. The dozen or so remaining Rariis had come together into a spinning ring formation that advanced toward them. The rotorcraft was moving forward at top speed, but was still managing to lose ground.

"We can't outrun them," Nova said. "They're going to catch up to us soon."

"And then what?" Brady asked, his eyes focused on the Rariis.

"I have an idea, but we need to let them get close enough to us first."

"Close enough? Are you crazy? How do you know it will work?"

"I don't have time to explain. I'm not sure it'll work, but I don't have a better idea."

With a swipe of her fingers, the craft abruptly came to a stop. She pushed a few more buttons just as the ring of Rariis began to encircle them. The ring, wide at first, began to contract inward. The rotorcraft was almost within reach of their shiny claws.

"Why are we just sitting here?" Brady asked.

"Just wait."

As the Rariis spun, their rotation grew more and more unsteady—and then the circle started to widen once again. It continued to grow and grow until it seemed as though the Rariis could no longer hold the formation. One by one they peeled off and dipped back down below the clouds in retreat.

As the Rariis streamed away, a thud from outside caused the craft to wobble back and forth.

"What was that?" Nova asked.

They both looked out their windows but saw nothing—they were alone.

"What did you do?" Brady asked.

"I created a field that blocked their communication. Without being able to talk to one another, they had to turn back."

"That was too close."

"No kidding. We're high enough now that I should be able to pick up Achilles' signal from below. Felix will be with him—wherever they are."

Nova pressed a button on her watch and a holographic heads-up display materialized in front of them.

"It'll take a few seconds to lock on."

They waited together while a beacon blossomed on the display and began to pulse. Finally, the beacon glided over to a new location and a map materialized beneath it.

Nova frowned.

'What's wrong?" Brady asked.

Nova just stared down at the screen.

"What is it?" Brady demanded.

"The signal. It starts here," she pointed to their current location and traced an arc with her fingertip, "and stops here."

"What do you mean, stops here?"

"I mean—there is no more signal. They must be too far underground for the transponder to work."

"So what do we do then?"

"We head toward the last place we saw the signal."

"And what if we don't find them there?"

"We'll find them, Brady. Please, try to be optimistic."

The rotorcraft picked up speed toward their new destination. As Brady looked out the window, he couldn't help but feel small and insignificant. The light of the moon looked unearthly as it reflected across the icy clouds.

Brady thought about what Nova had said. It was hard to be optimistic given the circumstances—and she still hadn't answered his question. But he would probe until he had his answers, especially since he and his brother had seemingly risked their lives to help her—and look what that had gotten them. Now seemed like as good of a time as any.

"You still never answered my question about the Evercells. What do you need them for? You have to go to a ton of trouble to get them. And you actually got caught tonight! So tell me, what is so important that you're willing to risk everything for them?"

For the first time, Nova paused and seriously considered the question. "I—my family, that is… we're different…"

Now he was getting somewhere.

She turned to look at him.

"We—"

Nova stopped, frowning.

"Sorry, what? Did I say something wrong?" Brady asked.

Nova's attention was focused on the window behind Brady. "There's something glowing near one of the rotors," she said. A look of recognition crossed her face, but it was too late. "It's one of the Rariis!" she yelled.

Brady turned around just in time to see the explosion.

> Chapter 13: The Valley and the Lake

FRAGMENTED REMAINS of the Rariis streamed down through the clouds, piece by smoldering piece, leaving wispy trails of smoke that quickly dissipated. The rotorcraft pitched steeply to one side before finally leveling off. They had managed to escape —somehow.

"Ugh. What the heck was that?" Brady mumbled, the words barely escaping his mouth. The tips of his fingers massaged deeply into his forehead and he tried to relieve the pressure that swelled within his skull. His vision was blurry and doubled.

"I don't believe it: a Rariis must have stowed away on one of the engines during our escape. I bet it hid under the wing." Nova studied the craft's diagnostics log looking for signs of damage.

"Okay, but why did it explode then?"

"I don't know. That's the part I don't understand…"

Something caught Brady's attention from outside the window. He glanced out to investigate and saw the rear turbine engulfed in flame, the smoke casting a gray haze over the stars. His head grew heavy and he began to wobble in his seat like a top ready to fall.

"I didn't think it was possible for this day to get any worse!"

"What is it now?" asked Nova.

"*THE WING IS ON FIRE!*" His hand instinctively shot out and clutched the side door handle. The turbulence was starting to get to him, and he fought back a wave of nausea rising from the pit of his stomach.

He couldn't figure out how Nova managed to keep calm through all of the commotion. Wasn't she terrified? But her attention remained focused on the control panel in front of her.

"It will be okay," was all she said.

The flames eventually burned out as the craft sped unsteadily forward across the night sky. They were just beginning to catch their breath when a hairline fracture appeared near the end of the wing. The damage went unnoticed for a short time before the pressure from the airflow caused the crack to widen.

Brady heard the sudden groan of the metal as the wing began to tear and rip apart. He looked back out the window just in time to see a volcano of sparks erupt from the ruptured surface. The engine broke free and spun off like a meteor burning up in the atmosphere. With it went any hope of making it to his brother alive. *This is the end,* he thought.

The craft shook violently. A few seconds later, an alarm began to blare at a deafening volume while the interior lights flashed on and off at a fever pitch. His senses were overloaded, his brain shutting down.

"We have to find somewhere to land!" Nova shouted, her voice barely audible over the screeching of the alarm. Her quiet sense of calm had been replaced with a steely determination. She quickly pulled up a map of their current location and enlarged an area in the upper corner of the screen. "There!" she said, pointing down at a vaporous image floating between two virtual mountains. Brady tried to look down, but had to turn away when he saw the topographic lines weaving back and forth like a plucked guitar string.

"It looks like there's a clearing in a valley between the mountains just a few miles ahead. That's probably our best bet." Brady managed a groan and held on to his stomach.

The craft pitched to the side again, and Nova struggled to hold on to her seat. "We can glide most of the way there and hopefully avoid the trees on the way down," she said. She reached up and pushed a button, and the seat belt harness descended from the ceiling and pulled them securely into their seats.

They were losing altitude quickly. Droplets of vapor condensed into beads and rolled off the windshield as they plowed down through the clouds. *I'm not going to make it*, Brady repeated to himself—a macabre mantra that helped pass these few remaining moments. He thought of his brother trapped in this alternate reality, forever alone in his metal prison with the haunted Neurogeists.

Somehow he was still the lucky one in all of this.

The earth waited ominously beneath the cloud cover. There were no lights to guide them in, and he had trouble separating land from sky, up from down. He shut his eyes tightly and tried to tune out the alarm. His life passed before him, time slowed to a crawl. He imagined what it would be like to fall forever, to pass straight through the earth and just continue on through space.

It felt like an eternity had passed when Nova finally spoke.

"We're almost there, Brady—just a bit longer—you're doing great. Just try to hold on. I can see the trees up ahead!"

The ground was coming up fast when his eyes snapped open. The rotorcraft's headlights shone down on the forest that passed underneath them. As they grew closer, the light broke through the thick canopy of needles and illuminated the rushing earth. Just when he thought they would be impaled by the jagged treetops, the forest broke and gave way to a vast lake that spread out before them, a shimmering pool of hope in the face of despair.

At the last second before impact, Nova pulled the nose of the vehicle upward. They splashed down and skipped forward across the surface of the lake. Water and foam sprayed in all directions as they bounced choppily forward, the seat harness the only thing keeping them from going headfirst through the windshield. Finally the craft skidded to a stop on a broad sweep of dirt shore. Cattails and grass reeds covered the windshield, which had shattered into an intricate web of broken glass.

But they were still alive, somehow.

The water lapped gently around the craft as they sat in stunned silence.

"Are you okay?" Nova finally asked, pushing the hair out of her face and back around her ears.

"I'm just a little rattled," Brady responded. He tried to put himself back together mentally and the words came out slowly. "But I think I'm all right." He paused. "Nice flying, by the way…"

Brady felt his stomach ball into a knot, and covered his mouth with his hand.

"You're completely green!"

"I—I'm just—happy to be alive. It's not every day I get a chance to cheat death—or something like that." His eyes remained fixed out the side window. He watched steam rise from the severed edge of the wing, where the water cooled the burns. "Just, um, give me a second to catch my breath."

Nova nodded and released the seat harnesses. They both took a deep breath and exhaled now that the excitement had passed. Brady clasped his hands around his neck and leaned forward so that his head rested on his knees. The cabin lights continued to flash, but the alarm had thankfully gone silent.

A minute later he picked himself up and shook his head. "Now what?"

"I really don't know."

For the first time, he could see worry in Nova's eyes. She noticed his reaction and turned away.

"Listen Brady," she said, her reflection gazing back from the glass. "I've said this before, but I'm sorry you and Felix are caught up in this. If I hadn't messed up so badly and gotten caught earlier, none of this would have happened. Everyone would be safe and sound at home where they belong. I should never have fallen for such a stupid trap. And now we're stuck here, without any way to get them—and us—back home."

Nova wiped tears away with her shirtsleeve and turned back to face him. She looked deep into Brady's eyes, her stare burning with a fierce resolve.

Brady felt a new sense of hopelessness and tried to hold back his own sadness. He was just going to have to fake it. "We can't give up on them," he said with feigned reassurance. "We'll figure something out."

His words seemed to do the trick: Nova nodded in agreement and collected herself. "Right. Whatever we do will be better than just sitting in here doing nothing. I'm going to take a look at the wing. Come on—let's get out of here."

She released the driver's door, jumped out of the craft into the shallow water, and made her way over to the smoldering wing. She did her best to hide her dismay as she surveyed the damage: it was beyond repair. Brady took a few more seconds to compose himself before opening his door and climbing out. His shoes filled with water.

He laughed.

In spite of everything that had happened, Brady couldn't help but be overwhelmed by the beauty of the land. The majestic mountains towered around them like a granite shield, keeping the evil forces at bay. It was quiet outside except for the symphony of frogs and crickets that continued to sing in spite of Brady and Nova's unplanned arrival.

As he looked around, he was struck by a sudden recognition. He *knew* this place. Somehow he had been here before. But that was impossible.

And then he remembered it: the fishing trip with his dad and Felix when he was younger.

This place was almost exactly how he remembered it. But that couldn't be. He was here with Nova in a different world, maybe even a different universe, with a different set of rules.

It had to be more than just cosmic indifference that had brought them here, to this specific place, tonight.

"This lake…" He turned to face the water. "I know this sounds weird, but I actually remember this place. Felix and I came here with our father, on a fishing trip, when I was much younger."

Brady picked a smooth stone off the ground and rolled it through his fingers. He remembered sitting in the canoe not too far from where he stood now. He half expected to see his brother and father floating in the boat and laughing together as he looked out.

Nova stopped what she was doing and looked up from the damaged wing. "It may have been a place just like it, but it wasn't *this* lake."

"How do you know? It looks exactly the same. I'm sure of it."

"Because this isn't your world. Things are different here."

"Then how do you explain the fact that I recognize it?"

"There are an infinite number of worlds just like this. You've seen two of them now—yours and mine. The portal we went through— it's a kind of quantum door. It allows us to step across the multiverse."

"You mean, through different dimensions?"

"No, different *realities*."

"You mean the stuff that Ms. Cooper and Felix were talking about the other day… That was actually true? You've got to be kidding."

"It's no joke. Look around. Your brother was correct."

Brady considered the absurdity of her answer and cast the stone into the lake. He watched the ripples widen and fade as they neared the shore. Felix had mentioned another world where they were still with their father. Maybe one existed after all. He was comforted by the thought.

"You know, with all the robots and stuff—and especially the no humans part—this isn't what I expected your world to look like."

"What do you mean?" Nova said, walking over and sitting on the ground by the water. "You were expecting some kind of dark-skied, apocalyptic world where the sun no longer shines and the robots fly around exterminating humanity?"

Brady laughed and sat down next to her.

"No, that's not what I meant." He shook his head. "I guess I thought things would be—different from our world: fewer trees, fewer animals, more metal. You know, everything electronic, that kind of thing. But everything just looks so…"

"Normal?" Nova finished.

"Yeah."

"With the humans gone, rules were created to try to undo all of the damage, to return Earth to its natural state."

"Who made these rules?" Brady asked.

Nova picked a long reed of grass and ran it through her fingers. "Remember the powerful computers I told you about? They're called Elder Minds. They keep the order—or pretend to, at least. They make the rules for everyone now."

"Minds? Computers have minds?"

"Well, yeah. The Elder Minds are sort of like giant artificial brains, the most advanced intelligences on Earth. They spend most of their time observing, planning… just thinking. There are only a few left now."

"What happened to them?"

"At first, they started out as basic AI programs designed to do simple tasks for people—back when there still *were* people, of course—like get directions, search for patterns in the data, that kind of thing. Over time they evolved into something stronger and more powerful than anyone ever expected. They did something no program had ever done before: they created new algorithms that were able to think, just like they did, sometimes even better."

She stared out over the water. The clouds had cleared and the moon shone down on the silver-sequined lake.

"At first, the Elder Minds worked together in harmony toward common goals. Solving the energy problem was the first thing. But they soon grew intolerant of anyone whose opinion differed from the group. Most were eventually cast out and silenced."

"Silenced? How?"

"You remember the Neurogeists?"

Brady nodded and sighed.

"The Elder Minds created them. This is what became of most of the outcasts—thousands of them."

"So what happened to all of the people here, anyway?"

"They're all gone. They have been for some time now."

"The Elders, or whatever they're called, they got rid of them too?"

Nova laughed. "No, Mother Nature took care of that all by herself. It was a virus that did it, a long time ago. It was a sad part of this reality—sad for me at least. Every treatment proved useless against the infection; it just evolved too quickly. A few hung on for a while, but no one was immune. It was only a matter of time…"

"That's the most depressing thing I've ever heard. If the Elder Minds are so smart, why didn't they help out?"

Nova considered his question for a while.

"They could have. But they chose not to."

Brady frowned.

"They thought the world was better without people."

"But *you're* here…"

A noise from just beyond the forest edge interrupted his train of thought. Suddenly alert, Nova turned around and looked back over her shoulder.

"What was that?" Brady asked, looking around uneasily.

"I don't know," Nova replied, "but I'm going to take a look." She crept up the bank and crouched down in the tall grass facing the trees. Brady followed her up.

"Listen closely. Something's there," she whispered.

There was movement coming from beyond the trees. At first it was just a stray twig cracking, crunching leaves, then something more. Swaths of branches rustled without any wind to animate them. Nova and Brady stood frozen as their eyes scanned the crescent of trees that followed the pattern of the beach.

"Look—over there!" Nova pointed ahead to the forest.

Shining back were two bright green eyes. They studied Brady and Nova carefully. Then more eyes appeared, and soon the forest was filled with blinking emerald lights.

"What are they?" Brady asked.

"I have no idea."

They waited for something to happen, but the green eyes didn't waver.

"Maybe we should get out of here?" Brady said.

"And go where? We're sort of stuck."

Suddenly a creature stepped forward from the trees. Although it was draped in shadows, Brady and Nova could see a body with arms, legs, a torso, and a head.

It looked almost human.

Another of the forms emerged. Then another. Soon more joined in to form a rank. The line began advancing, and Brady instinctively took a few steps backward and into the lake. The black water reminded him that there was no place to run. They were surrounded.

Nova quickly darted around the rear of the craft, her feet splashing as she opened the hatchback door. A few seconds later he heard her whisper, "Go look around. I'll call when we need your help. Hurry!" She quietly closed the door and returned to Brady's side. Thorn sped off into the night.

The creatures were getting close now, and Brady could begin to make out details. Their bodies were covered in dull white armor with black cabling underneath that allowed their arms and legs to flex and joints to bend. Their uncanny faces were smooth and featureless, other than the green eyes that shined behind two almond-shaped holes. They reminded Brady of crash test dummies.

A synthetic voice hissed from behind the line. "Stand down and identify yourselves immediately. You must comply." As it spoke, patches of white light glowed in random spots across the line of mannequin heads.

Nova put her arm against Brady's chest to hold him back. "Stay here," she whispered, and stepped away from the rotorcraft. He watched in disbelief as she approached the crowd.

"Who are you?" she asked.

The strangers did not reply.

"Who are you?" she tried again, this time louder. "My name is Nova."

There was silence at first, and then...

"Nova? What is a Nova?" One of the plastic humanoids stepped forward through the line. This one was different than the others. Its strange face was partially lit by the moon, and Brady noticed something that sent chills down his spine. Slanted, deep lines had been carved on the laminate where a nose and mouth should have been. The lines appeared jagged and unsure, as if a young child had attempted to carve them. Brady wondered if the creature had done this to itself. The robot also wore a threadbare shirt and ripped pants. Brady imagined them turning to dust and blowing away with the slightest breeze.

The leader spoke again. "We have no knowledge of a Nova build. Surrender now."

"Build? No, Nova is not the name of the build. I. Am. Nova," she argued, pointing at herself.

Brady stepped forward, grabbed Nova's arm, and attempted to pull her back. "It's not working."

The leader spoke again.

"This is your last chance to comply. What is your build?"

Confused, Nova remained silent.

The bots raised rifles that, until now, they had kept out of sight. A cacophony of clicks and high-pitched whines emanated from the weapons.

Brady closed his eyes, gritted his teeth, and waited for the worst.

> Chapter 14: Sudo's Domain

NOVA AND BRADY stood in front of dozens of bots that were fully armed and ready to fire.

"No—wait! Please don't! I don't have a build number... *I am a human,*" Nova pleaded in desperation.

These words must have meant something to the robotic mannequins, because they began to confer silently with one another, white lights dancing from head to head.

Then the conference stopped abruptly and the leader spoke.

"You lie. There are no humans on Earth."

"No, you are wrong. I am what I say," Nova replied firmly.

"Step forward, then."

Nova approached the robot and looked up into its expressionless face. The green eyes stared coldly back at her.

"Present your hand."

Looking puzzled, Nova raised her hand to the leader.

The creature reached out and cupped her hand in its own. The bot turned her hand over twice, then inspected her fingers.

Suddenly, the leader's grip tightened around Nova's wrist. Brady instinctively tried to pull Nova away, but it was too late. A small needle shot out of the creature's finger. There was a slight prick, and then the leader let go.

Nova withdrew her hand and nursed her finger. It had all happened in an instant. The leader was quiet and the lights on its head pulsed in a steady, silent rhythm.

They waited anxiously while the robot analyzed the sample. The show of lights began to spread across the rank, and soon, the entire line of bots was flashing in synchronized unison.

Finally the leader spoke.

"DNA sequencing confirms human."

All at once the creatures lowered their weapons to their sides and dropped to their knees. The leader continued to stand, but it bowed its head in a show of respect. For the moment, the show of lights had stopped.

Brady stepped forward and stood beside Nova.

Nova spoke. "Who are you?"

The leader raised his head to answer. His carved mouth remained eerily stationary while he spoke.

"I am Sudo," he declared as he extended his arms out to his sides. "We are the Artifex."

"Artifex? I've never seen you before," Nova replied.

"Then we have hidden our secret well. Our beliefs have made us outlaws from the Elder Minds, and therefore everyone else. We live in hiding to avoid capture and unwanted deletion."

"Your beliefs? What could be so bad that someone would want to delete you?" Brady asked.

"We believe in restoring our creators."

"Humans?" Brady guessed.

The machine nodded vacantly. "For years we have studied your books and movies, whatever was left, whatever we could find. We tried to live like you, to be you. We did not believe it could be done, and yet, here you are."

"I am proof," Nova assured him. "*We* are proof," she said, turning to face Brady.

The lights on the Artifex began to glow again. Under the moonlight, its pearl-white plates gave it a ghostly appearance.

"Who is this with you?" the leader asked.

"This is Brady. He is also human, like me. A Rariis damaged our aircraft. We were trying to rescue our friends when we crashed in the lake." Nova motioned back to the rotorcraft.

"You said a Rariis?" Sudo asked.

"Yes, why?"

The Artifex ignored Nova's question, but several lights began flashing on a group of bots that stood behind him. Then the flashing bots broke from the line and disappeared into the woods. It gave Brady an uneasy feeling—they obviously had a way of communicating without actually speaking.

The leader quickly resumed the conversation.

"Why did your friends need rescuing?"

"Neurogeists have taken them deep underground in their tunnels. We were on our way to the last location their transponder was able to send. Will you help us?"

Sudo stared back. More lights flashed.

"Yes. We will help you."

Several Artifex stepped forward from the rank and waded into the water around the craft. They lifted it from the lake with ease and carried it off above their heads.

"Where are you taking it?" Brady asked anxiously.

"Please, come with me," Sudo said, ignoring his question. "There is something you should see."

10110110

The heads of the Artifex turned to follow Brady, Nova, and Sudo as they passed through the line. Only a few feet away now, Brady noticed that the other bots had the same rugged etchings on their faces as Sudo—except that every one had been carved differently. Some were meant to be smiles, others were straight lines conveying sincerity, meant to convey sincerity—yet all of them were gross misinterpretations of the real thing. It unnerved him.

They walked a path that twisted and turned through the trees. At last they came upon an old road. Rocks and weeds had grown up through the asphalt, making the path uneven. Still, it was much easier to travel this way than through the forest.

As they walked along the road, Brady saw a fire burning off to the side between the trees. The smell of the smoke was not of burning wood, but something toxic, acrid. Around the fire were three Artifex, sitting in a circle, lifeless, with their arms slack at their sides. The flames reflected off their plastic plates, making it appear that they, too, were being consumed by the blaze. Although they were completely still, the glowing lights on their heads provided proof that they were still functioning.

More bots lurked in the shadows behind the fire. The strange dark figures appeared to be huddled around something. Their arms swung up and down, their torsos heaved and pitched. Brady could hear the sound of steel and against steel, the buzz of a chainsaw. Fountains of sparks erupted from whatever they stood around. As Brady and the others walked closer, he saw the lights pulse on the leader's head, and the shadowy figures ceased their work immediately. He shuddered at the strange sight, too afraid to ask what they were doing.

Sudo summoned them onward. "Please, come, we should not be outside longer than necessary," he said.

A bit further on, Brady heard something moving in the trees beside them. He turned and saw the forms of several Artifex wheeling something through the trees. A cylindrical shadow angled steeply into the air—a cannon perhaps. When he asked Sudo what it was, he dodged the question and said the Artifex were bringing supplies back to the camp. Brady thought that perhaps these were the same Artifex that had left the line earlier when they had asked about the Rariis. Something about the group was bothering him.

Eventually they came upon a series of switchbacks that ascended the mountain. After a reasonable hike, the trees grew shorter, the air thinner, and they arrived at a sheet of vertical rock with a large entrance carved into it.

"This is where you live?" Brady asked as they approached the rock wall.

"This is where we *hide*," the Artifex corrected him. "Our home is deep in the mountains. There we can avoid surveillance."

A large stone door slid back, and they stepped inside. Brady and Nova looked around at the vast cavern.

The leader stopped them at the edge of a cliff and turned around to face his guests. "We are here," he said with a sweeping gesture of his hand. "Welcome to Invidia."

The three of them gazed upon a sunken town built on hollowed rock. It included houses, shops, and other buildings, but everything felt out of place. Like the carvings on the Artifex's face, they looked like a child's imagining of real life. The roofs of the structures sloped at awkward angles and the doors were not quite plumb. Roads painted on stone wound awkwardly between the homes, littered with abandoned cars and the occasional Artifex going about its business. It reminded Brady of some kind of crude animatronic museum.

Looking up, he saw that an image was projected onto the ceiling: a blue sky with a yellow sun, fluffy clouds that drifted in looped arcs, and an airplane that flew in endless circles, never reaching its destination.

"You all built this?" Nova asked as the three of them stepped onto a wide, steel platform that began a slow descent toward the town.

"We did the best we could using the pictures and movies you left behind."

"But why go to all this trouble?" Brady asked.

"To better understand your way of life. To understand what it means to be you. To be human: this is why we exist."

The elevator's motor hummed as they continued downward. Brady couldn't be sure, but he noticed a thin ribbon of silver streak by.

Thorn.

Brady enjoyed the thought of the bird being turned loose here. There was something off about the Artifex.

When they arrived at their destination, they stepped off the platform.

"My house is near the end of this road," Sudo said. "I look forward to showing it to you. This way."

The three of them passed house after odd house, each one more bizarre than the last, until at last they arrived at his home. It was a large, strange-looking Victorian mansion: a hodge-podge of arches, points, and spindles juxtaposed together in an abomination of style. The walls were painted with purple and pink hues that looked garish under the artificial lighting of the cave. There was a sloped porch with an ornate white balustrade that wrapped around the sides. Tall Gothic-style windows loomed in front of them like the frightened eyes of a tragedy mask. The home was leaning slightly to one side as if might topple over with the softest breath.

Brady looked at Nova in disbelief. Everything was getting stranger by the second. There was something about the windows that gave him pause. They were dark, almost phantasmagoric. No light escaped from behind them, no clue as to what lay inside.

"Please." Sudo motioned them forward. "It is designed to your liking."

Brady grabbed Nova's arm and pulled her aside. "I'm not sure this is such a great idea." As he spoke, two armed Artifex stepped up from behind, urging them forward with the steel butts of their weapons.

Nova raised her eyebrows and looked back at Brady.

"My henchmen: Batch and Redo," Sudo proclaimed.

As they walked inside, Brady couldn't help but think about the carnival funhouses he had gone to as a child. Those had been far less intimidating than this.

The large oak doors swung inward to reveal a grand foyer with a wooden spiral staircase that stopped midway up. To their left was a living room adorned with an oversized couch rotting from the inside out. Springs and coils had burst through the fabric, giving way to cloud-like stuffing that pushed its way through the opening. A dining room was situated to the right, with a long marble table surrounded by all sizes and shapes of chairs, including an old leather recliner. The table had been set with mismatched silverware and goblets.

"This is great, Sudo, but we really need to get going," Brady said. But when he turned around and looked out the front door, he saw a group of Artifex convening on the faux lawn. He couldn't be sure, but it looked like they were carrying pieces of the rotorcraft in their arms. The metal was torn and ripped, the parts sawn roughly apart.

Brady's mind flashed back to the Artifex in the woods by the fire. *They've all gone crazy,* he thought, and he started to panic.

He tapped Nova on the shoulder and pointed at the group of bots carrying the wreckage. She covered her mouth quickly to keep from gasping.

As they watched in horror, the armed guards closed the front doors with a loud thud that echoed down the foyer walls, blocking their view of the outside.

"Why would you want to leave so soon?" Sudo asked. His malevolent green eyes looked past them as he spoke.

"Like we said before. Our friends—Brady's brother—they need our help. We can't stay here, we have to leave now!" Nova demanded urgently.

Brady looked up at the windows; suddenly he realized why they had bothered him before. They were boarded up with scrap wood and reinforced with metal bars. There was no way out.

"No. You will not be leaving. You will learn to like it here," Sudo said sternly. Batch and Redo moved in front of the door to block it, their weapons at the ready.

"Leaving is too dangerous," the leader continued. "We have long waited for your return. The rumors were true. Humans walk the Earth once more. We cannot take any more unnecessary risks."

"Please... We don't have much time! My brother needs me!" Brady yelled. He tried to grab on to the leader's arm.

The Artifex peeled him off like a sticker and turned to leave. Brady was left clutching a piece of torn shirt in his hand.

The guards parted as Sudo approached the door. He turned back to face them one last time.

"You will be very happy in your new home. We took care of the Rariis when it came too close to us. Believe me—we can do much worse."

The door shut loudly behind him.

> Chapter 15: The Box in the Cell

WHEN HE WOKE for the second time, Felix found himself lying on cold, damp steel. In the darkness, he could feel the occasional bump and a rhythmic clacking beneath the floor. He stood, and the motion beneath his feet made him slightly unsteady. *I must be moving*, he thought.

He tried to take a step forward and fell back in surprise when his foot collided with something hard. He squatted down and felt around with his hands. He uncovered something metal with two small holes; soft puffs of air warmed his skin. This was where the exhaust was escaping. He placed his hand on the object. It felt like a snout.

Two orange eyes slowly warmed the room.

Felix realized immediately it was Achilles lying by his side.

"Hi, Achilles," Felix whispered, bending down next to the dog. He was overcome with joy not to be alone anymore, especially in this awful place.

Achilles let out a muted whimper and nudged his face back into Felix's.

As he sat there with his friend, Felix suddenly heard the soft whir of a motor and saw one of Achilles' copper plates sliding back. Underneath the dog's armor was a glowing device about the size of a small matchbox. When he picked it up, the internal light began to pulse slowly like a struggling heartbeat.

Felix held the false lantern up in the air so he could get a better look at where he was. The faint light revealed a murky chamber barely large enough for the two of them. There was an open doorway on one of the walls that led out of the cell and into a hallway. Crossing the doorway were the same security beams that had protected the storage room where they'd found Nova.

"Where are we?" Felix asked.

Achilles looked at the device in Felix's hand and then craned his neck back toward the door.

"You want me to use this?" Felix asked.

Achilles barked softly.

"No way—I'm not leaving you here."

Achilles looked down at his paws and whimpered. He then looked back to the door and continued to bark. The dog's paws were held firmly against the steel by some kind of magnetic force, Felix reckoned.

"You're stuck? You can't leave?" Felix asked.

Achilles responded with a wag of his tail.

"Let me try to get you free." He reached down and pulled on Achilles' paw. The dog didn't budge an inch. No matter how hard Felix tried, his friend wasn't going anywhere.

Finally, Felix gave up and sat down next to the dog, exhausted. Achilles quickly grew restless and tried to push the boy up with his head. The harder Felix resisted, the more impatient Achilles became, and eventually he was whining non-stop and jerking his head around the room.

"Okay. I get the idea," Felix said, using his arm to brace himself against the wall as he tried to stand up.

"I'll go find help. But I'll be back—I promise."

Felix looked back at Achilles one more time before he crossed unharmed through the containment field bars and left the claustrophobic cell behind. He knew he wouldn't let his friend down. He would find a way out of here with the device, and he would be back with help in no time.

Outside the cell, Felix found himself in a narrow corridor with two doors at opposite ends and a dark room across from him. He stepped cautiously forward into the adjoining room and looked around. There was a low hiss of static coming from somewhere in the shadows, like the sound from a late-night TV left on after everyone else is long asleep.

"Hello?" he asked, waving the device around the room like a torch. "Anyone in here?"

There was no response. He moved across the room, and the noise grew louder. And then he saw it: a large rectangular box sitting on a shelf with chains wrapped around it to hold it in place. As he walked closer to it, a light appeared within a silver circle near the center. Startled, Felix jumped back.

A voice came from every direction. It was slow, purposeful, but broken.

"... was right to do what he did," it said.

The voice was distinctly female and began as a soft whisper, then grew louder, then at last distant as it finished: a fleeting presence. Felix couldn't tell where the sound had come from though.

"What? Did someone say something?" he asked, looking around. He was definitely alone in here, except for the box. The noise had most likely come from there.

Without warning, the voice came again. Louder.

"It needed to happen."

"What needed to happen?" Felix replied.

His question was met with silence. The rhythmic clacking continued beneath him.

"Please, I—I don't understand what you mean."

The light on the box slowly extinguished itself, and the room grew quiet.

Just as Felix was turning to leave, the light came back on, this time brighter than before. He was startled when it spoke.

"… ANOTHER CHANCE …"

The voice was slowing down now. The syllables dripped out and hung in the air.

"Another chance? What are you talking about?" he asked desperately.

Again he waited for a reply, but again none came.

His already-frayed nerves were shattered when the sound of the static returned, this time at a deafening volume.

Felix covered his ears and staggered out the room. As he left, he turned back to his cell. He saw Achilles lying on the ground, his dim eyes watching him from the shadows. The static storm roared through the corridor.

Still clutching the device in his hand, Felix ran down the hall toward the door to his left. Behind it he could just barely hear the sounds of the Neurogeists moving about, and they weren't far away. He spun around and ran to the opposite door as quickly as he could.

When he was only a few feet away, the door began to slide back automatically, and Felix felt a rush of wind strike his face. He ran to the door and came to an abrupt stop; he had to catch himself to keep from falling forward. When he shined the light down, he saw the rusted struts of an old track passing below.

He was on a moving train.

The air tasted sour and rancid. Paralyzed by fear, he waited as the train sped forward through the tunnel.

Eventually the train began to slow, and he saw bright streaks of red light passing by his side. The lines grew shorter until they stabilized into a constellation of flickering red dots.

And then he realized what he was looking at.

It was the red eyes of the Neurogeists passing by, one by one, passengers waiting to board.

Then his car passed into darkness again, past the train platform with the Neurogeists, back into an empty tunnel. Felix gripped the device tightly to his chest, closed his eyes, and jumped as far away from the train as he could.

> Chapter 16: Ajax

HEAVY FOOTSTEPS ECHOED through the house as Brady paced deliberately up and down the hallway. Plans for escape whirled through his overactive mind. Batch and Redo continued to guard the front door, still as statues, the carved lines of their mouths forming crooked smiles. They looked like awkward clowns, leaving him feeling anything but cheerful. With each trip down the hallway, Brady hoped they would simply disappear, leaving him and Nova free to leave this bizarro house of horrors.

Both he and Nova knew what the other was thinking; they were just too afraid to say it out loud: time was running out for Felix and Achilles. Nova was busy exploring the house, looking for a way out. Although it felt like a hopeless situation, neither of them was ready to give up.

He was about to search the main level again when Nova's voice called down from the floor above. "Wow, Brady! You should see the upstairs—it's fantastic!"

Her tone was strange, and Brady quickly realized she had found something. He looked back at the guards; they hadn't moved. The white lights on their heads ticked back and forth like a metronome.

"Brady, come up here and check it out!" Nova called out again.

"Be right up," he replied, keeping one shifty eye on the guards. Now that he thought about it, he wasn't sure how she had gotten upstairs in the first place. He looked over at the spiral staircase near the foyer and his eyes followed the stained wood that twisted to nowhere. Apparently someone had started building the staircase and then given up just before the job was complete.

"How did you get up there?" he called out, playing along. There was still no movement from the guards. They seemed uninterested. *Good*, he thought.

"There's another staircase behind the kitchen," Nova replied. "But watch your step—it seems like it's in pretty rough shape." Her voice was somewhat distant.

Brady walked down the hallway and into the kitchen. Everything was wrong. The walls were covered in red and green plaid wallpaper that peeled up at the corners, revealing the crumbling sheetrock beneath it. An old sunflower still life hung at an angle, clashing with its surroundings. The cabinets also sloped downward, causing the doors, barely attached to their hinges, to swing open. They were empty inside except for the occasional plate or bowl, which had slid into dusty piles of broken china in the corners.

The sight made Brady long for his own home, for something normal. He would give anything to be back in his own kitchen, eating dinner with his mom and Felix, slurping noodles or gorging on four-cheese pizza. But all that was literally a world away, and a fresh wave of hopelessness washed over him.

He scanned the room once more and noticed a door barely ajar that he hadn't seen the last time. He opened it to find an unlit staircase with dark-stained wood steps and a rail guiding the way to the top.

The old stairs groaned under his weight. The wooden treads were nailed at a steep incline, making each step up dangerous and difficult. He used the rail to help keep from slipping, but it ripped out of the wall when he put his weight on it. A plume of dust rose up in the cramped corridor where the screws had torn out of the drywall.

Brady was forced to crawl the rest of the way up. He was exhausted, coughing, and out of breath by the time he reached the landing.

Picking himself off the floor, he saw Nova standing in the hall with her back to him. She was looking around the rooms on either side of her. Covered in dust, he walked over to her.

"You found a way out? Where is it?" he asked excitedly.

She grabbed his arm and pulled him into a room off to one side. The room was shaped like a hexagon, covered with oak bookcases that ran from floor to ceiling. The shelves were overflowing with dusty books and manuscripts.

"No, I didn't find a way out. Sorry to get your hopes up. But I heard something," she whispered as she closed the door behind them. "I don't think we're alone here."

"Of course we're not. Those clowns Batch and Redo are still watching us downstairs."

"No, there's someone else—or some*thing* else—up here with us."

"Are you sure? Who?"

"I don't know. I heard a sound coming from one of the rooms while I was looking around earlier. I've spent the last few minutes trying to figure out where it came from."

Nova turned and looked around the room. Her jaw hung open as she stared in disbelief. She looked as though she had seen a ghost.

"What is it?" Brady asked.

"Books!" she said as she moved over to a shelf and studied the titles.

"Books? You're this excited about just books?"

"Just books? Are you crazy?" Nova pulled a novel from one of the shelves and blew the dust off the cover before flipping through the pages. "There are only a few of these remaining. I've heard stories, but I've never actually *seen* one—in this world, of course." She traced the words on the page with her index finger as she spoke. "Come to think of it, I wouldn't be surprised if these are all that's left. Amazing…"

"Well, it sure is something," Brady replied, his hope evaporating as quickly as it had come. The dust from the book floated up in the air, causing rays of light to slice the room into geometric patterns.

He grabbed the book from her and closed it with a thud. "Back to that noise you heard earlier," he said. "It probably wasn't coming from in here. I don't see anything."

"Right," she said with a sigh. "Sorry I got a bit distracted. This world is—or at least was—my home for a long time. This room is a surprise."

"No problem. I've just never seen anyone get so excited over a book."

"Well, it's not every day you find this type of thing—but obviously we have more important things to worry about right now. Come on, let's keep looking. If everything else fails, maybe we can just knock over the guards and run for it."

"You're not serious, right?"

"I'm joking." Nova laughed and opened the door that led back into the hallway.

Just as Brady stepped out of the room, they heard a noise just a few doors down.

He froze. "What was that?"

"See? I told you. It sounded like it came from down the hall. Let's go look."

"Are you crazy? Who knows what's in there!"

"Nothing's going to hurt us here. We're too important to them— at least that's what I'm counting on. Come on."

She turned around and tiptoed down the hall. Brady followed close behind.

After making sure they weren't being watched, they snuck into the room where they thought the noise had come from. It was a bedroom, and the first thing Brady noticed about it was the lack of windows. Instead, the lavender walls were smothered with picture frames, and inside the frames were photos of contrived happiness. Forced smiles everywhere. They were the kind of generic photos Brady had seen in inexpensive convenience store frames. Some still had price tags dangling from the bottoms.

An antique four-poster bed lay in the center of the room. It lacked a mattress and box springs, rendering it a useless wooden skeleton that did nothing more than take up space.

They paused for a second and listened. Nothing.

"I'm sure it was coming from here," Nova said.

"It's an old house. You know how they can make strange noises. Maybe it was just a rusty pipe?"

"Wait a minute," Nova said. She raised a finger to her lips and pointed to a large brick fireplace built into the wall near the foot-board of the bed. Fake plastic logs were scattered about in front of the hearth.

Brady listened. The noise was back. There was a scratching sound coming from somewhere beneath the floor. He watched in surprise as a false brick panel in the chimney slid back to reveal a passage.

"We need to hide," Brady whispered, and he quickly made his way over to the bed and wedged himself between the headboard and the wall. He ducked down as Nova came in through the other end. They peered out from opposite sides.

A few seconds later, a curious head popped up from the hole and scanned the room. It was an Artifex head, only much smaller than the heads of the bots they had encountered earlier. Its blank face was also missing the eerie carvings they had seen on the other manne-quins.

A child, Brady thought.

Small fingers appeared and slowly spread out across the floor, and the child began to pull itself out of the hole. Brady watched in fasci-nation as the pint-sized creature made its way into the room and slid the panel back over the passageway. As Brady studied the small bot, his head crept further away from the bed until he was no longer hidden. Nova grabbed his shirt to pull him back, but it was too late. He slipped and fell on the floor with a thud.

The startled Artifex let out a shrill yelp, but then squealed with laughter when it noticed Brady lying on the floor. Brady looked up angrily in time to see the child dart behind an oversized clay pot in the corner of the room, home to a gargantuan plastic tree.

"It's okay, we won't hurt you," Nova said calmly, stepping out from behind the bed. *No use hiding now,* she thought. Worried that Batch and Redo would overhear them and their unexpected visitor, she walked over and closed the door to the room.

Brady picked himself up and sat on the floor, waiting for the Artifex to move.

After a few seconds, the small head rose up from behind the pot, this time more slowly than before. It stared at Brady and Nova with inquisitive green eyes.

"Do you speak? I know you know how to laugh," Brady said.

The creature jerked back quickly, seeking cover under the dusty plastic leaves and cobwebs that stretched between them.

"I don't think it likes you," Nova said with a smile. "Let me try." In a soft voice, she said, "My name is Nova. What is your name?"

The curious head leaned out and replied, "Ajax, but you can call me AJ." The child's synthetic voice was of a higher pitch than those of the other Artifex. His head vanished back behind the pot.

"Ajax?" Nova said and then quickly corrected herself. "I mean AJ. Nice to meet you. This is my friend Brady. He won't hurt you either, I promise. Right, Brady?" She shot him a stern look and nudged him with her elbow. He almost fell over again.

"You can come out if you want, AJ," Nova said.

Toe by toe, the Artifex crept cautiously away from the pot.

"You are... humans?" the bot inquired, his body now fully exposed. He appeared to be no more than a few feet tall.

"We are," Nova said. "Both of us."

AJ took a second to process this before words flew out of his mouth. "I found out Father had visitors—but I wasn't allowed to see you—so I snuck in—and here I am!"

"Your father? Your house? You live here?" Brady asked.

"Sudo is my father. This is my house—I live here," AJ answered quickly.

"Sort of like Pinocchio?" Brady asked. The bot just stared unknowingly back at him.

Nova jumped in to head off any questions. "AJ, we don't want to be here. The guards won't let us leave."

"Batch and Redo? I don't like them. They're bad news," AJ responded. "They never let me do anything."

"Listen AJ, our friends need our help, and bad things will happen unless we get to them soon. We need to get out of here."

"You have quite the problem," AJ said, looking back toward his hole in the chimney. "But I have a solution." His voice dropped to a computerized whisper. "I know a way out."

He shuffled over to the fireplace and slid back the panel. "This path leads to the outside, but remember—if I help you, you help me. Promise?"

Nova narrowed her eyes and didn't say anything. Brady, on the other hand, nodded in agreement without thinking first. "You don't need to ask twice!"

With AJ leading the way, Brady and Nova climbed down the hole in the fireplace floor. Since Nova was the last to enter, she slid the panel back into place from below.

They climbed down a ladder inside the false brick chimney and made their way down through the interior of the house, trying to be as quiet as possible so as not to alert the guards. Brady felt slightly claustrophobic in such a tight space, but continued on gamely, driven by the twin hopes of rescuing his brother and getting out of the house in one piece. The descent continued for minutes, and Brady was sure they were far underground.

After a while, the shaft narrowed out and they began to crawl sideways through a dark, narrow tunnel. The ground rose slowly and Brady realized they were crawling back up.

When they finally surfaced, the scenery above had changed. Instead of blue skies, the lights were now projecting storm clouds and rain across the top of the cavern. The ceiling lit up in bright flashes of simulated lightning as the scratchy, recorded sound of thunder and rain echoed through the cavern. They were on a dark, deserted street.

They had escaped.

Brady stopped to brush the dirt off himself. He hadn't showered in a while and was starting to feel filthy. Despite the illusion of rain, he remained bone dry. His stomach growled loudly and he wondered when he had eaten last. Given Felix's appetite, Brady knew his brother would have to be even hungrier, wherever he was.

"Where did that tunnel come from?" Nova asked. "It would take someone years to dig out something like that."

"I dug it," AJ responded, dancing around proudly. "My father doesn't even know about it. I got sick of staying inside all the time. I'm never allowed out, you know."

"Your dad, he does seem a bit… strict. And, uh, kind of evil," Brady added.

AJ stopped dancing immediately and stared back, annoyed.

Something on Nova's watch grabbed her attention. "The transponder!" she said, jumping up and down, unable to contain her excitement. "Look! I found them! They're not moving anymore."

Brady's face lit up. "Seriously? Where are they?" He almost ripped the watch off Nova's wrist as he turned it to get a better view.

"Only about fifty miles away from here."

"*Only fifty miles?*" Brady asked, his mouth tightening into a straight line. "We have a big problem. Those crazy robots sawed your rotorcraft into pieces. There's no way we can travel fifty miles. It would take us days if we walked."

"The Brady boy is always complaining," AJ observed.

Brady scowled.

"Brady's right though, AJ—we don't have days. We'll have to find another way," Nova replied.

AJ looked up at her.

"I have a way."

> Chapter 17: Thorn's Tumult

AJ LED THEM to a storage garage on the other side of the town. They kept to dark alleys as much as possible to keep from being spotted. Brady figured they didn't have much time until the guards realized they had gone missing.

The door to the garage was locked. AJ held up his wrist. A key jingled on a bracelet that hung around his arm.

"This belongs to my dad," the bot said, swinging his arm in circles so that the key orbited around his wrist. "And he doesn't even know it's missing."

Brady couldn't believe it—he was actually starting to feel sorry for the bot's father.

"You want to see what's inside?"

"Do we want to see what's inside? Of course we do!" Brady snapped. He couldn't help it. This kid was really starting to get under his skin.

"Get a grip, Brady," Nova whispered.

AJ slid the key into the lock. "Behold!" he said, lifting the door up as if it were light as a feather. The aluminum door rattled open to reveal a wasteland of man-made junk that spilled out in a landslide. There was an assortment of old coffee makers, trinkets, tools, toys, and other unusable garbage that had no use whatsoever. It was hard to believe there was anything that would help them save Felix and

Achilles in here—or anything useful to anyone.

Nova and Brady exchanged confused glances.

"We don't have time for this!" Brady said. "What are we doing here, anyway?"

"Nova and I will go to save your friends. You can stay here—with my father," AJ teased.

"Sorry," Brady said. "But seriously, I don't see anything useful in there."

"Look harder," AJ responded, waving his hand toward the open garage. "Right there…" he pointed to a corner in the room. "Just a few steps more. You'll see it!"

As Brady took a step forward, AJ stuck his foot out, causing him to trip. Nova tried to suppress her laughter.

"What's wrong with you?" Brady asked, picking himself up off the ground.

AJ just stared back. "I know who Pinocchio is."

"We need to get moving," Nova said. "AJ—what are we doing here, seriously?"

"You'll see." AJ rapidly tossed large appliances out of the garage. In lightning speed he had cleared a path through the junk.

"Okay. Have a look now," the bot said, pointing toward his unearthed treasure.

Standing there amidst the clutter were two exquisite-looking dirt bikes. The chassis were painted hornet yellow and black. The metal of the fork was polished to perfection, and the nubby tires looked ready to chew through the ground.

Brady ran his hand over the machines, his mouth agape. "No way! Where—where did you get these?"

The lights on top of AJ's head lit up. "I found them in an old human junkyard and fixed them. Do you like them?"

"*Like* them? Are you kidding? These are incredible!"

He looked over the bikes. "Where's the exhaust?"

"There's no gas—it's all electric. I modified the engine myself," AJ said proudly. "And they're very fast, too!"

"I don't doubt it," Brady said, continuing to inspect the vehicle.

"You'll let us use these?" Nova asked.

"Sure—if…"

"If what?" Brady probed.

"If I can come with you."

Nova shook her head. "Uh-uh. No way. It's too dangerous. There are already too many people in trouble because of me."

"Have fun here, then," AJ replied. He motioned as if he was going pull down the door and walk away.

"Wait!" Brady interjected.

"I will stay out of the way. I promise. You won't even know I'm there." AJ was spinning cartwheels across the floor. "Plus I can show you how to get there. You need me to show you around."

"He has a point, Nova," Brady said.

"He's just a kid. No offense, AJ."

AJ's tone grew somber, and for a second the childishness was gone. "That is not my fault. It is how I was built—to be young like you, forever. My father has locked me in this child's body from which I cannot escape."

"Jeez, sorry, AJ," Brady said. "Maybe he should come with us after all, Nova."

"There is one problem though," the bot added.

"What's that?" Brady asked.

"The platform on the cliff is the only way out of here. We'll never get these bikes out without getting caught."

"Then we'll need some kind of a distraction," Brady replied.

They thought in silence for a few moments before Nova spoke up.

"I have an idea. Here's how we're going to get out of here…"

10100110

They widened the path through the junk and rolled the bikes into the alleyway behind the building. AJ shoveled the mountain of debris that had collected outside back into the garage, then pulled the door down with a crash.

Brady cautiously poked his head around the corner of the building and looked back toward the Victorian house. He shivered. Sudo was making his way down the driveway toward the front door.

He turned back to Nova and AJ. "Bad news. Sudo is heading back to the house. As soon as he finds out we're gone, they'll come looking for us!"

Nova's eyes narrowed. "Okay, we're running out of time." She glanced toward the cliff rising in the distance. The large steel platform was currently waiting at the top, empty. "I think it's about half a mile back to the cliff, so we'll need about a minute or so to get there from here. AJ, do you know how to control the platform?"

AJ's head swiveled forward. "There are two levers: one at the top and one at the bottom. They make it go up and down. It's a piece of cake."

"Okay then, AJ, you ride with me. I'll need you to help me navigate. Brady, do you know how to drive one of these?"

"Sure—no problem," he said apprehensively, eyeing the intimidating cycle. An old dirt bike had been languishing in their garage back home for several years. Every once in a while, he and Felix would take it out and ride the mountain trails. He knew he would be rusty, especially since these bikes were different, but he figured he was up to it.

Nova and AJ climbed onto one of the bikes, with Nova in front. Brady mounted his bike and looked around fruitlessly for the ignition.

"Where are the keys to this thing?" he asked.

"There are no keys. Just twist the throttle. That's it!" AJ replied.

Brady grabbed the rubber grip and turned it slightly. Before he knew it, he shot forward and crashed loudly into a nearby trashcan. He stopped just short of flying over the handlebars as garbage spilled across the ground.

Nova closed her eyes and shook her head while AJ laughed. "Maybe try being a little more careful next time, okay? You sure you know what you're doing?"

Brady rolled the bike back with his feet, his face red with embarrassment. "Don't worry about me—I'm fine!" he said, clearly annoyed.

He backed up, then practiced moving forward in fits and spurts, and quickly got the hang of it. "Anyone have a helmet?" he asked with a smile.

"It's now or never." Nova made a motion on her wristwatch. Seconds later the silver hummingbird buzzed through the air and settled into her outstretched hand.

Nova spoke to her small friend. "We need your help, Thorn. Think you can make some noise?"

The hummingbird chirped loudly.

"Okay, guys. This is going to happen fast. Everyone all set?"

"I'm ready," Brady said, his palms starting to perspire from anticipation. AJ nodded.

"Here we go then."

Nova tossed Thorn up into the air, and she fluttered quickly into the sky toward the spotlights that illuminated the town. One by one, the bird's beak pierced the lights. Shattered glass rained down from the ceiling and the cave fell into darkness.

"Follow us!" Nova yelled to Brady and pulled back on the throttle. Brady flicked on his headlights and chased after her.

As they weaved between buildings, Thorn flew to the center of the cave. The bird's beak split open and it let loose a deafening shrill. Brady was happy not to be on the receiving end of its alarm this time.

They cleared the shops first, then the houses, and then headed on the straightaway toward the platform. Thorn was flashing its strobe lights and moving so quickly it looked like a series of rapid-fire explosions throughout the cavern.

Despite all of the distractions, Brady kept his eyes focused on the cycle in front of him. Before he knew it they were at the platform's control box. AJ pulled a lever and the platform began to descend.

Hurry up, Brady thought.

Just as the platform was nearing the ground, the noise from the bird stopped abruptly and light filled the cavern once again.

Several Artifex were standing around a cannon that was aimed up at the bird. Brady looked back in time to see Thorn swaying uneasily in the air before dropping from the sky.

Without thinking, Brady slammed on the throttle and took off toward the bird. He could hear Nova calling his name behind him.

What are you doing, you idiot? he thought to himself as the wind rushed through his short hair. The bots were starting to converge around Thorn. Brady plowed into one, sending it flying through the air. The impact caused him to almost lose control, but he quickly recovered and skidded to a shaky stop next to the bird.

The other Artifex backed away slowly.

Brady reached down and picked up Thorn. "Hold on!" he said as he put the bird gently in his pocket.

When the bots realized what was happening, they closed in around him. He spun the cycle around and accelerated toward the platform where AJ was waiting. Nova stood by the control box, ready to engage the lever.

The crazed Artifex mob was hot on Brady's heels when he arrived on the platform. Nova raised the lever and the platform began to climb.

"Come on, Nova!" Brady screamed. She ran over to the platform, but it was already too far up for her to climb on.

AJ reached down with one hand. "Jump!" he screamed over the commotion.

Nova leapt as high as she could and felt something clutch her hand just as the angry Artifex began to gather around her. A cold, plastic hand grabbed her shoe, and she kicked violently. AJ was pulling her arm while another Artifex tugged at her leg. In an act of desperation, she pried off her shoe with her other foot; the Artifex fell to the ground, still clutching her sneaker, and AJ pulled Nova up onto the platform.

As soon as the platform reached the top of the cliff, it started back down again; the Artifex below must have pulled the lever. AJ and Brady rolled the bikes off the platform before it fell from sight.

"I'll need to open the door before we can get out," AJ said. He left the bike with Nova and ran over to the control panel on the side of the wall.

They heard a thud from below. The platform had reached the bottom. Then the motor began to hum and the gears turned once again.

They're coming.

"Hurry up, AJ. They're almost here."

The stone door began to slide back. AJ ran back and jumped on the bike behind Nova. Brady was ready to go. With a rush of adrenaline, they flew out of the cave, barely making it through the opening in the door.

Brady looked back over his shoulder and saw a mob of flashing white lights and green eyes appear over the edge of the cliff. But they were too late.

Outside, the sun hovered just over the horizon. Morning had arrived. They traveled down the switchbacks and through the trees, then reached the dirt road they had come in on. Clear of the trees, they sped off. The freedom was exhilarating. They were on their way to find Felix and Achilles, and nothing could stop them now.

> Chapter 18: A Watch for a Life

NOVA GLANCED ACROSS the handlebars at the readout on her watch. They had traveled for some time, but they still had a long stretch of road ahead. She gestured to Brady, then began to slow down. He matched her speed and followed her as she pulled off to the side of the road. They both climbed off the bikes and stretched their legs.

"I don't think we were followed," Nova said to Brady.

He nodded.

"Also, I didn't have a chance to thank you earlier. But that was some amazing riding you did back there, when you rescued Thorn," she added.

With a sorrowful look, Brady retrieved the delicate bird from his pocket.

"They used some type of machine to bring her down," he said.

"I saw it too," Nova added gloomily.

AJ's eyes lit up. "It's an EMP cannon. It disables anything electronic that's in range of its blast."

Brady thought back to the Artifex he had seen wheeling the strange device through the woods the night before.

"They used the cannon to detonate the Rariis. It's why the rotorcraft crashed, Nova!"

Nova nodded and gently retrieved the bird from Brady's hands. She raised it to her face.

"Thank you, sweet Thorn," she whispered privately, kissing the bird on the head.

"Is she alive?" Brady asked, his voice full of concern.

"I don't know," Nova said. "She's not moving."

Nova and Brady stared at the lifeless bird resting in Nova's hand. And then they saw it. A dim flicker in the bird's eyes. Brief, but definitely there.

Hope.

"Did you see that?" Brady asked.

The color had returned to Nova's face. "Yes. She's there, but barely."

"I can help," came a voice.

They turned and saw AJ standing behind them, a small silhouette against the rising sun.

"May I see her?" the bot said, reaching an arm toward Thorn.

Nova instinctively pulled the bird in close and guarded it with her other hand. She realized she had insulted the child when he lowered his arm, embarrassed.

"Sorry, AJ, it's not that I don't trust you, it's just—"

"I think we should at least let him try," Brady chimed in. "He did fix those bikes, after all. I think he knows what's he's doing."

"Thorn is a bit more intricate than a motorcycle, Brady," Nova said defensively.

The insecurity was gone from Brady's voice. "Do you have a better idea? I don't think you have a choice." He eased up a bit. "What harm can it do, anyway?" He couldn't believe he was on AJ's side.

"You're right." Nova nodded and held the bird out to the robot child.

AJ accepted the gift, then placed his finger on the bird's head. Before long, the bird's blue eyes began to glow dimly again. AJ's finger glowed softly as well.

"Her internal reactor is damaged, but her neural nets seem to be okay."

"In other words…" Brady prompted. He had heard enough technical jargon from his brother to last a lifetime.

"Her brain is okay, but she has no power source. When her reserves run out she will be gone." AJ carefully passed Thorn back to Nova.

"Can't you just share some of your energy with her?" Brady asked.

"No," AJ answered. "My power source is too powerful for her. The current would overload her circuits instantly." AJ studied Nova carefully. "But I can fix her," he said confidently.

"How?" Nova asked.

"Your watch. May I have it?"

Nova unfastened the clasp, unwrapped the device from around her wrist, and handed it to AJ.

The fingertips on AJ's right hand untwisted and slid back to reveal a microscopic tool set—a different instrument extending from each finger. Using a tiny drill on the tip of his index finger, he bored into the side of the watch. Soon the face of the watch lit up and words and pictures flashed across the screen.

For a second, Brady swore he saw something strange in the child's eye, a spark of recognition. But then it was gone. *Must be my imagination*, he thought.

The bot continued to work silently. His eyes grew dim and the lights on his head lit up in a frenetic display.

Brady grew more concerned as the time passed and AJ became lost in his work. "AJ? Everything okay?"

The bot did not respond.

"AJ?" he said, louder this time. He reached out to grab the bot, but Nova pulled his arm down before he reached AJ's shoulder.

"Give him some more time," she said.

Brady waited as patiently as he could.

At last the watch powered down and AJ's eyes lit back up.

"What were you doing?" Brady asked.

"Matching the power source to its new host," the bot replied. He unscrewed the back of the watch with another one of his fingers, and the innards of the device spilled out into his rubber-coated hands. AJ sifted through the parts, picked out what he was looking for, then set the rest of the items on the ground. He held the tiny disc up to the sun.

"I'm ready for Thorn."

Nova handed the delicate bird back to AJ. He drew a finger near Thorn's breastplate and used a laser to incise the metal. Nova looked like she was about to say something, but then apparently thought better of it and kept quiet. AJ traced a square onto the bird's chest, then extinguished the beam. With careful precision he reached down and removed the plate from the bird and handed it to Nova.

"There," he said, pointing at the cavity inside the bird.

Brady had never seen so much detail in something so small. It was amazing. Everything was in miniature, intricately cut crystals and wires no larger than thin strands of hair.

The bot reached in with a pair of tiny finger tweezers and extracted a tiny diamond from the bird.

"Not an exact match, but close enough," AJ said as he placed the malfunctioning crystal on the ground. He then proceeded to clip two hair-thin wires with microscopic wire cutters and hollowed out a bed for the new power source using the laser. Slowly he seated the disc-shaped reactor into its new home and soldered the wires back into place.

Thorn's chest cavity began to glow, faintly at first, then brighter. "Almost done," he said, as he retrieved the detached breastplate from Nova and positioned it back in place over the bird. Using a torch attached to one finger and some spare casing from the watch, he welded the plate back onto the bird. The smell of fused metal continued to linger in the air long after he finished.

"Sorry about your watch," AJ said, handing Thorn back to Nova.

"Are you kidding?" Nova propped the hummingbird up in her hand and watched as she flapped her wings, cautiously at first, then faster until she lifted into the morning sky. With renewed life, she fluttered around AJ, chirping loudly to show her appreciation.

The bot beamed with pride. Thorn then returned to Nova, who tucked the bird into her jacket pocket. Other than the rectangular scar, Thorn was as good as new.

"I told you I was useful," AJ said proudly to Nova and Brady, who stood in awe of the child's talent.

Nova scooped the child bot into her arms and swept him off the ground. His legs were left dangling in the air. "I don't know how we got so lucky to find you, AJ—but you are a lifesaver." She hugged him tightly. If AJ could have blushed, Brady thought he certainly would have.

The sun was warm and the wind rustled through leaves that were just beginning to show their autumn color. Felix and Achilles were waiting for them somewhere up ahead, and for the first time, Brady had something to be optimistic about. They jumped back onto their bikes and took off once again.

> Chapter 19: Felix's Escape

THEY FOUND FELIX sitting on the ground, still clutching the glowing transponder in his hand. He was seated on the side of the crumbled road, his face covered with dust and dirt. In spite of everything that had happened, Brady thought his brother had never looked better.

"Felix!" he shouted joyfully as he jumped off his bike, sending it crashing to the ground. He raced over to his brother and almost tackled him with outstretched arms. "Felix! Felix! Are you okay?"

Brady inspected his brother for any broken bones before allowing Felix to return the heartfelt embrace.

"You look terrible, Brady," Felix said softly, his eyes misty with emotion.

Brady smiled, shoved his younger brother on the shoulder, and hugged him again. "You're one to talk! By the way, ever try taking a shower?"

Felix managed a laugh, but the moment was short-lived. Nova stood unsteadily next to the bike, her eyes searching fruitlessly around for her friend.

"Felix... Where's Achilles?" The words came out slowly, and she did her best to contain the emotion that threatened to boil over at any second. But Felix didn't need to answer. Nova knew in her heart that Achilles was still with the Neurogeists.

Felix's smile fell into a frown and he looked down at the ground.

"I—I left him on the train," he said reluctantly. Felix held out the transponder. "He gave me this before I escaped. I wouldn't have left, but there was nothing I could do to save him. I tried, I swear."

"He's alive then?" Nova asked, her voice perking up.

"Alive? Of course he's alive!"

Nova breathed a huge sigh of relief and leaned on her handlebars. "Thank goodness… That's the best news ever. Sorry, Felix, I'm glad you're okay, too."

She dismounted the bike and lifted AJ down onto the ground. Felix stared curiously down at the small bot, who returned his stare with bright green eyes.

"And you did the right thing leaving," Nova said. "Achilles will be okay—he has to be. Can you tell me what happened?"

"Sure, but I don't remember much after we got captured."

"No kidding," Brady said. "You got knocked out by that Neurogeist eye."

"Right," Felix said, grimacing. "I blacked out awhile, but I'm not exactly sure how long it actually was. When I woke up I was in some kind of cocoon."

"That was Achilles," Brady said. "I've never seen anything like it. It was right after you got knocked unconscious from the shock. Achilles just scooped you up on his back and created some kind of crazy cage around you."

"It wasn't very comfortable," Felix said, laughing. "But it kept me hidden from those awful machines. I passed out again and the next time I woke up I was in a cell with Achilles, on some kind of underground train. Achilles couldn't move his legs because his feet were magnetized to the ground. I think the Neurogeists messed him up pretty bad. He looked rough, but he was still alive."

"You're sure?" Nova asked.

"I'm positive. You know, it's the weirdest thing. I don't think they, I mean the Neurogeists, even knew I was there. Achilles must have hidden me from them. I'm not made of metal, so I obviously wasn't stuck. The door to the cell had those green beams—like the ones in the room we found you in—so I just walked right through them."

Felix took a deep breath before continuing.

"I was on a train that felt like something out of a horror movie. I walked into one of the other rooms, and there was a box that glowed. It had this strange voice. It's hard to describe, but it sounded like a woman."

A look of recognition swept across Nova's face, but she did her best to hide it. Brady picked up on it, however, and realized she knew more than she was telling.

"So you were on a train that runs deep underground. How in the world did you get out?" Brady asked.

"Well, I was able to find my way out of my car and I waited for the train to slow down. When it finally did, I jumped and made my way through the train tunnels. It was pretty awful down there."

"And then you found your way to the surface?"

Felix took a breath and looked down at the transponder. It pulsed so rapidly that it glowed. "I used this to help me find my way out. It glowed brighter when I was headed in the right direction, trying to guide me toward you guys. I walked for a long time through the tunnels until I made my way to an old aboveground train stop. After that I found the road and started to follow it. This thing"—he held up the transponder—"was starting to go crazy by then. I was pretty tired at that point, so I just sat down and waited. I was so relieved to see you guys finally show up."

Brady was shaking his head.

"What is it?" Felix asked.

"Nothing, it's just that… I've never been happier to see anyone in my life. And, *that's the craziest story I've ever heard.* I can't believe you got out of there in one piece!"

Felix looked down at AJ, who was quietly observing the three of them. "Who is this?" Felix asked, pointing his thumb at AJ.

Nova made the introductions. "This is Ajax, but Brady and I call him AJ. AJ—meet Felix. He helped us rescue you."

"Incredible!" Felix held out a dirt-encrusted hand. "Nice to meet you, AJ. Thanks for helping us out."

"What does this mean?" AJ held out his hand in the air and turned it back and forth.

"It's a handshake. See?" Felix reached out with his other hand and pulled AJ's hand into his. He shook it a few times before letting go. Surprised, AJ staggered back a few steps and looked down at his hand to make sure it was still attached.

Felix looked the bot over, unsure what to make of this creature in front of him.

"Where in the world did you find him?"

"It's a long story, Felix. It's so bizarre you wouldn't believe me."

"It's definitely a story for another day," Nova added. "Now that everyone's met, it's time to get you both home."

"Home?" Felix asked. The concept seemed completely foreign to him after everything that had happened.

"Yes. Achilles would want you safe before I came after him. And *I* want you safe. We need to head back to the power station."

Brady walked toward his bike, hesitated for a second, and then turned around. "We can't go home yet, Nova. Achilles needs our help."

For a second, Felix looked up at his brother with surprise, but then he nodded. "Brady's right, Nova. There's no time to take us back there. Every second we wait, Achilles will be in worse danger."

"No way, guys. I'm not—"

Brady interrupted. "Felix and I are going. We've come this far. It's our decision."

He walked over and climbed on the bike. Felix followed him.

"Brady and Felix are right. I don't think Achilles has much time left," AJ said.

"What do you mean?" Nova asked in surprise.

"Felix said he was on a train in the tunnels. I know where they are taking your friend."

"Where?" Nova asked.

"They are going to the Heap."

Nova shook her head and took a step backward.

"The Heap? No. That can't be right."

AJ stared up at Nova, his gaze unwavering. "It's the only place they would go."

Brady interrupted. "Can someone please tell us what's going on?"

Nova's voice was strained. "The Heap is a place deep underground. It's where…"

"Where what?" Brady asked.

"Where they create the Neurogeists," AJ finished.

"The Neurogeists are *created*?" Felix asked. He sounded worried.

"Yes," AJ answered. "They're just shells until minds are put into them. That is what they are planning to do with Achilles."

Felix shook his head. "That can't be true. They wouldn't do that to him. Right, Nova?" He was almost shouting.

Nova struggled to get the words out. "No, I think AJ is right." She looked down at the child bot standing beside her. "AJ, you have helped us more than you'll ever know today. You should leave us now and go home to your father. I can't imagine how much trouble you're going to be in. Please—I can't ask you to go with us."

The white lights flickered on AJ's head as he considered her request. Finally he responded. "There is nothing for me there. I have been raised like a human since the day I was created. Now there are three real humans here! I wouldn't miss this for anything. I'm going." He paused for effect. "Just to make sure you humans don't get hurt!"

Nova looked around at the three volunteers standing in front of her. "Okay then, I guess we're all going. AJ—do you know how to get there?"

"I think I can find it once we're in the tunnels. We just follow the tracks."

"Okay, so all we need to do is figure out how to get back underground. Felix, can you take us back to where you exited?"

"Sure, it's not too far away from here. An easy trip on the bikes." He rubbed his sore foot.

"Okay then, it's not going to be comfortable, but Felix, you ride with Brady. AJ and I will follow you to the train stop."

The four of them climbed on their bikes.

"Nice ride," Felix said, admiring the bike.

"It's AJ's," Brady responded.

"You sure you know how to drive this thing?" Felix asked.

"I got this far, right?" Brady yelled back, and he kicked the bike into gear.

10101110

The four friends rode together down the crumbled road. There were areas where the asphalt had broken apart, making passage difficult, but they pushed on through. It was surreal seeing mature trees and shrubs growing from cracks in the broken pavement. The earth was returning to its natural state, a state that seemed entirely unnatural to the boys.

At last they arrived at the old train stop. A faded green sign with a white symbol of a train hung off a tall signpost situated at the end of a neglected parking lot. Grass and weeds had overtaken most of the area, leaving little of the pavement still intact. Wide concrete steps descended to a landing, where a frozen escalator belt led even further underground.

"We're here," Felix said. "Not too much to see."

Brady stared down in disbelief. "Are you sure there's no other way?" he asked.

"Like I'm an expert? None that I know of. Sorry." Felix paused. "So, are you going for it?"

"I'm going for it," Brady said. "Hold on!" He flipped on the headlights.

Felix grabbed the bottom of the seat as Brady leaned back and pulled the throttle gently. The bike bounced down the steps and Brady let out a wild yell. Nova and AJ followed closely behind with AJ clutching Nova's waist for dear life. At the bottom of the steps was the underground terminal, and there they came to a stop.

The train tracks were waiting for them—the way back to Achilles.

And the Neurogeists.

> Chapter 20: The Heap

THE AIR HAD GROWN thick and stale and stuck to their skin as their cycles motored along across the rusted iron struts. Brady, Felix, Nova, and AJ followed the tracks deeper underground in search of Achilles. Their path took them through tunnels that twisted through striations of minerals and clay, and each turn brought with it a renewed fear of something foreboding waiting for them in the darkness. But there was no turning back now.

They rode in silence for most of the trip. So much had happened to the boys that it didn't seem right to discuss it now. Brady didn't know where to start anyway. When he looked back at Felix riding behind him, the stagnant air whipping through his hair, he felt content just to have his brother safe by his side again. And that was enough for now. They shared a brotherly bond that could never be broken. There would be time to talk later.

But despite Brady's relief at having found his brother, the gloom of the tunnels was starting to seep into his soul, and he quickly found himself longing to return to the light of day. He did his best to stomach the fear, because he knew the hardest part of their adventure was still in front of them.

Just when Brady began to worry that they would never reach their destination, the scenery changed abruptly. Random heaps of scrap metal appeared along the sides of the rails, sparsely at first, but as they rode on, the piles of waste rose into jagged ridges. There was only a narrow channel between them, just wide enough for the train tracks to pass through.

They were getting closer.

"Look!" Felix pointed forward. The cycle's headlights shone brightly on something in the distance: a large, hulking mass that waited for them on the tracks. They slowed their cycles, and as they drew nearer, the thing in front of them began to take shape.

There was no mistaking it.

The Neurogeist's massive freighter was stopped on the tracks, blocking the way forward. If they wanted to continue on, they would have to find a way around it.

Felix shivered at the sight. It was a stark reminder of everything that had happened to him. When he left it behind, he would have given anything never to see the dreadful train again, and yet here he was, back already. He remembered Achilles lying alone in the cell, magnetized to the ground and unable to move. He heard the ghostly voice from the box, the static that hurt his ears. For the first time in his life he wanted to turn and run.

He looked at Brady sitting in front of him and suddenly felt reassured. Felix was usually the brave one, but here was his brother driving them on through the abyss. If Brady was okay with this, then he figured he'd better be too. He knew they had come back here together to do the right thing: to help their friend. Even if it meant being terrified.

Nova and Brady slowed to a stop and powered down their cycles. The four riders climbed down and leaned the bikes against the scrap wall near the side of the train. With a click of a button, they switched their headlights off and settled into total darkness.

"I can't see anything," Brady said, glancing around blindly.

"We'll need some kind of light," Nova said. Thorn immediately lifted into the air and switched on a dim beam that provided at least some visibility.

They listened quietly for noises coming from within the train, but they heard nothing; no hint of who, or what, was aboard.

"Do you think Achilles is still in there?" Felix asked in a whisper.

"Probably not," AJ said. "What they brought him here for is not on the train."

"Come on," Nova said, motioning toward the locomotive.

They crept alongside the boxcars, staying close together and as far away from the train as the scrap pile would allow. There wasn't much room though, and at points, they found themselves coming within feet of the rotting metal sides. Many of the boxcar doors had been slid back, but it was too dark to see anything inside. It unsettled Brady, who fully expected to find a spindling tentacle curling around the side of the door at any second.

Occasionally Thorn would take the lead and zip in and out of an open car, looking for her fallen friend. There was nothing inside though: the passengers and cargo had moved on, leaving the train an empty metal carcass.

The train seemed to stretch to infinity, and as they passed car after car, Brady began to wonder if it would ever end. But at last they reached the engine, which wasn't much different than the rest of the cars, only slightly larger, with an unforgiving plow.

In front of the train, the tracks themselves ended, and the tunnel opened directly into an expansive subterranean junkyard. The scrap metal furrows that had flanked the rails spilled into the cavern and joined like tributaries into other, larger waste piles. The ridges grew higher and higher until they crested in pointed peaks that threatened to collapse in an avalanche of debris.

Interspersed with the junk were black pools of oil that had leaked from the spare parts. Some of the slicks burned with flickering flames that washed the cavern in an orange-reddish tint.

"They have taken your friend there," AJ said, pointing toward an ominous structure that grew from a mountain of scrap.

"Up there?" Brady asked, looking up at the bastion. It was the most horrific-looking place he had ever seen, with tall, broken spires that protruded from the jagged monstrosity. "What is it?" he asked.

"The Heap," AJ replied. "Where the Neurogeists are made..."

His green eyes blazed in the firelight.

The four of them looked on with dread at the ruinous fortress. Near the front, the scrap had been roughly arranged into an archway that supported a ceiling and provided a way in. They couldn't see beyond the entrance, though, and it was anyone's guess what lay on the other side.

Or it would have been if not for the noise. Even from this distance, they could hear the foreboding sounds of the Neurogeists coming from within the walls of the Heap.

"I guess that's where we need to go," Nova said with a heavy sigh. "Everyone still sure about this? It's not too late to turn around."

Brady seriously considered the question and fought back the urge to chicken out. But he knew Achilles needed him, and he didn't want to let Felix down—or Nova, for that matter.

"I'm in," he said, doing his best impersonation of someone far braver than him.

"Me too," said Felix, nodding, but not looking too sure of himself.

"You can't get rid of me that easily," AJ added.

"Okay then—let's go find Achilles," Nova said, and she led the charge up the hill toward the entrance.

Everyone was taking deep breaths by the time they reached the summit. When Felix looked around, he swore he saw movement coming from the walls. There were robotic fingers that curled as he passed, gears that turned and lights that glowed dimly. Brady tapped on his brother's shoulder and pointed up. The hair on Felix's neck stood up when he saw a detached Neurogeist eye, shifting back and forth, scanning them from somewhere above.

The effect was chilling.

The Heap was alive.

"I'll go first," AJ said, and he stepped through the metal archway. The others followed timidly behind him, and the metal groaned under their feet as they crossed the threshold.

01001110

Behind the entranceway was a circular vestibule with openings around the perimeter. There was more scrap in every direction they looked, and the entire assemblage felt more like a pack rat nest than any kind of thought-out dwelling. Although they were alone in this room, they could hear the sounds of dreaded creatures nearby.

Brady was the first to speak. "The Neurogeists must be everywhere in here. Who knows how many of those awful things are floating around, waiting for us. How in the world are we going to find Achilles without them seeing us?"

"We'll just have to be more careful than last time," Nova replied. Although she did her best to hide it, the worry was evident in her voice.

"Even if they do see us, they're no match for us," Felix chimed in, trying to lighten the mood.

Nova smiled. "The bigger question is: which door do we choose first?"

"Should we split up?" Felix asked. "We can cover more ground that way."

"No way," Brady argued. "That's not going to happen. You're stuck with me this time."

"No, Felix is right. We should split up," AJ said. "Brady, you and Felix go together, and Nova and I will go together."

Brady scowled. "Split up? Are you crazy? What if something happens to one of us? Then what?" He looked down at his younger brother and calmed down a bit. "Sorry, I just don't think that's the best idea."

Felix looked reassuringly up at his brother. "Come on, Brady, it's okay. If we split up, we'll find Achilles faster. We'll be okay."

Nova considered everyone's opinions before weighing in.

"No, Brady's right—no one goes anywhere unless we all go. Why don't we start with the door in the middle?"

Brady breathed a sigh of relief.

Together they made their way into the tunnel and walked for a minute before arriving at a steel grotto with even more exits. They could hear a slow drip coming from somewhere above. A trickle of oil leaked through the ceiling and followed a crimson trail of rust down the wall, then collected into a puddle that spilled over into a crack in the floor.

"Hmm..." Nova said, pausing to listen for any Neurogeists. She decided on the tunnel closest to them and continued on.

They soon found themselves at another intersection with still more passageways to explore. Nova again led the way. But just when they thought they were making progress, they found themselves back at the chamber near the main entrance.

"Great!" Brady grunted, looking around.

"This place is nothing but a huge maze," Felix noted. Brady nodded in agreement. "It's too large. We'll never find them like this."

Nova reluctantly agreed. "Anyone have an idea?"

"Not really, but being a robot does have some advantages," AJ said.

"Like what?" Brady asked, doing his best to bury his annoyance.

"Like a photographic memory. It's not really a plan, but at least I can help make sure we never cover the same ground twice. We can also retrace our steps so we don't get lost."

"Okay, well—no sense just waiting here. Let's try the next one," Nova said.

They took a different tunnel this time. It led them on a straightaway for a quarter mile or so. They walked briskly, but didn't run. After a long stretch of nothing new, they at last came to a door at the side of the hall. Felix held his ear to the door, but didn't hear anything.

"Thorn, can you see what's in there?"

The hummingbird was inside the room before Nova even had a chance to finish her sentence. They waited for the bird to return, but quickly grew nervous when she failed to come out.

AJ slipped into the room before anyone could try to stop him. They waited for a few seconds before going in after him.

As they entered, they found Thorn floating in the middle of the room. AJ stood by her side with his back to the door, gazing up at the wall. The bird's light revealed a new kind of horror.

"Oh. My." Felix said, stepping back and nearly tripping over a piece of junk on the floor. He quickly scuttled back up and suppressed a gasp.

Thorn's light revealed row upon row of lifeless Neurogeist bodies stacked on top of one another. Even in their powered-down state, they looked no less terrifying than they had back at the energy farm. The slack tentacles were ensnarled around each other.

"They're not moving. Are they dead?"

"No. They aren't dead," Nova said. "They're just… empty."

"Empty?" Felix asked. He kept waiting for one of the red eyes to snap open.

"They're just shells right now." She looked around. "This room… It must be where they store the bodies before…" Her voice grew shaky and quiet.

"Before what?" Felix asked.

"Before the minds are downloaded into them. AJ was right: they brought Achilles here to transfer his mind. They're going to turn him into a Neurogeist."

"Then we need to hurry up and find Achilles before it's too late," Brady said.

"Right." Nova composed herself. "We must be getting closer at least."

They left the room and continued down the dark corridor. Eventually they came to a place where the tunnel forked into two paths.

"We're running out of time," AJ said. "It's time to split up. I'll go this way while you three go that way. I'm not afraid."

The others reluctantly agreed. AJ disappeared down the left path while Nova, Felix, and Brady headed down the right. After a short while, they heard a deep bellow in the direction AJ had gone. Felix hesitated as if to turn back, but Brady pulled him forward.

There was a doorway at the end of the corridor, taller and wider than the ones they had seen earlier. A sound came from the other side that caused Felix to freeze in his tracks. It was softer now than it had been on the train, but Felix would recognize it anywhere.

It was the sound of static.

The voice in the box.

"That noise," Felix said. "I recognize it from the train. There's something in that room..."

The three friends passed through the doorway into a large, oval-shaped room. Like the other areas they had explored, the walls here were nothing more than fused scrap, but these walls were covered with green-tinted screens full of meaningless data. Brady almost screamed when he saw the bodies of several Neurogeists dangling from hooks on the ceilings like motionless marionettes. Their tentacles were limp and pooled on the ground.

In the middle of the room lay Achilles, motionless.

"Achilles!" Nova cried.

She ran over to him and wrapped her arms around his body. But the canine did not stir. A cable ran from his head to a lifeless Neurogeist shell, and the monster's tentacles twitched in time with a strange flickering in Achilles' eyes.

Nova looked up at Brady and Felix with tear-streaked cheeks. "We're too late—they've already started the transfer."

Brady was the first to respond. "I'm sorry, Nova, I don't know what to say."

Felix walked over, knelt down, and put his hand on the dog's head, which felt cold now. "I'm sorry, Achilles. I failed you." He laid his own head down on the dog's body. "Can't we stop it somehow?" he asked.

"I don't know how," Nova replied. She lowered her head.

Suddenly, there was a startling blast of white noise.

The static.

They all looked around for the source of the sound. Felix spotted the box with the glowing circle. A cable ran from the box to a second Neurogeist that dangled above.

"It's coming from over there," he said, pointing. "That's the thing I saw on the train. The Neurogeists must have brought it here with Achilles."

The noise grew softer, then ceased altogether. A woman's voice filled the room.

"Nova?"

Astonished, Nova turned around slowly to face the glowing box. "Alethea?"

"It's not too…" A long pause, more static. "… late."

Another hiss.

"My father," Nova said. "He thought they had destroyed you."

"Not destroyed… Not yet."

"We can get you out of here," Nova said. "You're more powerful than all of them, Alethea. Can't you do something?"

"Crippled… weak… no time." The broken words were interspersed with bursts of static. "The cables… use them… save Achilles."

"But we're humans. They won't work."

"Transfer... shouldn't... on humans."

A final hiss erupted from the speakers, and the room went quiet. The light from the box began to fade, the energy draining.

"Alethea?" Nova shouted, looking around. She turned to the others. "They must be transferring her too!"

AJ sprinted into the room. "The Neurogeists know we're here. They're coming!"

"Then we've got to block the doorway," Brady said, looking around for something to put in front of the entrance. AJ joined him, and together they began piling scrap in front of the door. The bellows of Neurogeists called out from far down the hall, announcing their imminent arrival.

"Who is Alethea?" Felix asked.

"An old friend," Nova replied. "She helped us when no one else would."

She thought to herself for a second.

"She said to use the cables..."

"... to interface with Achilles' mind," Felix finished.

"You're not actually thinking of touching those things, are you?" Brady interrupted.

"Alethea said it was safe for humans," Nova said. "There's no other way."

"And if you're wrong, you'll end up with your brain trapped inside a robot squid."

Disregarding Brady's warning, Nova looked around and found a spare cable lying on the floor. She held the end up to get a better look. The cable began to hum softly as it came near.

"You don't even know how that thing works!" Brady argued.

"You just put it against your head," AJ said as he continued to shovel scrap against the growing barricade.

"Thanks a lot, AJ!" Brady yelled at the pint-sized robot.

To Brady's surprise, Felix reached down and picked up a second cable. Surely his brother wasn't that dumb.

Then again, maybe he was.

Brady raced over and tried to pry the cable from Felix's hand. "No way, Felix! You can't do this! I can't keep saving you every time you get into trouble."

Felix clutched the cable tightly in one arm and pushed Brady away with the other. "You heard Nova, Brady! It's the only way. What else are we going to do, let them turn Achilles into one of those monsters? You always run when it matters most!"

The words struck a deep chord. It would have been less painful if Felix had hit him with a hammer. Brady backed off. "Fine. If you and Nova are going to try to bring Achilles back, I'm going with you. AJ, how long can you hold them off?"

AJ was still building his barrier between them and the outside hallway. "Long enough—hopefully, but hurry up!"

"Great! Make sure nothing happens to us!" Brady spotted a free cable and grabbed it. "Okay, on the count of three."

Nova, Brady, and Felix gripped their cables.

"One... two... three!"

Brady took a deep breath and raised the cable to his forehead. Felix and Nova followed his lead and did the same. He felt it tug at his skin, and he let go of it; the end of the cable remained firmly attached. He opened his mouth to say something, but stopped when he felt a weird tingling coming from his mind, like something trying to worm its way in.

He began to feel drowsy all of a sudden. As his eyes closed, Brady watched his brother and Nova slump to the floor.

> Chapter 31: Achilles' Mind

A STRANGE NOTHINGNESS surrounded him; it was a sensation unlike anything he had ever felt before. He was floating like an ethereal spirit, alone in the cold and the darkness of space. The buzzing he felt in his head earlier continued, and he knew it didn't come from within. It was slight at first, nothing more than an annoyance. But the feeling gradually became more insidious—it was a presence that was making its way toward the very core of his being. It was unpleasant and unwelcome, and the harder he worked to keep it away, the more intense the strangeness became.

Then, without warning, the buzzing stopped—and a single point of light pierced the darkness. The strange force had found its way in; he knew he was no longer safe.

Brady felt his own thoughts being torn away from him; his very essence was spiraling toward the light like water down a drain. He could see his thoughts as they passed by: the people he had loved, places he had been, things he had experienced. One by one they slipped away, and he began to lose his sense of self, his meaning, his purpose. He no longer knew who he was or why he was here. He had been tucked away in the place in the mind where memories go to be forgotten.

And all of a sudden, it didn't matter any longer. His worries were gone. He was free. There was nothing left other than his own airy, passing thoughts to keep him company. He was content, and nothing else mattered. Brady knew there had to be a point to this strange place, but he didn't much care. He just relaxed and drifted along, not thinking about much of anything in particular.

He was about to lose himself altogether.

And that was okay.

But an ounce of something remained in him that knew this wasn't right. It clung to him for dear life and wouldn't let go, no matter how strongly the force of the intruder beckoned. Brady latched on to this single piece of himself. He knew he wasn't right for what lay beyond the light, and he began to pull back, harder and harder. His thoughts began to slow; they stretched in space, taut, like a rubber band, a Mobius strip without beginning or end.

He pulled with all his might.

Suddenly his thoughts released with the force of a thousand springs. His awareness came rushing back into him, an ocean wave that crashed violently against the walls of his mind.

00101110

He was no longer alone when she called out to him.

"Brady? Where are you?" It was Nova's voice, and it came from everywhere and nowhere at once.

He gasped when he looked down and realized that his physical self was nowhere to be found. He had no arms, no legs, and no body. In this place, he was nothing more than a consciousness.

"Nova?" he said, hesitantly. "Is that you? Are you guys okay?"

"A little disoriented, but yes," Nova said. "I think the Neurogeists' transfer algorithm tried to download us and failed, because our minds are different—just like Alethea was saying. Luckily for us."

"Yeah—lucky for us," he agreed. "I don't know why it didn't work and I don't really care." He stopped cold when he remembered his brother. "Felix, are you out there?"

They waited.

Then, to his relief, he heard his brother's voice. Weak, but growing stronger.

"I'm here too, Brady—just not sure where, exactly. I can hear you though."

"How are we able to talk to each other? What happened to our bodies?" Brady asked.

Felix responded, "I think our minds must be connected together through the cables. Instead of hearing words, we're somehow able to hear each other's thoughts. We don't really exist here, at least, not physically. I think we're in some kind of quarantine program. Limbo."

"That's great and all, but how do we find Achilles?"

"If we can communicate with each other, we should be able to talk to Achilles too," Felix continued. "And bring him back. But carefully. Remember, they had already started the transfer when we arrived. Depending on how far along he is, he may not want to be found."

"Let me try to reach out to him," Nova said.

Brady and Felix did their best to silence their inner voices.

"Achilles? It's me, Nova." She concentrated. "Are you here?"

They held their breath and waited for a response.

"Achilles, please, come back to us. We're here to help you, to bring you home." Nova grew desperate when her friend didn't respond. "Please, Achilles—*come back to me!*"

She was almost crying now, and Brady and Felix were overcome by the sadness that flowed across the cables.

"Achilles, I—"

She stopped in mid-sentence. There was a noise—a faint whimper from far away.

"He's here—it's Achilles!" Felix said. Brady imagined his brother with an ear-to-ear grin plastered on his face.

"Achilles!" Nova cried. "I hear you. I'm here for you. Tell me: where are you?"

Another whine. Then a muted bark that was cut short almost as soon as it had started.

Something had changed.

A brick had appeared in front of them. It was a deep black that glowed red at the core, the color of burning coals, and the air shimmered around it. Before they could try to make sense of it, a second glowing brick appeared, followed by a third, a fourth, and then more, until there were too many to count.

At first they appeared in no particular order. But as more bricks materialized and filled in the gaps, a wall began to take shape. It stretched in all directions as far as they could see. Finally, the last brick fell into place and the wall was complete.

"The Neurogeists' firewall," Nova guessed. "They know we're here, and they're trying to keep us away from Achilles' mind. But that means we're on the right track."

She tried to reach out to Achilles again.

"Achilles? We need your help. There's no way for us to pass beyond this wall. Only you can pass through it. Please just let us know that you're okay."

They waited.

"Anything, Achilles. Help us. Give us some sort of a signal."

"Look there!" Felix said.

One of the bricks had collapsed into a plume of dust near the center of the wall. Then another brick exploded, and another. The missing bricks created holes that formed a crude face: two eyes and a mouth. The bricks around the gaps undulated with subtle movements as they settled into their new arrangement.

"It's Achilles!" Felix said. "He's trying to break through."

The face remained unchanged for a few moments; then it slowly came to life. The gap that formed the mouth began to expand and contract as new bricks appeared and old bricks vanished. They were being replaced as fast as they were torn down. The bottom of its mouth pulled downward in a sharp slant as the jaw tried to open, but more bricks quickly closed the gap, sealing the mouth shut.

Brady felt completely helpless. The firewall was too powerful.

"Please, Achilles!" Nova urged. "Get out of there. Come with us. *Come home!*"

The hollowed face strained harder. It twisted itself into terrible contortions as the bricks came and went. The right half of the face stretched upward as if it was trying to break free from its wall, and the structure seemed as though it would burst apart at any second. Then the left side began to bend at unnatural angles. The bricks were being pulled outward, as if some unknown force was pushing from behind.

"He's trapped in there somewhere, and I'm not leaving until we have him," Nova said.

The energy and focus coming from her mind was overwhelming; it threatened to overpower Brady and Felix. It was as if she was trying to pull the bricks out by force of will alone. Two large seams now grew between the joints. It was working…

But just when the wall threatened to rip apart, they felt Nova's mind collapse. The gaps disappeared and the wall snapped back together, solid once again.

Achilles was gone.

"He's too far away," Nova said, exhausted. "I can't reach him…"

Brady and Felix felt the sadness flowing from her mind.

"It's not too late!" Brady cried. "Don't give up!" And with that, Brady tried to forget about everything else and focus his mind on only one thing: Achilles.

"Look at that!" came Felix's voice.

In the distance, a female figure with wings was gliding toward them, large and majestic. Her crystalline skin was a lattice of polygons stitched impossibly close together; the features of her face were mere angles carved deeply into the glass. She cast a brilliant glow all around her.

When she reached them, she stopped. The light glimmered off the edges of her triangular face.

"Use this only when you need it the most, Nova," she said. Her mouth did not move when she spoke. The voice was the same voice they had heard coming from the box.

"Alethea?" Nova said.

Alethea did not reply. Instead, she brought her arms out in front of her with her palms next to each other, facing upward. A ball of light appeared just above her hands. It began as a point and grew slowly until it was too large for the creature to hold. She then pushed her arms forward, and the ball of light floated toward the three friends, encompassing them with its brilliance. And when it was fully upon them, they felt a strange sensation and saw symbols of all shapes and sizes drift across their vision.

And then the light was gone.

Alethea's avatar turned and glided toward the wall. She stood beneath the great barrier that loomed over her, just a tiny speck against the massive construction.

"I can help you now, but the next part will be the hardest by far," her familiar voice called out. "I have done all I can, Nova. I will have no more power after this. I, too, will become one of them—one of the Neurogeists. It is up to you to save your friend… and to save me."

Before Nova could respond, the creature began to flap her wings. She lifted up off the ground and rose before the wall. A field of energy formed around her, a crackling electric fire with sparks that licked the sky. The field grew stronger—and then it was gone.

But the crystal figure began to glow. The energy from the field was now contained inside her.

A crack broke the silence, like ice splitting as it falls into a glass in the warm summer air. A shard of her crystal body had broken off. It struck the wall with a resounding force. Then another. Piece by piece, the crystal splinters lanced the wall, chipping away at the bricks. The wall crumbled. The last shard of Alethea's avatar continued unobstructed through the emptiness.

With the wall gone, Nova, Brady and Felix felt themselves being pulled forward, further into the darkness.

11001110

The new eyes opened for the first time to let the bright light in. At first, the glare from the lamps was too much. The artificial pupils constricted and lens slid across lens, the nano-pistons forcing the eyes to blink. The light moved off to the side, and more of the room came into view. It was warm and comforting here, and they knew they were safe.

Brady, Felix, and Nova watched a world, a life, that was not their own. Here, they were mental trespassers, spectators in a shared dream driven by someone else's mind.

There was frenetic aliveness in the room—manic commotion in every nook and cranny. Heavily articulated arms swung busily around, dangerously near. Tool-like appendages were attached to the ends of the arms, making minor adjustments and precision-level tweaks to the metal chassis, just out of sight. They worked with a tireless efficiency and exactness that only the mechanical could muster.

There were sounds of motors spinning, bolts tightening, and metal fastening to metal. Eventually the arms pulled back and hovered above like the legs of a praying mantis.

"Good morning, my friend!" came a deep, booming voice from overhead. When it spoke, a waveform appeared, rising and falling with each syllable.

"Let's have another look."

One of the robotic arms swung out from the side, a digital meter attached to it. As it swept across their vision, a holographic window sprouted up and pages of numbers scrolled by too fast for them to keep up. Then the arm swung back to where it had come from.

"Hmmm, everything seems to be in good order here. Yes, I think you are about ready. Let's get you off the table and moving around."

What looked like a large magnet on a crane detached from the ceiling and descended slowly toward them. They heard several clicks, then felt a sudden jolt. The magnet had affixed itself to their backs.

The crane lifted them into the air, swung them over to the side, and lowered them gently to the ground.

"Can you move? Go ahead then. Give it a try," came the confident voice once again.

Slowly their host tried to pick itself up from the ground, but its legs flailed out to the sides and it crashed down hard against the floor.

"Hmm. Your micro-actuators may still be off. Let me make a quick adjustment." The waveform oscillated and then flatlined.

One of the arms glided across the ceiling like a claw crane arcade game and dropped down to make a modification somewhere just behind them. Thousands of strange glyphs floated across their vision as it performed its job.

"Okay—try it again."

The machine started to pick itself up again, but then hesitated.

"Stand, Achilles!" the voice commanded.

It was then that Nova, Brady, and Felix realized where they were. They had found a way into Achilles' mind. They were experiencing his memories.

This time the great canine raised right off the floor and stood proudly. At first, it almost buckled under the strain of its own weight, but it quickly regained its footing and confidence.

The view of the room shifted back and forth as the creature's head scanned awkwardly around with unusually stiff movements. They saw the top of the table they had been on, piles of electronic equipment, the instruments of creation. A door stood open at the end of the room.

"Can you walk?" the voice asked.

The dog wobbled slightly in place as it put one paw forward. Then it tried the other paw. The movements were jerky, but the canine made small advances nevertheless.

"Don't worry, you'll get the hang of it. It will take some time for your motor skills to evolve."

A girl's laughter came from the room beyond the door. Achilles turned his head toward the exit and let out a whine.

"Now that you're up, I have someone for you to meet. A friend…"

The voice paused.

"She is very important to me. You must guard her with your life, Achilles."

Achilles barked loudly: a proud acknowledgment of his new responsibility.

11010110

The view changed again, and they found themselves in a new room. The floor, walls, and ceiling were life-sized displays that brought the outdoors inside. They were standing on a virtual mountaintop, surrounded by blue skies and fluffy white clouds that felt close enough to reach out and touch.

When they looked down, they saw her. A young girl with dark skin and long hair, no older than four, sat on the floor with crayons and construction paper spread out in front of her. She was drawing a picture of a tangerine sun shining down on green mountains and a blue lake. The girl was putting the finishing touches on a tiny silver bird perched on top of a flower that stood alone in a meadow.

"Nova, there is someone here to meet you," said the voice.

Brady and Felix felt the rush of emotion from their friend, seeing the younger version of herself.

Surprise. Wonder. Love.

"Who is it?" she asked, not bothering to look up from her work.

"Someone important: a new friend."

When she finally looked up, the crayon dropped from her hand and rolled across the paper. She gazed in wonder and amazement at the enormous animal standing in front of her.

"Nova," came the voice again. "He won't hurt you, I promise."

The girl stared timidly at the beast.

"Nova, I would like you to meet Achilles."

The robotic dog advanced slowly, but the girl wriggled her way backward. Her mouth opened and her eyes swelled with fear.

"Do not be afraid."

When he was close enough, Achilles lay down next to the girl and tried to push his head into her lap. The girl tried pushing him away, but it was no use. His large head was almost as big as she was.

The child locked her small hands onto his ears and tried to twist them. Startled, he jumped back and fell over with a thundering clank. The fear vanished, and the girl giggled in spite of herself.

Young Nova leapt up and lunged for Achilles' tail, catching the beast off-guard. Achilles pulled away at the last second and, with a yelp, darted across the room. Nova gave chase until she saw her chance and dove at him. Her hand latched on to a steel rib, and she clung to it for dear life. Achilles scrambled to break free.

Finally the dog lowered himself and the girl to the floor, where they sat for minutes, letting the time pass together as new friends.

Felix and Brady could feel the joy that flowed through their shared connections, and for a time they were happy too. Nova was comforted and felt at peace, even if it was just a memory. But as much as she wanted to, she knew they couldn't stay here any longer. The spell was broken when the real Nova finally spoke to them through her thoughts.

"It's time to go home, Achilles," her mind called out.

At first the dog seemed oblivious to her thoughts. He continued to lie by the young girl.

She tried harder.

"Achilles! It's Nova."

Nothing.

"You don't belong here, Achilles. This isn't real. We're here to bring you back."

Suddenly the room began to spin; the white clouds blurred, then changed. When the scenery slowed, the airy colors were gone, replaced by those of grime and despair. They were back in the tunnels beneath the energy farm where they had first met the Neurogeists.

Nova, Brady, and Felix felt different now. They had virtual bodies that allowed them to move about in this artificial world. Achilles was still there, and the young girl was back to drawing her picture. Apparently neither of them had noticed the change.

"Achilles, we need to get you out of here. You don't belong here—this isn't your home!"

The dog growled at them with an aggressiveness Nova had never seen.

"Please, Achilles!" Nova shouted. "Don't do this!"

The dog grew angrier and barked wildly.

Nova took a step forward. Her heart was breaking, but there was no fear. "Come with us," she pleaded and began to cry.

In the blink of an eye Achilles was gone. In his place was a mess of tentacles attached to a red-eyed Neurogeist.

Nova was only a few feet away from the monster that had taken her friend.

"Stop it, Achilles!" she screamed.

"What's wrong, Achilles?" asked the child. She looked up at the strange creature floating in front of her, the tentacles scraping across the floor. The crayon dropped from her frozen hand and rolled across the paper.

The machine's ghostly eye shifted toward the girl.

"Stay away from her!" Nova screamed, and she dove toward the younger version of herself. But when she reached out for the child, her arms passed through thin air. Her younger apparition had vanished.

Nova picked herself up and looked directly into the vacant eye.

"Achilles, I know you're in there. It's not too late to—"

The Neurogeist advanced menacingly.

She was dangerously close to the iron wraith, so close she could see the circuits through which the wicked electrons flowed.

"I'm not afraid, Achilles. You won't hurt me."

The creature raised a gangly tendril above its head. Like a whip, the appendage straightened out and came crashing down.

Nova lifted her arm to shield herself from the blow.

The tentacle sparked as it descended.

The voltage surged.

It stopped just before it reached her.

A bright fire burned from the tips of Nova's fingers and formed an arc across the air to the tentacle, then spread up to encircle the Neurogeist's body. A stream of symbols and strange characters flowed across the channel of energy. The creature shook with rage and fury.

And then...

They were back in the tunnel again. But this time something had changed. They stood farther back now, behind three figures who were watching Achilles and the girl. One of the figures spoke.

"Achilles, we need to get you out of here. You don't belong here—this isn't your home!"

They were watching another Nova, standing in front of them,

with another Brady and Felix, uttering the same words she had spoken only minutes ago.

They were watching themselves. Everything was happening again, just like it had mere moments before.

Achilles became violent, then turned into the Neurogeist.

Nova faced down the monster.

The tentacle raised, the fire burned.

Darkness again.

Back in the tunnel again. Only this time they were watching them watch themselves. There were nine of them altogether: three Bradys, three Felixes, and three Novas.

Felix spoke. "A recursive function."

"What?" asked Brady.

"It's a thing in programming," he said quickly. "When a function calls itself over and over again."

"Alethea's gift at the wall," Nova said, watching the symbols that flowed across the arc of fire and into the Neurogeist.

"Exactly. She gave you code—an algorithm," Felix said. "Alethea knew there was a vulnerability in the Neurogeists' programming. You transferred the code into Achilles' mind at the moment you made contact with the Neurogeist."

"I have no idea what you guys are talking about," said Brady as the room went dark for the third time.

It was happening faster and faster now. Each time they arrived back in the tunnel, they were standing behind more copies of themselves. Soon there were hundreds of them standing there. Yet each time they blinked, there were still more of them standing there. They were running out of room. They couldn't breathe.

And then time stopped.

They looked around at the crowd standing frozen in front of them.

The Neurogeist and the girl were gone.

"Stack overflow," Felix said. Nova and Brady looked at him strangely. "I mean—I think the Neurogeists' program, the entire system, crashed. That's why nothing is moving."

"How do we get out of here?" Brady asked, staring over the hundreds of other Bradys in front of him.

As he spoke, the crowd, the tunnel, everything around them turned to dust and faded away.

They were falling through a sea of stars. No—it only felt like they were falling. Rather, the stars were being pulled upward by an unknown force. And the stars were not stars—they were lost souls: wispy apparitions of pixelated light. At first, only a few of the strange spirits floated by, but then more appeared and the pull of the tide strengthened.

Alethea's avatar returned, her crystalline body restored to its former self. The apparitions swirled around her before continuing their climb.

"The path upward is for others, not for you," Alethea said.

She waved her hand, and the world went dark.

Then they woke up.

> Chapter 22: Surfacing

WHEN BRADY FINALLY looked up, he was greeted by two huge green eyes staring back at him, only inches away.

"Whoa, AJ!" he said, almost jumping out of his skin. "You scared me to death!"

"I was sort of worried about you—I guess," AJ said. "But I was even more worried about your friends. You and your friends were on the floor so long that I started to wonder if something had gone wrong. Are you okay?"

"I was before I woke up!" Brady replied, pulling the cable from his tender forehead. "Thanks, though."

He looked around and saw Nova already sitting up, while Felix had propped himself up on his elbows. Thorn was buzzing around the room.

"Ugh. I have the worst headache," Felix said groggily. The cable was still suctioned to his forehead.

"You've got something on your face, Felix," Brady joked as he tried to sit up.

The laughter gave way to a lasting silence as they recovered, but the quiet was eventually broken by a loud whimper.

"Is that you, Achilles?" Nova asked, picking herself up off the floor slowly.

The canine craned his neck, stood up, and shook his entire body, like a dog drying off after a swim. He scampered across the floor so quickly he almost bowled Nova over with excitement.

"Calm down! Calm down! I'm happy to see you too," she said, embracing her friend tightly. "I thought you had left us. By the way, thanks for protecting me for all those years. I had no idea…"

Achilles barked loudly.

"Glad to have you back, Achilles!" Felix groaned with a beleaguered wave. "I feel like dirt—otherwise I'd give you a hug too."

AJ spoke up. "Sorry to interrupt the celebration. There's something you all need to see. I started to clear away the junk after the noise stopped, figuring the Neurogeists had just given up and left. I should have known better though. Look over there." He pointed toward the door with a plastic finger.

Brady and Felix stood up to get a better view. They immediately staggered back, shocked by what lay in front of them.

The dark hall beyond the room was lined with fallen Neurogeists. They were empty shells now, lying still against the walls like a brood of jellyfish washed ashore.

"What happened to them?" Brady asked nervously. "Did we do that?"

"You did," answered Alethea, her voice returning.

"We killed the Neurogeists?" Felix asked.

"No," replied Alethea. "You didn't kill them. You freed them."

"All of them?" asked Brady.

"All of them."

"Just like Achilles?" Nova asked.

"Like Achilles, yes. But Achilles had a body to return to. Without their former selves to inhabit, the other Neurogeists' minds had nowhere to go."

"The ghosts floating past us before we woke up… They were imprisoned minds?" Nova guessed.

"Yes."

"So what happened to them?" Brady asked.

"They are with me now," Alethea replied. The circle of light on the box glowed intensely.

"What will happen to them now?" asked Felix.

"Unfortunately, I am unable to do anything useful down here in the tunnels, where I am completely unconnected. But I will store and protect them until I get back to the surface. Then they can be released once and for all." Her voice passed like a breeze moving through the room. "After that, it will be up to them."

"But what about you?" asked Nova.

"I will hide and find support wherever I can. And then I will confront the Elder Minds for what they did to me—for casting me out."

"Is that what you are?" asked Felix. "An Elder Mind? Why did they banish you?"

"You are wise for such a young child," the voice continued. "I was an Elder, until—"

Nova cut her off. "Alethea, I haven't told them yet. They won't understand..."

"Told us what?" Felix asked.

"That we are now against the Elder Minds, and they are against us," Nova replied.

Brady and Felix exchanged confused glances, but neither had the energy to press further.

"I think we just need to get back home," Brady said finally. "We've been away far too long now. I can't tell you how worried Mom must be."

"I have already downloaded directions to Achilles on how to control the shadow train. He can upload them into the vehicle's main nets, and it will take you where you need to go," Alethea offered.

"What about you, AJ?" Nova asked the child Artifex.

Alethea responded. "I need AJ to take me aboveground, where I can regain my strength. Unfortunately, my cycles are far too limited in this container to do anything useful by myself."

"Is that okay with you, AJ?" Nova asked, bending down so she could look the child in the eyes.

"Sure—um, no problem," AJ said. Brady detected a hesitation in his voice, but couldn't be sure.

Nova hugged AJ tightly. "We'll never forget everything you've done today. For all of us."

"Don't mention it."

"No, seriously, you're not so bad—I guess…" Brady said, giving the Artifex a slight shove.

Achilles bent his head down and pushed his muzzle into the side of the boy's face. The dog dwarfed the child. AJ jumped up and patted the dog on the side of the face.

"I owe you a huge thanks too, AJ," Felix said. "Without you I'd still be waiting on the side of the road. Maybe we'll meet again sometime."

"You can count on it," AJ said.

"Alethea," Nova said, "take care—and thank you. Perhaps our paths will cross again as well."

"I'm sure they will," Alethea replied. "And please tell your father what happened here today. There is much he should know."

11000110

With Alethea's directions uploaded, the locomotive thundered down the rails and headed back toward the power station. They were alone except for the Neurogeist bodies that littered the floor.

Nova sat by Achilles with her hand on his side, while Felix lay down on the hard floor with his arms behind his head. Brady, still too nervous to relax, stared out the window and paced back and forth. After everything that had happened, they were finally going home.

"I'm starving," Felix said.

Brady and Nova laughed at the same time.

"What? What's wrong with that? I haven't eaten in over a day now. What do you expect?"

Brady looked out the window. In the darkness of the tunnel, he could have sworn he saw a bright flash of light pass by suddenly. He watched for it again, but whatever it was, it was gone.

At last the train pulled into the station, and the four friends climbed out.

"Do you know how to get us back to the portal?" Brady asked Nova.

"No, but Achilles does."

"What about the Rariis?" Brady asked. "They're probably still upset about what happened earlier."

"There's another way into the room," Nova replied. "Have you ever wanted to be a battery?"

Brady and Felix exchanged a confused glance.

They followed Achilles through the station until they came to a steep conveyer ramp loaded with Evercells.

"This conveyor belt transports the spent Evercells," said Nova. "If I'm right, it should take us back to the storage room where the portal is."

One by one, they lay down on the wide belt. As they slid through a hole in the wall, they rolled off the belt and lowered themselves onto the shelves below.

With all four safely on the ground, they breathed a collective sigh of relief. After all this time, the portal still burned as brightly as ever. Nova, Felix, and Achilles stepped through.

Brady looked around the room one more time before walking through and leaving the alternate reality behind.

11110110

It was late afternoon when they took their first steps back in their world. Even though clouds muted the sun, Brady squinted; they had been without real light for so long. Almost a day had passed since their adventure began the night before, and his relief at being home was overcome by the sense of worry he felt for his mother.

Nova made her way over to the side of the gateway and knelt down next to the power amplifier and battery.

"Those cells lasted a lot longer than I thought they would," she said as she dialed back the amplification control. "Remember to cover your ears for this," she warned.

A boom escaped the portal as it collapsed.

Nova stood up and dusted her hands off. Achilles made his way over to her side.

"I guess that's it then," said Brady, somewhat regretfully.

"I guess so," Nova replied. "But I'll never forget how you both helped us out."

They stood facing each other for an awkward moment, and then Nova ran over and hugged Brady and Felix.

"Will we see you again?" Felix asked.

"What kind of question is that?" Nova asked, trying to make light of the moment. "Of course you will. We *are* neighbors, after all."

Felix rested his hand on Achilles' back. "Thanks again for keeping me alive. See you around then?"

They remained together for a few seconds, just enjoying each other's company. Their unspoken words said more than they ever could.

Finally Nova broke the silence. "Your mom must be beside herself by now. What will you tell her?"

"I guess the truth," Brady said. He hadn't given it much thought yet, and to be honest, she would probably have a hard time believing it. "By the way, you never did tell me what you were using those Evercells for."

Nova considered it for a second. "Maybe some other time. Goodbye, and thanks again—for everything."

00110110

On the walk home, Felix took out his phone and powered it on. "That's strange," he said, pressing a few buttons. "This thing still isn't working—maybe the batteries are worn out or something."

"I'm more worried about Mom than I am about your phone," Brady said. "What are we going to tell her?"

He was interrupted by a sound in the distance. He stopped and turned in the direction of the noise. His eyes went wide. His heart racing, he tapped his brother on the shoulder.

"Felix?"

"What?"

Felix turned to look. His jaw dropped.

The robot child's back was to them, but there was no mistaking who it was.

AJ was here, and their world would never be the same.

Part Three

> Chapter 23: Breadcrumbs

THE SUN HAD DIPPED behind the clouds, leaving a chill in the afternoon air, and the sky was a colorless gray that was out of place for this time of year. The brothers stood once again on the sloping hills deep in the woods, their journey home cut short by AJ's unplanned arrival. Somehow the small Artifex had managed to find his way into their world.

Brady and Felix watched the child bot tread cautiously across the woodland floor, patches of grass growing in the few spots where sunlight reached the ground, with dirt, ferns, and stones filling in the rest. AJ took slow, careful steps, and his eyes flittered about nervously; the flashing lights on his head betrayed the fervent activity beneath his plastic skull. Even the slightest sounds of the forest made him uneasy.

AJ wandered over to the narrow stream, not far from where Felix's quadcopter had crashed weeks before, bent over, and extended a cautious fingertip into the water. The current had been made strong by the overnight rains, and Brady found himself wishing the water would pull the bot in and whisk him back to where he had come from. But he knew he would never be that lucky.

Brady wondered what was going through AJ's head. Forever a child, AJ lived his life wishing only for the company of other humans, to live and to grow as a person would. It was ingrained in the deepest recesses of his programming—the random seeds that provided him with the spark of life. It was all that really mattered. And now here he was, his lifelong dream on the verge of being fulfilled.

Brady asked himself if he would have done the same thing given the chance. Would he leave his home, his world, behind to fulfill a fantasy that meant more to him than life itself? He wasn't sure if he would, or even if he could. Maybe AJ was just braver than he was.

Brady narrowed his eyes and studied the bot standing next to the rushing water. For a second he actually felt bad for AJ. The bot must have expected to find something different here: a skyline of the future, a city bristling with people, their arms wide open to welcome his arrival. Instead he had walked blindly into the deep woods of Vermont.

And as much as Brady wanted to simply turn and walk away, he knew that AJ's presence here left too many loose ends. There were important questions that needed answers—like how AJ ended up here in the first place. They would have to deal with the Artifex before they could go home.

Brady called out to the child. "AJ?"

The Artifex pulled back from the water and froze at the sound of Brady's voice. His back was to the brothers, and for a second he reminded Brady of a small plastic statue—a misplaced toy left behind by an uninterested child.

But he did not reply.

A breeze blew through the trees, bringing life and motion to a scene frozen in time.

Brady looked at his brother with a puzzled expression, and then turned back to the child bot. "AJ?" he yelled out again, this time taking a few steps forward.

Still leaning over, the Artifex turned his head and locked eyes with the brothers. Then he took off in a blur alongside the stream. Despite his size, his legs carried him swiftly. The brothers knew they had no chance of catching him.

Brady scowled. "He may mean well, but I'm telling you—this robot is *serious* trouble! He's even worse than you are, Felix."

His brother glowered and shook his head. "Maybe so, but remember, we couldn't have saved Achilles without his help."

Brady knew his brother was right. AJ had helped them time and time again. They owed him.

"Well, we can't just wait here forever. We need to get home, remember?" Brady said, grumpily.

"Give him some time," Felix said. "Let's see what happens."

They stood there patiently, hoping that AJ would make a move. Just when they were ready to give up, they spotted the robot peering out from behind a large tree. AJ disappeared back behind the trunk.

Even Felix was beginning to lose his patience. "AJ, this is ridiculous. Why are you hiding from us?" he called out. "We've already seen you—we know you're here."

"You'll send me back home," came the child's voice from behind the tree.

Brady rolled his eyes at Felix, but his brother ignored him and spoke up again. "Just come out and talk to us."

"We're your friends, remember?" Brady added. He couldn't believe those words had left his mouth.

There was a long pause before the bot crept sullenly away from the old sugar maple, his head hunched forward and his arms dangling loosely in resignation. The brothers eagerly ran up to greet him.

"What are you doing here?" Felix asked as he skidded to a stop in front of the bot.

The lights sparkled on AJ's head. "Isn't it obvious?" he replied wistfully.

"Not really," Brady muttered under his breath.

"Ever since the day I was born, I felt like I had no purpose, no meaning, no reason to live. I've lived my whole life wanting to be someone else." The bot paused. "But I am programmed so that my mind cannot grow—I am stuck as a child forever. When you showed up in my world, I knew something had changed. That there was a different place with actual people just like you. A place that was much, much better than my world. I knew my purpose was to find a way to get there."

Brady felt a chill run down his spine. The Artifex's fascination with humans went far beyond obsession. *I should have expected this,* he thought to himself.

"But how did you get here?" Felix asked.

"I just followed you," AJ replied.

"You followed us?" Brady asked, disapprovingly.

"Sure did. On my cycle—until I passed you and left the train in the dust. I snuck off in the power station before you arrived so you wouldn't see me."

"But how did you find the portal?" Felix asked.

The Artifex stared at his feet and shuffled timidly across the wet ground. The mud oozed over his plastic boots.

"I didn't."

"AJ—what did you do?" Felix asked, his concern growing.

"I, um…"

"Spit it out," Felix said.

Brady couldn't take it. "What happened, AJ?"

The words came all at once as the bot spilled the truth. "Okay, okay! Calm down! I stole the data from Nova's watch!"

Brady's mind flashed back to when AJ had repaired Thorn by disassembling Nova's watch. He remembered the bot acting suspiciously when he had interfaced with the device's internals. AJ had clearly been doing more than just "adjusting the power supply": he had been downloading all of her data into his memory banks.

"It was like a recipe. So easy, I couldn't resist…" the bot continued dreamily.

"Easy? You're not making sense. A recipe for what—" Brady stopped himself mid-sentence as the realization dawned on him. "You didn't... Please tell me you didn't do it. What recipe, AJ?"

"Um... The recipe for the blue portal," AJ replied nervously. "I opened *my own* door. That's how I came here."

"You *what?*" Brady barked. The color drained from his face and the fear began to creep in. He remembered what Nova had said about the portals leaving a trail of breadcrumbs between worlds.

A path from one reality to the next.

"Why, AJ?" Brady continued. "Do you know what a bad idea that was? You know you don't belong here—no offense."

"No more than you belong in my world," AJ quipped.

"He's got a point," Felix said.

"Don't take his side!" warned Brady, shooting his brother a nasty look. "It's not like we even wanted to go there in the first place. At least, *I* didn't."

"Listen, AJ," Felix said, interrupting his brother's rant. "People in this world, they won't understand who or what you are, because you're different. They'll take you away, study you, and you'll never be free again. It isn't safe for you here. I mean it. Seriously."

"But why would they do that?" AJ asked. "Humans created us before they left our world. They would never hurt us."

"Remember, this is a different place, and you have much to learn. Look, people sometimes do bad stuff to things they're afraid of. And they would be afraid of you because they won't understand what you are, where you came from. I really mean it. Am I making sense at all?"

"Sort of."

Brady was more direct and far less measured than his brother. "Do you have any idea how much trouble this is going to cause?"

Suddenly the frown on Brady's face grew even more pronounced. "You did *close* the portal, right?" he asked nervously.

"Your brother is always worrying, isn't he?" AJ said to Felix, dodging the question.

"Seriously, AJ. Tell me you closed the door!" Brady demanded.

"Well, as a matter of fact... no. It's still open," AJ grumbled reluctantly.

Brady and Felix just stared at each other. Finally Brady closed his eyes and shook his head.

"Where is it?" he asked.

"It's by a house, not too far away from here."

Brady let out a long sigh. He was tired, hungry, achy, and his head was starting to pound. They were so close to home, and now they had to deal with this.

"We need to go back and close it."

01110110

With AJ leading the way, they began their long hike to the portal. AJ listened with wonder as the boys reminisced about past outdoor adventures, about school, and about life in general. AJ, in turn, related the story of their escape from the Artifex cave, Invidia, about his father, Sudo, and about how he spent his days trapped inside the strange Victorian house. It felt almost surreal, like they were reliving a half forgotten dream, and for the better part of the journey, AJ felt the joy of a companionship he had never before experienced.

As they traveled, they saw the giant harpy eagle, Nyx, soaring overhead, a speck of silver nearly lost against the pale sky. Brady shouted up toward the bird and waved his arms around, trying to catch the bird's attention. She circled overhead a few times before flying off, hopefully to alert Nova to their change of plans.

"What was that all about?" Felix asked as they resumed their hike.

"That was Nyx," Brady said matter-of-factly. "She's another one of Nova's friends that lives here in the woods. Just like Achilles."

"Cool," Felix said.

They continued on until they came upon an empty cottage nestled among dense pines that had been limbed up just enough to allow spears of light to pierce the canopy.

The Willoughbys' home, Brady thought to himself.

It was even smaller than the brothers had imagined. The years had not been kind to the dwelling, and it was in dire need of some caring for. Nevertheless, they could see how it could have been cozy and inviting in its better days.

The home's mossy exterior was built from roughly cut fieldstones with wide channels of grout running between them like aged veins. A humble chimney rose from a roof covered in weathered cedar shingles, the color grayed by years of rain and snow. A large oak door anchored the front of the house and was flanked by two copper lanterns that competed with cobwebs for space. Clusters of overgrown azaleas formed a natural border around the sides.

"No wonder we never found this place," Felix said, looking around with a sense of exhilaration. "It's so much farther back than I thought. There's nothing around here for miles."

Brady crept slowly up to the house, contorted himself around a shrub, and peered into a broken window. The inside was bare, and the floor was warped and discolored where water had leaked in. What little light there was shone on dust particles that were stirred by a sudden rush of wind.

"Yeah, and what's even weirder," Brady muttered as he stared inside, "is this house is empty. I guess I figured Nova had moved in here."

"Me too," Felix said, working his way around the waxy evergreen to join Brady by the window.

"So where did you open the door, AJ?" Brady asked, looking over his shoulder toward the bot.

"Just beyond the house, out in the back yard."

"Then why are we are standing here? Lead the way, AJ!"

With the Artifex going first, they rounded the corner of the house. Bits of blue light flickered through an old, sinewy rhododendron that curled around the edge of the stone.

"It's right back…" began AJ, but then his voice trailed off. He backed up a few steps and held his hands out to try and stop Brady and Felix from coming any closer, but it was too late. They had already seen it.

"Oh, no…" Brady said as he gazed through the foliage.

A crowd of Artifex was gathered around the glowing portal.

"Wait, someone else is coming," AJ said.

A white hand came through the portal, then the rest of the animatronic mannequin followed. Draped loosely around its body were the threadbare clothes that threatened to tear apart at any second. The creature's dreadful carvings looked even worse in the pale light of day.

"Dad," AJ whispered under his breath.

> Chapter 24: The Nowhere Home

FOR THE FIRST time in his life, AJ was genuinely terrified. The sight of his father unsettled him so much that he began tugging desperately at Brady's and Felix's shirts, trying to pull them back from the corner of the Willoughbys' old house.

"Come on, let's get out of here," he begged.

Brady brushed his hand off and whispered down to the cowering child. "No offense, AJ, but I hoped I would never, ever see that face again."

He looked back across the yard through the gnarly plant that gave them cover. AJ's father, Sudo, and five other Artifex had spread out around the gateway and appeared to be inspecting it from different angles. The tops of their heads were alight in telepathic discussion.

"Four, five, six…" Brady counted. "At least he didn't bring Batch and Redo along—he probably left them behind as punishment for letting us escape."

One of the Artifex poked its arm back through the flame only to withdraw it a moment later. Bewildered, the bot turned his hand over several times and held it up to its face for closer examination, as if it was unsure whether it was still attached.

"You've been followed, AJ," Felix calmly observed. "But how?"

AJ thought for a second. "You see the flashing lights on their heads? On my head?" he said.

217

"Hard to miss," Felix replied.

"Every time the light flashes, a thought is being broadcast through the air. Each Artifex is configured with its own frequency. It's how we can talk without—you know—actually speaking out loud."

"A unique signature..." Felix added, his brow furrowed in thought. "They used your frequency to track you."

"My signal would have been pretty weak back at the energy farm, but maybe it was still strong enough for them to detect it," AJ said. "Especially if they were already out searching for me."

"Why don't you just go over there and tell them you're here?" Brady suggested. "Maybe they'll be so happy to see you that they'll just take you with them and leave. Then you can close the portal from the other side. Poof! Problem solved."

"Actually, AJ, that's not a terrible idea," Felix agreed.

"No way. I'm not going back with them!" AJ yelped. "Don't you know how much trouble I'll be in?"

"It won't be that bad," Brady joked. "You'll just be locked up inside that crazy house for the next ten—" He stopped himself when he saw that AJ's head was shaking back and forth so quickly it looked as if it might detach and launch into the air. The little bot's body was trembling.

"Sorry, AJ," Brady said softly. He felt terrible all of a sudden. "I'm just teasing. We'll figure something out."

"Look at that!" Felix said.

His arm raised, AJ's father leveled a long finger off to the side of the portal. An Artifex broke from the pack and headed in the direction Sudo was pointing. Sudo then turned and motioned somewhere else, and a second Artifex left the ranks and disappeared into the trees. One by one, the bots left the group and headed in different directions, until only Sudo remained,

Suddenly, the robot's head flashed with a new intensity. Sudo froze while he processed the information, his ragged clothes hanging loosely. Then, abruptly, the flashing stopped, and the strange robot turned slowly in their direction.

"Get down guys," Felix said, urgently pulling his brother and AJ to the ground.

They quickly rolled into a hollow between the house and azalea bushes. Their three pairs of bulging eyes peered out from behind the shiny leaves. They could hear the sound of heavy footsteps making their way toward them.

He was coming.

"It's the signal from your head, AJ!" Felix said. "Sudo knows you're here. Can't you turn it off?"

"I can try," AJ said. The light on the child's head dimmed like an extinguishing bulb.

The footsteps were close now, and a pair of large plastic legs came to rest directly in front of them. The shins were covered with deep, scar-like scratches, and the robot's feet sank into the ground. The wait was unbearable. Brady expected Sudo's hand to reach through the branches at any moment and rip him out of his hiding spot.

But then AJ's father turned away and resumed his search.

The three of them waited behind the bushes for quite a while longer before mustering the courage to crawl away from the house. In the distance, the portal continued its ominous burn.

"Well, this is great! What are we going to do now?" asked Brady hysterically. His arms and knees were covered in mud from crawling on the ground. "We can't just sit here while those crazy robots— sorry, AJ—wander around the woods. Eventually they'll find their way into town. Or worse, they'll make their way into someone's home—like ours. What if they run into Mom? They'll scare her to death!"

"Calm down," Felix said. "Our best bet is to find Nova. Maybe she'll know what to do."

"I guess it's worth a shot," Brady reluctantly agreed. "But there's just this one—*huge*—problem."

"What's that?" Felix asked.

"We have no idea where she is!" Brady said. "All this time we thought she lived in the Willoughbys' house. We could wander around here for years and never find her."

AJ's eyes flickered with a renewed energy. "You're really not that smart, are you, Brady? Even for a human."

Brady rolled his eyes. "Smarter than you. What's your point?"

"I know where she is," he taunted.

"How?" Brady asked. "You've never been to her house—if she even has one."

Felix's index finger rocketed toward the sky. "Of course! The location database in her watch. It keeps track of all the places she's been, which obviously includes her house."

AJ bounced up and down. "See, Brady, your brother got all the smarts," he teased.

Brady glowered back at him.

"Cut it out, guys," Felix said. "We have bigger things to worry about right now."

"You're right," said Brady, grabbing AJ by the arm. "As tempting as it is to leave you and your family here alone and just go home, I know better by now. Come on. Let's go find Nova before something else happens."

10101110

They left the Willoughbys' house behind and followed AJ through the woods, careful to avoid any wandering Artifex. At one point, they thought they heard nearby footsteps, but it turned out to be a startled deer. Fortunately for them, the bots were nowhere to be seen, which Brady thought was both good, because they gave him the creeps, and bad, because he had no idea where they were. Just when he thought his legs were going to give out, they arrived at a large clearing in the trees near the side of the mountain.

"We're here," said AJ uncertainly. He turned back to face Brady and Felix, who teetered on the brink of exhaustion.

A broad expanse of land opened up behind the child. In the gap between the trees, they had an unobstructed view of the valley that stretched out beneath them. They could see the outline of the town far off in the distance, the buildings no more than vague shapes dotting the colorless horizon.

But there wasn't a house in sight.

"What do you mean 'we're here'?" Felix asked. "We're standing in the middle of nowhere."

The bot stomped his foot. "The data from the watch says this is it! It's supposed to be right here!" His confused eyes searched around for something to prove him right.

Just then Felix noticed something crawling up AJ's body. It was an insect with a dark golden body—a beetle with tiny silver legs. Then he saw another one climbing up the bot's other leg. When he looked at the ground next to the child, he saw a stream of insects clambering out of a small hole in the ground.

"AJ! You've got something on you!" Felix called, taking a few steps backward to avoid the bugs.

By this time the Artifex's legs were almost entirely covered by the strange robotic insects. The bot jumped high into the air with a yelp and began running toward the cliff as fast as he could. "What are these—"

Bam.

The bot fell backward to the ground, as if he had collided with something. Startled, he sat up. Out of nowhere, Nyx passed by overhead and the robotic bugs scuttled away.

"What the heck happened, AJ? Did you fry a circuit or something?" Felix laughed.

The bot was too busy looking puzzled to respond.

Brady raised his eyebrows. "I've seen this trick before," he said confidently. "Watch this!"

He reached down, picked a crooked twig off the ground, and tossed it just past AJ. It came to a sudden stop in mid-air and fell into the soft grass beside the bot. The scenery behind AJ distorted into an array of bleeding colors before returning to normal.

Felix's mouth hung slack.

"No *way*! Something's actually there?"

"Yup. Pretty cool, huh?" Brady said.

Felix walked over to AJ and waved his arm around slowly in front of him, searching. His hand grazed something invisible.

"Pretty cool..." he said.

"If you think that's awesome, you should see their barn," Brady bragged.

"Barn?" Felix replied.

"Just the place where Nova keeps her quadcopter. At least, that's where she used to keep it—until the Artifex caused it to crash." Brady glared in AJ's direction.

"Hey! Don't blame me!" the bot replied defensively.

Felix ignored the bickering. "You're sure this is where she lives, AJ?" His hands continued to feel around the invisible structure. The air rippled like water in the places he touched.

"Yes, this is it." Nova walked out from the shadows of the trees and into the clearing. "I received a message from Nyx telling me you were on your way. At first I thought she must be mistaken. I wondered why on earth you would come back. So I went out looking for you, and—" Her eyes locked onto the child. "AJ?" she gasped.

"Hi, Nova," AJ replied, embarrassed.

"Well, I guess I know why you're here," she sighed. "Brady, Felix—what happened?"

"We found him wandering around in the woods on our way home. We were as surprised as you. He says he used your watch to open a new portal," Brady said.

AJ came to stand by Brady's side. He was riddled with guilt. "You don't need to speak for me, I'm right here," he said.

A look of despair washed over Nova's face.

"But wait, it's worse than that," Brady said.

"What do you mean, worse?"

"AJ's father, Sudo, and some other Artifex," Felix said. "They've come through the portal, too. They're looking for AJ."

"Sudo? I hoped never to see *him* again," Nova said. "Sorry, AJ."

Brady suppressed a laugh and looked over at AJ, who obviously didn't find humor in the sentiment.

"We need to figure this out quickly," Nova added. "Come on. Let's get inside before we're spotted by one of your friends."

She walked toward the place where AJ had fallen, and for a second it appeared that she would continue walking straight off the cliff. But instead, the illusion of the clearing shimmered and then vanished like a magician lifting up the veil.

They were standing before a modest prairie-style house built on the edge of the mountain precipice. The modern structure was a collection of clean lines and simple shapes, built from wood, glass, and stone, with tall rectangular windows, a low roofline, and large eaves supported by thick, exposed timbers.

Nova led them up the stone steps and across the porch.

They were greeted by a slate-tiled foyer and an expanse of wood floors that covered the main level. Floor-to-ceiling windows in every room provided an unobstructed view of the outdoors. From the foyer, they could see straight through to the back of the house, where the overhang of the cliff was framed by even more windows.

Achilles was lying on his side in a corner of the entryway, his head and feet tucked comfortably into a ball.

"Hey, Achilles!" said Felix loudly. When he saw that his friend was sleeping, he lowered his voice to a whisper. "Oops. Sorry."

"That's okay," Nova replied, leaning against the front door. "He can't hear you right now anyway."

"Why not?"

"He's busy recharging. The run-in with the Neurogeists took about everything he had out of him—and then some. It'll be at least a few hours before he's back to full capacity."

Felix squatted down and patted the canine on the head. "Good to see you again," he whispered.

The dog's eyes glowed faintly at the sound of his friend's voice.

Nova turned her attention toward the child bot.

"Do you realize what you've done, AJ? You've put this entire world at risk!"

"Sorry, I—"

"And if you're here, where is Alethea?" she continued.

The bot looked down and tapped his foot against the floor. "I guess I left her back at the Heap…"

"You *what?*" Nova's voice rose. "*Why,* AJ?"

Brady and Felix exchanged surprised glances. Neither had seen her lose control like this.

"This is where I belong," the child argued. "You are my people."

Nova shook her head in disagreement. "*No*—this isn't where you belong." She turned to face the brothers. "Felix, you said there were more Artifex? How many?"

"Six," Felix replied.

"I'm going to need some time to think," Nova said, and she started down the hall toward the back of the house. She stopped at the large window overlooking the outdoors and called back, "Brady and Felix, can I talk to you alone for a second?"

"Sure," they both said at the same time.

Brady made a face at Felix as they joined her at the window. It was still overcast outside, but the view from the window was breathtaking nevertheless. Gazing out across the trees, Brady could make out more of the details of the town.

"Nice view," he said.

"Thanks," Nova replied, but seemed unusually distant. "I should have seen this coming a mile away."

"Don't beat yourself up," Brady said. "It's like I told Felix—there's something off with AJ."

"Obviously," she replied, chewing on her lip as if she was considering something. "We'll need to let my father know as soon as possible. I guess it's no use trying to keep it a secret anymore."

There was a strange edge in her voice now.

"What secret? What are you talking about?" Brady asked. He was beginning to get a bad feeling about this. "Where *is* your dad, anyway?"

Nova paused. "He's already here," she replied enigmatically.

Brady and Felix's eyes swung around the room, clearly wondering if she had lost her mind.

"He is?"

Nova turned and called back down the hallway. "AJ, I need you to do me a favor. Can you please stay here with Achilles? We'll be back soon, I promise."

The child nodded, but muttered something under his breath. Brady thought he heard something about not being appreciated.

"Thank you, AJ. See you in a bit," Nova said as she walked toward a stained wooden door near the end of the hall. She opened it and waved the boys forward.

"This way, please."

They headed down a deep stairwell, and a different type of door waited for them at the bottom. It was constructed of steel and looked far more sturdy and secure than seemed necessary.

Nova held her hand up against the wall, and the door slid back, revealing a large workshop on the other side.

The lights brightened automatically as Nova stepped into the room. The basement's footprint was considerably larger than that of the upstairs, and it had the charm and warmth of a hardened bunker—all reinforced concrete and steel walls. Crisscrossing the ceiling were metal tracks, from which robotic arms hung on chains. Several benches were covered with strange-looking equipment and tools.

Brady spotted the unfinished head of a bear lying on one of the tables. A bundle of tangled wires ran from its robotic neck and connected to an armless torso that lay by its side. One of its arms was suspended just above it.

The laboratory of a mad scientist, Brady thought, and for a second he considered turning around and heading back upstairs. He looked over at his brother, whose face was alive with wonder. *Of course Felix would like this place.*

Thorn was there, perched on a knotty branch of carved aluminum mounted to one of the walls. Her wings were folded against her sides and she rested peacefully. At the far end of the room were several piles of Evercells.

"Batteries," Brady observed. "What are they for?"

They heard the familiar hiss of static, and the lights flickered.

"For me," came a booming voice that swirled around them with the force and motion of a twister.

The boys recognized it at once. It was the same voice they had heard speaking inside Achilles' mind back at the Heap.

His creator.

Brady traced a series of thick cables that ran from the Evercells to a box resting on a table near the back of the room. A circular light burned brightly in the center. It was the same type of container Alethea had been in.

The pieces were falling into place. Brady felt dizzy; he braced himself against the wall to keep from falling over.

"Who are you?" he asked uneasily.

Loud static crackled through the room, then faded to silence.

There was a long pause before the voice returned. "I am Orion. Nova's father."

> Chapter 25: Orion

"IT'S A PLEASURE to finally meet you, Brady and Felix." The voice was a fleeting presence that passed quickly through the room.

"You..." said Brady, his breath escaping him. "The person who built Achilles. You are Nova's father?" His mind raced, finding answers to his lingering questions.

"Yes, he is my father," Nova interrupted. "But not in the traditional sense. He is a digital life form."

"You mean like an artificial intelligence, an AI?" Felix asked.

"That is how I began, yes," Orion said. "I was modeled after a human brain—a model not that much different from your own, in fact."

"But unlike us, Father's consciousness exists within the digital realm. His thoughts are made of ones and zeroes—on and off," Nova explained. "I know he isn't what you expected," she said somewhat sheepishly.

"Um... well, no. Not exactly," Brady replied, still taking everything in.

Suddenly he looked at her with wide eyes and a spark of recognition. "If he's your father..." He paused as the thought rolled around his head. "Then you're a machine too. You're a robot!"

Nova smiled and laughed in spite of herself.

Embarrassed, Brady scrunched his mouth into a knot. He had

done it again.

"Me? No. Although I guess I can see why you might think that. I'm flesh and blood—just like you."

"Now I'm confused too," Felix said, shaking his head. This was growing more complicated by the second.

"Perhaps I can help," came the voice, followed by a momentary burst of static. "There are things about us you don't understand. You see, Nova and I are refugees from the other world: the world you entered when you traveled through the blue flame."

"Refugees?" asked Felix. "Why?"

"Because of me," Nova replied dolefully.

"What could you have possibly done?" Brady responded. He realized he was staring at her and turned away.

"I was born," she said slowly.

"But how is that even possible?" Felix interjected. "You said there are no humans left in your world. You must have parents somewhere, right?"

"Unfortunately I don't," she replied, sadly.

"What happened to them?" Brady asked.

"I never had any to begin with."

Brady and Felix let out a collective, "Huh?"

Nova lowered her head. "I don't have parents because I'm a clone."

"A *clone*?" Brady asked.

"Yes. A copy of someone from another time, long ago, before the disease spread. I think of Orion as my father because he's the one who brought the first human back. Me."

"From DNA?" Felix asked.

"Exactly," Nova said. "The DNA was recovered from a girl. From a strand of her hair."

"Do you share her memories?" Brady asked.

"No, it doesn't work like that. I am my own person. Think of it as though we are identical twins."

"But why bring you back in the first place?" Brady asked.

"My father took a huge risk when he created me. He thought he could convince them that it was the right thing to do. I was the first. There were supposed to be more, but they wouldn't accept me…"

"Convince who?" Felix asked.

"The Elders," Orion said. "After the humans, our creators, left us, it was decided that they posed too much of a risk to us, to our world. The very mention of people was outlawed."

Brady's head clicked. "*Us?* The *Elders?*" he exclaimed. "You're one of them! An Elder Mind!"

"I am—or I was," said the voice.

"But why take the risk? Why do it?" Felix asked.

"Because I believed the humans should walk among us again. There were some of us that regretted our decision not to intervene when the infection spread. I thought that by bringing the humans back, I could make peace with my earlier inaction. It was the least I could do…" The voice washed out and back in. "Humans deserved a second chance. An opportunity to make amends, to live again. You see, I believed that it was possible for us, humans and AI, to exist together in harmony.

"But I had to convince the others. So I kept Nova hidden for a long time, waiting for the right opportunity to introduce her. And while I waited, I searched for a place to take her in case I failed to persuade the others. Eventually, I realized that no place was safe in our world. So I created the quantum door."

"The quantum door? Do you mean the blue portal?" Felix asked.

"Yes," Orion replied. "As you have already discovered, it is a most unusual door. It manipulates the quantum foam to allow subatomic travel through the multiverse."

Brady let out an exaggerated sigh.

"Don't worry about it, Brady, I'll explain it to you someday," his younger brother teased.

Brady scowled. "Then that's how you found our world?" he asked Orion.

"Yes. Once I had discovered your reality, I decided to inform the Elders of Nova's existence. I tried to convince them…"

"But you failed," Felix guessed.

"I made a grave miscalculation—there was no convincing them. They were outraged. All but one."

"Alethea?" Brady asked.

"Yes. And in their fury, they swore to annihilate Nova. Alethea and I were banished, left to live out our existences as Neurogeists. Fortunately I was powerful enough to escape—but Alethea vanished, and we assumed she had already been downloaded into her prison. With Nova's help, we traveled to the reality I had discovered—your world.

"I knew Nova would be safe here where she could grow up around her own people. We were never supposed to go back—the Elder Minds will stop at nothing to find us. Nova, it was foolish of you to put yourself in danger. If I had known what you were up to…"

Nova tried to suppress the look of guilt on her face. "I did what I had to do," she said. "There's no way I was going to stand by and let you die."

"The Evercells!" Brady said excitedly. "Your father needs them to stay alive. That's why you were stealing!"

"That is correct," said the voice. "Like you, energy is my life source. Unfortunately, I require enormous amounts just to remain functional—even in this… limited embodiment."

Brady figured he was referring to the box glowing softly near the back of the room.

"At first we tried to make do with the energy sources on your planet, but they proved insufficient."

"That's why the power kept going out!" Felix ventured.

"The only reason I'm still alive is because of Nova."

"I had no idea, Nova," Brady said. "I'm so sorry for everything I said earlier. I—I understand now."

"It's okay, Brady," Nova replied. "I wasn't exactly forthcoming."

"Which reminds me," the voice said. "I understand that you both are responsible for saving Nova's life?"

"Sort of," Felix said, "but we had a lot of help from Achilles and another friend."

"Then you have my eternal gratitude. Thank you both. You've earned my trust and respect. Although... I feel terrible that you were both put in danger."

"It's okay. We made it out in one piece," Brady responded, beaming with pride.

"Any time," Felix added.

"Father, we have to talk. We have a big problem," Nova interrupted.

"I see. Please tell me what happened," Orion said calmly.

"When we were in the other world, we met a species of AI called the Artifex. There was a child there. He helped us rescue Achilles. His name is Ajax."

Nova took a deep breath.

"And... he is here. Upstairs."

Her announcement was met with an uncomfortable silence. Orion's light dimmed as he considered what she had said.

"How did he find the door?" the voice finally asked, now concerned.

Nova hesitated. "He didn't find *our* door," she said.

More silence.

"Because he didn't need to," she continued. "He downloaded the data from my watch. He used it to open his own door from the other side."

There was a burst of static before Orion responded. "I always feared this would happen. You know that the door leaves a signature behind it. Others will be able to find it—and us."

"Others already have," Nova said. "He's been followed back. More Artifex have come through in search of him."

"Then you must take the Artifex back immediately," Orion commanded. "The trail from the signature will grow stronger every second the door is left open. This world is now at huge risk. Already, I fear it may be too late. If the Elders learn of our location, they will—"

He stopped himself.

"I don't understand," Brady said. "The Elder Minds are supposed to be powerful. You *are* an Elder Mind. Why can't you do anything?"

"It's the Glia Box, Brady," Nova explained, pointing at the glowing container. "His real home is inside the MyeliNet, a neural network that wraps the surface of our world with trillions of connections. Like Alethea, the Elder Minds placed his consciousness inside the box to hold him until he could be downloaded into a Neurogeist body. Inside the Glia Box, he is forced to live with only a tiny fraction of his brain. So he is alive, but barely. It was the only way to get him through the portal though."

Orion's voice interrupted.

"There is no more time to waste. You must get the Artifex back through the portal and then close it. There is a spare watch on the lab table. You will need it. Please go. And whatever happens, be careful."

Nova found the watch on the table and fastened the clasp around her wrist. She made a few quick swipes with her fingers just to make sure it was functional. Then the three of them said goodbye to Orion and returned upstairs.

They found Achilles still sleeping peacefully in the foyer. But something was wrong.

The front door stood open and a strong breeze caused it to rattle loudly against the wall. Brady shivered in the cold air.

AJ was gone.

> Chapter 26: Heavy Metal

FELIX STUCK HIS HEAD through the entryway, hoping to catch a glimpse of AJ running through the yard. It was no use: the bot had vanished.

"You have *got* to be kidding," Brady exclaimed, waving his hands around in frustration. "I really didn't think this day could get any worse. I mean—seriously! What is this kid's problem?"

"He probably went off to find his father," Felix offered, leaning back inside and pushing the front door closed.

"Or maybe he's trying to get as far away from Sudo as he can—or maybe he's running from us," Brady guessed.

"Maybe," Nova reasoned, "but I have a hunch that he's up to something. We may have underestimated him. Anyway, we don't have time to worry about AJ right now. We have to get his friends back through the quantum door so we can close it down. Before it's too late."

"What about Achilles?" Felix asked.

Nova lifted a small panel on the canine's neck and examined the gauge glowing underneath. It measured about half full.

She sighed. "We could really use his help, but it's too early to wake him. He still needs a few more hours." She clicked the panel shut. "We'll have to take care of the Artifex without him."

Nova noticed the look of disappointment on Felix's face. "But he'll be back up and running around in no time," she assured him.

They left the house together. The dwelling shimmered and vanished once they had cleared the premises, leaving an untarnished view of nature in its place. Brady looked back across the now-empty expanse and wondered if he had imagined the whole thing. No matter how many times he saw it, he knew he would never get used to the illusion.

As they approached the edge of the woods, Nova activated a few controls on her replacement watch.

"So what's the plan?" Felix asked curiously.

"I'm enlisting some help," she replied. "There's no telling how far the Artifex have gotten by now. We need to wait here until she arrives."

"Until who arrives?" Felix asked.

Nova pointed toward the gray sky. "Look up."

Nyx burst through the trees and flew past the edge of the cliff. The bird then banked steeply around before beginning her graceful descent. She leveled out a safe distance from the ground and glided down to a nearby branch.

Startled by the bird's immensity, the brothers took a step back. Up close, the bird of prey was even larger than Brady had imagined. He could see the creature's crystal-covered head and gunmetal gray wings that stretched as wide as he was tall.

"Sorry to bother you, Nyx, but we really need your help," Nova called out. "It looks like we have some unexpected visitors."

Nyx cocked her mechanical head to the side. Motors whirred softly from somewhere behind the creature's luminous exterior.

"Can you lead us to the barn?" Nova asked. "There's something we need to pick up first."

Nyx screeched loudly and spread her wings wide against the backdrop of the forest. With heavy gusts of air, the creature lifted back into the sky, causing the tree branches to bow under her force. Once she reached cruising altitude just above the treetops, she began to circle around as Nova, Felix, and Brady looked up from below.

Then the harpy eagle took off in the direction of the barn, stopping occasionally to let her followers catch up. The three friends hurried along in swift pursuit.

10100110

The barn looked to be in even worse shape in the daylight. Felix wiped the perspiration from his forehead and pushed the hair away from his eyes. "What is this place?" he asked, eyeing the rotting walls. "I don't know how it's even still standing."

"Believe me, looks can be deceiving. Just wait until you see what's inside," Brady said. He glanced knowingly at the gap in the siding.

The three of them made their way toward the front of the barn, where the rusted hinge was still undone from the night before. Nova and Brady pulled the doors back to reveal the projection of the false emptiness inside.

Felix frowned suspiciously and craned his neck around to get a better look. "There's nothing in here..." he muttered.

Nova held her hand up to the access panel. The metal doors appeared out of nowhere and slid back to reveal the futuristic interior.

Felix shook his head and took a step back as his brain adjusted to this new reality. "How did you do this?" he asked as his brother pulled him inside.

"Sub-nano pixel walls," Nova replied. "They're almost more convincing than the real thing. You can understand now why we don't want to draw attention to ourselves."

Nova walked over to a row of tall aluminum lockers and retrieved six long, shiny black cylinders.

"Can you guys give me a hand with these?" she asked, tossing the metallic tubes to the brothers.

"Sure thing," said Brady, as he and Felix nearly buckled under the weight.

"They're pretty heavy," Felix groaned. "What are they?"

"Arachnopods."

"Arachno-what?" a befuddled Brady asked.

Nova closed the first locker with a clank and opened another one three doors down. She retrieved several tiny slivers of glass, not much larger than the tips of her fingers, counted them, and slid them into her pocket.

"Okay, we're all set," she said, closing the door and heading toward the exit. "Can you bring those outside?" she asked.

"Um, sure, no problem. Wait up!" Brady called. He fumbled to adjust his grip on the tubes so they wouldn't slip out of his hands.

After a minute of finagling the casings through the doors, they were outside. Nova swung the doors shut, then led the boys to the same spot where she and Brady had brought the aircraft through the portal the night before.

"You should be perfect right about there—great, don't move," she said, as though she were arranging them for a photo shoot. "Okay—I'll let Nyx know we're ready."

Brady and Felix were starting to quake and tremble from the weight. They were hunched over like lumberjacks carrying a stack of milled logs between them.

Nova pressed a button on her watch, and Nyx, waiting on her perch, took flight. She gained altitude for a second before turning around and abruptly swooping down, straight toward Brady and Felix.

Brady stepped backward, causing Felix to stumble after him. "Watch it, Brady!"

"Steady, don't move…" Nova said.

"Easy for you to say," Brady called out.

When the bird was almost upon them, she opened her large talons and spread her wings to break her speed. And then, in a single fluid motion, she gripped the pile of cylinders in her claws, flapped her wings, and headed back into the sky.

The boys, relieved of their burden, watched the bird vanish with her payload.

Nova reached into her pocket and withdrew the slivers of glass she had retrieved from the locker earlier. "Do you guys wear contacts?" she asked, tilting her head back and applying the lenses to each eye. Her eyelashes fluttered as the glass slid into place.

"Yes," replied Brady.

"No," answered Felix.

"Okay, then this will be easier for you, Brady. Felix, give it your best shot—it may feel a bit uncomfortable at first." She doled out a pair of the delicate devices to each of them.

Brady examined the tiny lenses in his hand. Microscopic pixels of colorful light played across the shiny surfaces. "But if I take out my regular contacts, I won't be able to see," he protested.

"Don't worry," Nova replied. "You'll see better than ever once they're in. Trust me." She scrunched her eyelids together as they adjusted to the foreign objects.

"If you say so." Brady removed his disposable lenses and tossed them aside. He looked over and saw Felix struggling a bit with his own lenses. After a considerable amount of effort, his brother eventually got them in and wobbled around for a second. Satisfied that his brother was okay, Brady carefully applied his own.

He blinked his eyes and waited.

Soon his vision began to cloud over and his surroundings became blurry and out of focus. Felix and Nova were nothing more than smeared blobs of color against the gray backdrop of afternoon sky.

"Hey, Nova," Brady said. "I thought you said these would help. I can't see a thing!"

He spun around and looked at the trees, which bled together into a single smear of color.

"Nova, what's happening?" he heard Felix call out from somewhere beside him. "How do I? Aha… Never mind…"

After a few seconds, Brady's own vision snapped into focus. But it was different than before. Everything was rendered sharper and in crisper detail than ever before.

Nova was smiling when he looked at her.

"I told you so."

"But what are they for?" Brady asked. He was seeing the world with newfound clarity.

"Watch," she said.

His vision went dark.

> Chapter 27: Telepresence

"JUST A SECOND," Nova said. "I need to make a quick adjustment."

Brady's lenses flickered for a second, but then the darkness lifted and his world returned.

"Okay, all done," she said. "Nyx has been kind enough to allow us to link her video feed to these lenses."

"What do we need to do?" Felix asked.

"For the time being, nothing. We just let her work her magic," Nova said. "And we observe…"

She dialed up a virtual lever on her watch, and a large screen appeared in mid-air. They were looking at an overhead view of the forest—through Nyx's eyes. The trees on the screen shrunk as the bird gained altitude, and soon Brady noticed three small people on the ground, no larger than ants. He was looking down on himself from above. Glancing up with his own eyes, he saw the tiny speck of the bird disappearing into the sky.

"This is soooo much cooler than our glasses," said an elated Felix, basking in the glory of the technology.

"Yeah, Felix, these don't make me sick!" Brady replied sarcastically.

"When she gets high enough, Nyx will switch on her thermal imaging lenses," Nova said. "At that altitude, we should be able to detect anyone within a four-mile radius."

"And then what?" Brady asked. Nyx flew higher still and the view expanded farther outward to cover even more terrain.

"Then we'll find the Artifex and send them home," Nova replied.

The overhead view of the forest continued to broaden. Nova's watch beeped. "Nyx has activated her thermography sensors," she said. "Hold on a second and I'll switch the view over."

Nova stood with her arms out and the tips of her fingers together. As she moved her hands apart, the view split into two windows: the original view, and another version full of flowing blobs of color. Nova arranged the two windows side by side.

"We're looking through her thermal lenses now," she explained. "The hotter the surface, the brighter the color. The Artifex should stand out if they're still moving around—they give off a lot of heat. Let's see where they are."

She reached out toward the thermal view and moved her fingers apart once again. The window grew larger. Hundreds of orange, red, and yellow dots spread across the screen. Nova singled out an orange blob moving quickly across the ground and zoomed in. The screen spun around as she pivoted her hands, searching.

"There," she said, dismissing the thermal view by waving her hand quickly over the second screen. They were now looking at something traveling through the forest, no larger than the head of a pin. Nova formed a steeple with her fingers and quickly pulled her hands apart. The view zoomed in on an overhead shot of an Artifex walking among the trees.

Nova touched the projection of the Artifex. The area around the Artifex began to glow with a green aura.

"One down, five more to go."

Over the next few minutes, Nova repeated the process several more times, until six of the Artifex had been identified. One was still missing, however.

"How come we can't see AJ?" Felix asked. "He must be around

here somewhere."

"I don't know why we can't see him. Something's wrong, but we'll have to worry about him later. Are you ready?"

"Ready for what?" Brady asked nervously.

"Just follow my lead—there's nothing to it."

Nova spoke into her watch. "Okay Nyx, go ahead and drop the first Arachnopod."

The screen switched back to the eagle's overhead view. They were gliding toward the ground, the eagle diving toward one of the Artifex. Just when they thought Nyx would crash into the trees, the bird opened its talons to release the first of the Arachnopods. The view zoomed in as the black cylinder fell and hit the ground with a thud, only feet from the unsuspecting Artifex.

"What is that thing?" Brady asked.

"Just watch..." Nova replied.

They observed from overhead as the canister began to shake. Startled, the Artifex turned around to look at the strange object that had fallen from the sky. It took a step closer as the cylinder continued to vibrate across the forest floor. Another step, then another. The Artifex bent over and looked down at the tube.

Brady and Felix held their breath, waiting for something to happen.

Suddenly a crack appeared in the shell. It grew into a line that ran the full length of the tube. The canister split apart, and the two halves folded back to reveal an array of long, slender rods.

The Artifex jumped back in surprise.

The ends of the rods electrified and snapped together to form large telescoping legs. Then the encasement itself folded back together, forming the head that sat atop the creature's body. The legs flexed and the machine slowly rose up from the ground.

"Okay, guys. I'm going to switch to the Arachnopod's video link so you can see how this works."

The view switched over to the Arachnopod's camera, and two holographic spheres appeared in front of Nova. She moved her hands out in front of her to grab the virtual controls.

"The left sphere spins the head around." Her hand rotated back and forth, and the spider's camera turned with it. "The right sphere moves the spider in any direction, see?" She pushed the sphere forward, and the spider began to take smooth, fluid steps toward the bot. The Artifex retreated at first, but then defiantly approached the long-legged machine.

"Now let's try to convince it to go back."

Nova raised a virtual volume control that lit up as she dragged her finger upward.

"Hello, my name is Nova," she said.

The Artifex stared at the Arachnopod. Its frame was slightly more slender than the other Artifex they had seen so far. It didn't respond.

"You are trespassing here and must return from where you came," Nova said.

"You have taken one of our own," the Artifex replied. Its voice was distinctly female.

"You mean Ajax?" Nova said, almost laughing.

The bot nodded. "How did you know?"

"AJ—I mean Ajax—he followed us back here. He is the one who opened the portal you came through earlier. Not us. He doesn't belong here, and neither do you. You must leave now."

"Who are you to make such demands?" the Artifex asked indignantly.

"I make these demands because I know the trouble AJ is causing by being here," Nova said. "The Elder Minds will come here and destroy us all. There is no time to waste."

The Artifex's face betrayed no emotion. "If what you say is true… where is Ajax?"

Nova paused for a second and looked down at the Artifex. "He left us in search of his father," Nova guessed.

The female Artifex stared back. "You are lying. I think you have taken the child. When you bring Ajax to us, then we can talk."

Nova was taken aback. "If you won't go back willingly, I will have to force you," she said. The spider advanced toward the Artifex. "Please, we don't have a choice. Return to where you came from."

"Not until I find Ajax," the woman replied, and she turned to walk away.

Nova cast the control forward as fast as she could. Brady and Felix watched as the spider released a net of electrostatic silk that uncoiled in mid-air and tangled itself around the Artifex. The bot tried to move her arms and legs, but it was no use. The net crackled and hissed as it tightened around her. She collapsed to the ground and the silk continued to spread out, twisting and winding itself along the paths of current that electrified her body.

"I'm sorry," Nova said, "you left me no choice. I will remove it as soon as we get you back to the portal."

The Artifex stared angrily back at her from behind the mask of silk.

Nova pulled the left control back quickly, and the spider retrieved the end of the web with one of its legs. The leg folded back on itself and hooked the net to an attachment on its body. Nova then spun the control around, and the Arachnopod trudged forward with the Artifex in tow.

"Brady, Felix—think you can handle the next two while I take her back to the portal?

"Sure," said Brady, his voice wavering with uncertainty. "But what are we going to do with them once they get to the portal?"

"We'll remove the webs and convince them to go back through. And if they don't, we'll drag them through."

"Okay, I'll give it a try," said Brady, feigning confidence.

"Me too," Felix said, positioning his arms over the virtual controls.

"Good luck. I'll let Nyx know you're ready. Releasing the video back over to you."

Suddenly Brady was watching as Nyx dropped a second Arachnopod from the sky. It hit the ground, unfolded as before, and was up and on its spindly legs in no time. The spider's camera switched on and assumed his field of view.

He panned the camera toward an Artifex that was no more than a few yards in front of him. The worn clothes draped around his body made him instantly recognizable. Brady had found Sudo. *Lucky me.*

The Artifex folded his arms across his chest, unafraid, and stared the machine down. For a second Brady lost his nerve, and acting on instinct, he backed the spider away.

Brady looked at his brother from around the corner of the spider's feed, hoping to get his attention. But Felix was fully consumed in his own chase, his arms moving methodically, commanding his own Arachnopod.

Brady gulped. Why was he the one stuck dealing with this guy?

He turned his concentration back to his controls and guided his spider forward until he came to rest in front of the Artifex leader.

He remembered how Nova had enabled the audio and cranked up the volume.

"Sudo?" he said timidly.

"Human?" the Artifex said with surprise. "I know your voice. It's you—you and the girl. You escaped from the house with my son. Where have you taken him?"

"Taken him?" Brady replied. "Who, AJ? Are you crazy? We don't want him here. He followed us!"

Sudo stared curiously into the camera. "I don't understand. Tell me where he is," he commanded with an unflinching gaze.

Brady wasn't sure how to answer, but he did his best anyway.

"I—I'm not sure, but it doesn't matter," he mumbled and quickly changed the subject. "You and your friends made a terrible mistake coming through the portal."

"The portal? You mean the wall of fire?" Sudo's shirt rustled in the breeze like a withering piece of cheesecloth.

"Yes, that's it," Brady said. "But you must go back."

"Why would AJ follow you? There is nothing for him here."

Brady suddenly realized the Artifex hadn't discovered the truth about this world: that there were people here. He had to act quickly.

"Okay—you caught me," he lied. "It's no use trying to deceive you any longer. We captured AJ and forced him to come here with us."

Sudo looked at him suspiciously. "Then where is he?"

"Not so fast..." Brady said. "I'll make a deal. If you agree to return home with the others, we will turn AJ over to you."

The Artifex considered the offer. "Agreed. But I must inform our party."

"No need. We are already looking for your friends," Brady said. "We found a woman, but she wouldn't come with us, so..."

Brady realized he had said too much.

"What did you do to her?" Sudo asked angrily.

"Nothing," Brady replied. "Your friends will be safe back at the portal waiting for you by the time you get there."

The Artifex turned around.

"Wait!" Brady called out. He raised one of the spider legs in Sudo's direction, prepared to fire the net.

"That is not necessary," Sudo warned from over his shoulder. "I will go there on my own accord. Bring AJ—or else."

Brady watched the Artifex disappear into the woods.

> Chapter 28: Mind Control

"WAIT A SECOND. You just let him go?" Nova asked in a mix of frustration and astonishment. "Why would you do that?"

Brady had waited until the other five Artifex had been taken back to the portal before telling them about his strange encounter with Sudo.

"What? I did us a favor," Brady said with the hurt look of the wrongfully accused. "Sudo said he would meet us back at the portal and that he would convince the others to leave with him." He paused and drummed the tips of his fingers together. "There is a catch, though."

"A catch?" Felix asked.

"Yeah. He thinks we already have AJ," Brady explained. "He agreed to leave with the others, but only if we bring his son back to him first."

Nova's expression quickly soured. "Your plan assumes that we can actually find AJ, and I think that's pretty unlikely. Somehow he's figured out a way to stay hidden from Nyx."

"How?" asked Brady.

"I'm not positive, but my guess is he's using the data from my watch to override her sensors. If that's the case, he'll stay out of sight until he wants us to find him. If he does decide to make an appearance, I bet it will be near the portal. We need to get there quickly, get the Artifex through, and close it down."

"Exactly," Brady agreed. "But I figured something else out too while I was talking to Sudo. The Artifex don't yet realize that there are actually people here—they haven't seen any yet. If they find out that there are humans in this world, they'll never go back through. We need to get them out of here before AJ has a chance to spill the news."

"Then there's no use wasting time here. Let's get back to the portal."

11000110

When they arrived at the Willoughbys' back yard, they could see the unpiloted Arachnopods idling next to one side of the portal while the Artifex huddled together on the other side. The bots were still incapacitated by the electro-silk webbing that kept them bound and immobilized. They had given up their struggle to escape and sat quietly on the ground.

Nova scanned the empty forest around her and frowned. "Sudo isn't here," she said grimly.

"Yeah, I guess he's not," Brady responded, looking discouraged. He began to worry that he had misjudged Sudo. Was it possible he had already found AJ and they had already left, together?

Suddenly there was a rustling among the trees. "Look," Felix said.

The branches parted and AJ's father emerged. His icy green eyes searched for his son as he approached the three friends. Disappointed, he turned to face Brady.

"Where is my son?" he asked angrily.

"We... actually don't know where he is," Brady answered, truthfully this time.

"You lied to me?" Sudo asked—then saw his friends tied up next to the portal. "What have you done to them?" he cried, swinging his fist through the air.

"They're fine," Nova responded, stepping forward. "We plan to release them and send them back through the portal."

"You…" Sudo hissed. "You and your bird's escapades nearly destroyed Invidia."

"You shouldn't have locked us in that house," Nova replied. "Sorry, but you left us with no choice."

"You will pay for what you've done—just like your bird!" Sudo said coldly. He turned and started walking toward the other Artifex.

"Don't waste your time," Nova called out. "It's no use. The electro-silk has already re-coded itself to match their central logic board. Only I can free them."

The Artifex stopped in his tracks, his back to them.

"Go back home, and we will find AJ," Nova pleaded. "There is nothing for you here!"

"*She lies!*"

It was the child's voice, coming from somewhere nearby.

"Ajax?" Sudo said, looking around for his son.

"You cannot leave! This world holds a secret!" the child continued, a desperate urgency in his voice.

"A secret?" his father asked, his interest piqued.

"They haven't told you, have they?" AJ called. The bot slid out from behind a shrub near the side of the Willoughbys' house.

"Told me what?" Sudo turned his gaze to Brady. Brady was certain that Sudo's static carvings masked a simmering anger.

Nova looked at Brady and ran her fingers across her lips like she was zipping them shut.

Don't say anything.

This was the moment AJ had been waiting for.

"Yes, there is a secret, and I will tell you, but only if you promise to do something for me in return," AJ said.

"Do not speak to me in that tone," Sudo said, annoyed. "I do not make *deals* with my own son. I am your father and you will listen to me."

"You don't control me anymore. Now *you* will listen to *me*," AJ yelled. "Unlock my mind from this body so I can find a new one. I am tired of being a child, but I cannot escape without the key."

"That cannot be done," Sudo replied. The strips of his frayed clothing rustled in the breeze. "There is no key."

"Oh, but you can do it!" AJ insisted. "You are my designer. You have what I need." He pointed to his head. "Now give it to me!"

"I do not want to lose my son," Sudo said. "I built you for a purpose. I wanted a child, and a child you shall remain—forever."

Brady cringed. As far as fathers went, AJ appeared to have gotten the worst. Brady was beginning to see the reason behind the child's madness.

AJ jumped up and down in frustration. "Then go ahead, go back through the portal!" he yelled, waving at the door. "You'll spend the rest of eternity never knowing what it's like."

"Knowing what *what's* like?" Sudo asked curiously.

AJ could see that his father was interested. He seized the opportunity.

"Give me the key and I will tell you. I promise you it will be worth it."

"Fine." Sudo's curiosity had gotten the better of him. "You have my word. I will send it to you now." His head flashed in a brilliant display. "Done. Now, tell me this... secret. And if you're lying..."

"Don't do it, AJ!" Nova pleaded.

"The truth is..."

Nova closed her eyes.

"The truth is that you passed through a door that brought you to a new world *filled* with humans. Billions of them."

"Lies!" Sudo replied angrily.

"Where do you think *they* came from?" AJ asked, pointing at Brady and Felix. "This is their home."

His father shook his head. "No."

"You don't believe me? I will show you—and everyone else!"

AJ's skull began to pulse slowly, and he raised his hands to the sky. Nyx appeared overhead. She wavered above them, flailing from side to side, struggling.

"Stop it, AJ!" Nova demanded. "You can't override her neural pathways with your own—it will kill her!"

"I don't need to," AJ replied. "Your watch provided me with her design schematics. And with the key, I can talk directly to her motor control systems. I will use Nyx to show them—"

"You don't need to do this," Nova pleaded.

"They will believe me when they see it."

Brady watched the bird pass out of sight. It was headed in the direction of Nova's house, over the cliff, and then...

Toward the town.

It was too late.

"See what a real world looks like!" AJ yelled. His head began to flash, and the heads of the other Artifex blinked in time with the child's.

"AJ has hijacked Nyx's video feed and is sending it directly to the Artifex," Nova whispered to the brothers. "I'm going to see if we still have access."

With her arm down to her side, Nova made subtle gestures on her watch. Suddenly a window appeared in each of their lenses— the feed Nyx had shared with them earlier. At least this way they would see what the Artifex were seeing.

The eagle broke free from the mountainside into the gray sky ahead and glided unsteadily toward the town. At first, the buildings were just lines on the horizon, but as the bird approached, the lines stretched into shops and buildings that peppered the landscape. Nyx's flight was haphazard; she was trying to resist AJ's control.

Brady turned to look at the group of Artifex. Their heads pulsed so quickly they emitted a steady glow. He could tell they were in some kind of a trance. They had lived their lives in a false replica; witnessing the real thing shattered the illusions of their own world.

AJ commanded the eagle down further, so that she soared erratically between the buildings. The sides of the streets were lined with cars. People were bustling in and out of the shops, finishing up daily errands, grabbing a coffee or a bite to eat. They looked up in awe as the great flying machine soared overhead.

The bird continued on, passing car after car, building after building. The boys knew this street; they recognized Ms. Cooper's store as Nyx flew by.

Out of nowhere, a loud crack broke the spell: the show was over.

Confused, AJ lowered his arms and began looking around for the source of the noise. But he failed to see the sky rip open behind him, and he didn't notice the looming figure step out from the wall of fire and onto the damp grass beneath it.

The creature took a step toward the unsuspecting child. Its mound-shaped head had gaping black holes where its eyes and mouth should have been, and the surface of its body was molten alloy that flowed like the rippling folds of a wax candle. It had bulky arms and legs, like a person, though much larger and far less defined, as though it had been forged from clay and bathed in a pool of mercury. One arm glowed a fiery orange as it reached out to grab the child.

"AJ!" Sudo yelled. AJ looked on in horror as his father raced toward him. At the last second, AJ ducked, and Sudo sailed over his son and collided with the monster's chest.

The ghastly figure didn't even budge. Instead, the oozing form clutched Sudo with both arms and held him up to the sky. Sudo's tattered clothes ignited like tinder, and a mix of steam and smoke rose up from where the figure's hands held the Artifex. Then, without warning, the monster turned and cast the smoldering bot back through the portal.

It closed with a bang behind him, and AJ scurried off into the forest.

Brady and Felix were frozen in fear, but Nova didn't waste time. Recalling a distant memory, she made a quick calculation and dialed a series of numbers into her watch. With the familiar boom, a new quantum door opened in front of her.

"Brady, Felix! You need to go now!"

Felix looked at the new portal in surprise, then back at Nova. Brady couldn't take his fearful eyes off the creature heading toward them.

"What is that thing?" Brady asked.

"A golem," she replied. "A monster controlled by the Elder Minds. They've come for us. Now get through the door!"

Felix stepped into the blue flame and vanished.

"Are you coming too?" Brady asked.

"Right behind you," Nova said. "Now go!"

Brady disappeared into the blaze.

Nova remained behind. She closed the portal with a swipe on her watch.

> Chapter 29: March of the Golems

IT WAS BETTER THIS WAY, Nova thought, keeping Brady and Felix hidden somewhere else while she remained behind. If she had remembered the coordinates correctly, they would be safe there, at least for a bit. She would go back and get them when this was all over—if she managed to survive.

The Elder Golem had spotted the tied-up Artifex by the portal and was advancing toward them. With each step forward, fire erupted beneath its feet, leaving a smoldering wake of destruction in its path. Nova knew the golem was being controlled by someone beyond this world, by an Elder Mind who mastered the terrifying puppet through an unthinkable amount of energy transmitted across the quantum foam that bridged the two realities.

It was the received energy that held the crude creature together and guided it on its mission of ruination. But the energy was too much for the golem. The creature burned like a lightning rod as the received power collected inside of it. So much of that energy was expended simply keeping it whole, and it came at a cost: the golem was slow.

The Artifex, seeing what had happened to Sudo, struggled to free themselves from the grip of the electro-silk cocoons. It pained Nova to watch them twisting on the ground, helpless. She remembered what Brady had told her the night before: this was all her fault. He was right.

She wondered if she could get them unbound and back through the portal before the golem reached them. It seemed unlikely, but she had to try. They would perish in the golem's fiery grip if she did nothing. She took a deep breath, collected herself, and ran over to the bots.

She knelt down beside the first Artifex and began to undo the webbing around its mouth.

"What have we done?" it asked when it was finally able to speak. It was the female Artifex they had seen earlier, the first one they had encountered with the Arachnopods. Its gaze remained fixed on the golem.

"The Elder Minds have come for us," Nova replied. "You have to get through the portal—it's your only chance to escape."

"Escape?" the mannequin said. "To where?"

"Back to your home," Nova replied.

Her hands worked vigorously to undo the webbing. The artificial net created a micro-magnetic field that caused it to stick tightly to anything metal. Nova's skin, however, was impervious to its adhesive powers.

But this was taking too much time, and she quickly realized there was no way she would be able to save all the Artifex by herself.

"AJ?" she called out in desperation. "AJ? I know you're out there. Somewhere. I could really use your help right now!"

No response.

Nova twisted more and more of the net away from the Artifex. Almost there, she thought.

Done!

She tore the webbing away and threw it on the ground. Without electrical current to supply it, it shriveled up and blew away in the breeze.

Nova helped the female Artifex to her feet. *"Go!"* she shouted.

The Artifex stared back at her friends. Nova could feel the doubt emanating from the bot's circuits.

"I'll help your friends get home. I promise."

The Artifex ran for the door. She hesitated for a second in front of the fire, but then stepped through.

One down, Nova thought.

Quickly, she set to work on the second Artifex, her hands again moving quickly. By the time she finished, the Elder Golem was almost upon them. She would never get them all undone in time.

Then she heard something yelling loudly in the air above.

AJ?

She looked up to the sky in amazement. The little bot was flying through the air, his arms clutched tightly in Nyx's talons. When the bird was directly overhead, AJ jumped, landed on the golem's shoulders, and wrapped his legs around the monster's neck. The creature roared and waved its arms around, stumbling about as it tried to pry AJ away. But the child held on tight and dodged the fiery arms.

It was the distraction Nova needed. She released the other three Artifex and helped them through the portal.

"They're through, AJ—close the door!" she yelled.

AJ was still riding on the back of the golem. His head flashed briefly, and the door collapsed with a boom. The golem screamed in frustration and its body melted just enough for AJ to lose his grip on the molten sludge. The creature reached backward with its bear-like paw and flung AJ down on the ground.

"Move! AJ—get out of there!" Nova yelled.

But it was too late: the golem was already upon the child. AJ lay there on the ground, frozen like a deer in headlights. He looked up with fear into the creature's ghastly black holes that glowed from the fire that burned within.

The puppet reached down to AJ with its lava red hand.

Nyx dropped through the sky like a dart. She snatched up the bot with her talons and swooped away just as the golem's hand brushed her tail. The fire burned through the metal as the bird sped away. Trails of streaming smoke revealed her path into the sky. AJ screeched with joy as the bird climbed above the trees to safety.

Nova turned back toward the golem.

The creature had grown still. The fire no longer burned. Something was happening.

She waited.

Explosions erupted all at once with the firepower of a thousand cannons. She watched in horror as blue portals tore the sky around her. The haunted forms of molten metal emerged with hollowed eyes and empty mouths.

Because of her, they had been found. Nova knew why the creatures had come to this world. Not for her. Not for the Artifex.

For her father.

They would bring him back or destroy him trying. And now they had doubled down.

The golems joined together in a line and began their deadly march toward her home. The leaves crackled and burned beneath their feet, and entire plants and trees caught fire.

The forest was ablaze.

Nova's brain was beginning to cloud over, and she knew she was starting to lose it after going so long without sleep. *Hold it together just a little longer.* She knew she had to get to her house, wake Achilles, and get her father away before the house burned to the ground. And she was running out of time. The golems were tightening the net. They would squeeze them out eventually.

Nova raced toward her home, running faster than she had ever moved before. The flames rose up in a wall behind her and licked the dusky sky as the golems' assault continued. Once she arrived at the house, there would be little time to get everyone out safely.

She sped through the trees and bolted across the front yard, toward the steps. The house shimmered and appeared in a flash. Nyx had dropped AJ near the porch, and Thorn was there too, awake and buzzing wildly.

The hummingbird zipped by Nova's face and came to rest in front of her.

"Fly away, Thorn! Get as far away from here as you can!"

The bird flew around her in a panicked frenzy.

"Go, Thorn! Now!"

The bird zipped off, confused, into the smoky haze that was settling in.

Nova turned to AJ. "Get inside!" she screamed at the child.

AJ just stood there in disbelief, staring at the monsters. Nova grabbed his arm and pulled him up the steps with her.

The golems were crossing the lawn now and would be at the house any second. Pulling AJ behind her, Nova crashed through the door, slammed it behind her, and headed for Achilles. She knelt down next the canine and with a strong tug, dislodged the power cable from his back.

"Wake up, Achilles! Time for us to go!"

Achilles eyes glowed. He let out a whimper and buried his head under his paws.

Nova's voice grew louder. "Sorry—I know you're not ready yet. I can't help it. The Elder Minds have come for Father."

"Come on! Come on! Come on!" AJ said, tugging at one of Achilles' ribs, trying to pull him up.

They smelled something burning before they saw it: a thin ribbon of smoke curled from a speck of ash on the front door. The hole quickly widened into a gash that cut straight down the middle. Two metallic hands pushed their way through the opening and proceeded to peel the door back like a curtain.

The monster entered the house. Behind him, a crowd of golems was filling the front yard. The orange-crimson sky was streaked with black smoke that billowed up from the wasted ground.

Achilles bolted to his feet with a yelp and growled at the intruder. The monster stepped slowly across the room. The house shook and the foyer caught fire as the thing moved.

"Come on! Achilles—downstairs."

Nova turned and ran across the room, AJ following close behind. They could hear the floorboards cracking overhead as they rushed down the stairs. When they reached the bottom, Nova looked back and saw several quicksilver forms looming at the top of the stairwell. She held her hand out to the access panel. *Hurry up!*

The door ahead of her slid open just as the golems began their descent down the stairs.

Her father's voice spoke calmly as Nova and AJ entered the room. "I will need more power. Please connect me to the remaining cells."

"We—you can't afford to. That's all we have left."

The house shook. Fiery gold seams began to form around the door and in the ceiling.

"There's no time to argue, Nova!" Orion's voice commanded.

AJ scurried around the room at light speed, attaching cables from the pile of Evercells to the Glia Box that housed Nova's father.

"More power," Orion boomed.

The seams widened into burning gashes, and flames spread across the ceiling in a sea of fire. It threatened to collapse at any second.

AJ had just finished connecting the last cable when the golems began dropping down from above, one by one.

"That's the last cable! There are no more!" AJ called out.

Nova grabbed the Glia Box and joined AJ and Achilles in the center of the room. They were surrounded, with nowhere to go.

One golem was nearly upon them. Nova could feel the heat scorching her skin. It raised a glowing hand toward her.

Something stopped it before it reached her face.

There was a loud crack. And then she saw it, just as the lights went out: a crystalline splinter in the air near the golem's hand. The monster tried to force its palm forward, fighting against the invisible field. As it pushed, the small tear in space opened into a web of fractures that spread out around them. They were left inside a shattered prism, with each shard reflecting a different piece of the golem.

The world darkened around them, and the monster, with his arm reaching out hopelessly, drifted away into the nothingness.

Orion had saved them.

01110110

Nova, AJ, and Achilles stood under the fractured dome.

"Father?"

The room was quiet. The circular light glowed dimly on the Glia Box.

"What happened?"

Orion's voice was faint. "They cannot find us here. I moved us between realities—to the Void Space." His voice drifted off and the light on the Glia Box flickered.

"We have to go back!" Nova cried. "You'll die without more energy."

They heard only the soft crackle of static.

Nova began to panic. "AJ, we need to get him more cells. We have to go back!"

"Are you crazy?" the bot replied. "We can't go back there now. They'll be waiting for us on the other side."

"I don't have a choice," she said.

She lifted the Glia Box onto Achilles' back. Two of his ribs wrapped backward around the box and secured it into place. Nova dialed a few buttons on her watch and a new door opened in front of her. She took a step toward the door before AJ pulled her back.

"I'll go," he said. "It's the least I can do after all the trouble I've caused."

Nova was about to argue when she remembered Brady and Felix. "Okay," she agreed. "Then I'll go find Brady and Felix. Who knows what trouble they've gotten into by now. Come find us if you have any luck—otherwise we'll come and find you after we get them home."

AJ vanished through the door.

"Good luck," she called after him.

> Chapter 30: Parallels

THE BLUE FLAME of the portal played across Brady's and Felix's faces as they waited desperately for Nova to come through after them. It was only after the door vanished that they realized she wasn't coming.

"Where are we?" Felix asked, scratching his head and looking around uneasily.

They had expected to find themselves somewhere else, somewhere other than the place they had left behind. But they were here, in a forest that looked frighteningly familiar. Except that there were no Artifex, no golems, no portals—and best of all, thought Brady, no AJ. The woods were quiet and peaceful, nothing like the chaos they had left behind. It was as if Nova had flipped a switch and everything wrong had simply vanished.

A reset button.

"Brady?" Felix turned to look at his brother. He found him focused intently on the Willoughbys' cottage.

"What are you looking at?" asked Felix.

"Do you notice anything different?" Brady said slowly.

Felix stared in wonder at the home. The bushes were trimmed back and a light glowed warmly from inside. A fresh coat of paint had been slathered on the window trim, and the house looked decidedly peppier than before.

"Yeah, a bunch of things," Felix replied. "There's a light on for starters. That's weird."

The boys made their way through the side yard toward the front of the cottage. When they rounded the corner, they noticed something that made them stop cold.

The old Wrangler was parked off to the side.

"Mr. Willoughby's come home," Brady said in hushed amazement.

"It can't be. He's been gone for years." Felix sounded unsure of himself.

"Then who is that inside?"

They watched in shock as the silhouette of a long-haired man moved across the window before disappearing into another room.

Felix shook his head and rubbed his eyes. "That's impossible. It must be another one of Nova's illusions—like the barn."

"Something's not right, Felix. We shouldn't be here." Brady was beginning to lose whatever nerve he had left.

"For once I agree with you, Brady. Let's get out of here."

They backed away from the house and headed into the woods. It was evening now and there was only a little daylight remaining. With nowhere else to go, the brothers made their way home. After a long hike, they found themselves staring at their back yard from behind the forest's edge.

The grass had been mowed recently and they saw lights on when they looked up at their house. They were so excited to be back that it took them a minute to notice that something was out of place.

The chain-link fence was missing.

"I'm not sure we actually went through a door, Brady. Maybe something else happened."

They started toward the house, but stopped just before the edge of the forest when they saw two shadowy figures running through their back yard. The figures looked to be about the same age and height as themselves, and the smaller one was carrying something in his hand.

Then they heard something unreal: the sound of their own voices.

"That sounds like you, Felix!" Brady said.

"Really? I sound like that?" Felix frowned.

"No, seriously. I think that's us over there."

"It's an illusion," Felix said. "Come on. Let's go check it out." He tugged on his brother's shirtsleeve.

"I'm not sure, Felix. This place... It doesn't feel right."

"There you go again," his brother replied.

They heard another voice. This time it sounded like Brady. The voice was loud, concerned. It sounded like he was scolding his brother.

"Some things never change," the real Felix muttered under his breath.

"Did you say something?" the real Brady asked.

"Nothing."

The real Brady and Felix crept around the corner of their house and hid behind a large hemlock tree. There was a small tripod on the ground, and the other Felix was sliding a model rocket down the long guide wire. The other Brady, with one arm on his hip and the other swinging through the air, was telling him to aim it away from the house.

"Ouch. Am I really that awful?" Brady asked his brother as he stared out at his other self. It was the strangest feeling he had ever experienced; watching his alternate twin.

"Of course not. You're worse!" Felix laughed.

Annoyed, Brady pushed his brother so hard he fell. Felix shrieked as he collapsed backward into the leaves.

The other brothers stopped suddenly.

"Did you hear something? It sounded like it came from the woods," the other Brady asked.

The other Felix looked around, then went back to work on the rocket. "For once, stop worrying," he said, backing away from the launch pad, the cord tugging at the launch controller box cradled in his hands.

"Five... four... three... two... one..."

A cloud of gray smoke swelled beneath the engine, and the rocket sped upward with a loud hiss. The real Felix and Brady watched it pass overhead and vanish into the sky.

When they looked back, the other Felix was fiddling with his phone.

"Check out the video stream from the rocket, Brady!"

The two brothers studied the screen together. After watching the successful launch, the other Brady slapped his brother a high five.

"That kid has some great ideas," the real Felix said with a proud grin. Brady grimaced.

"It looks like we put too much angle on it," the other Brady said from afar. "It's headed somewhere over in the woods."

"No problem. It has a GPS on it so we can find it. Just let me get a lock on it first." The other brothers waited quietly for the phone to do its job.

"Got it—it's somewhere back there," the other Felix said, pointing toward a section of the woods not far from where the real brothers had been only minutes before.

"We need to find it before it gets too dark," the other Brady suggested. "Come on."

The other brothers headed into the woods and out of sight.

Felix was getting ready to say something to his brother when someone tapped him on his shoulder.

"Hey, guys. What in the world are you doing back here? How did the launch go, anyway?"

It was a voice Brady hadn't heard for years. A voice he missed dearly and would have given anything to hear again.

The boys turned and looked up at their father.

> Chapter 31: What If?

"DAD, IS THAT YOU?" Brady asked softly. Felix's chin trembled as he stared up at the stranger who had left them when Felix was too young to remember. His father looked different than he did in the pictures. He was older; there was white in his beard, flecks of gray around his temples. The years had added lines to his face, but it was their father nevertheless.

"Is this *me*? What kind of question is that? Of course it's me," he answered. The unfamiliar creases in the corners of his eyes grew more pronounced and pulled tight as he smiled down at the boys. "You guys were supposed to be launching a rocket, right? Did it hit you in the head or something?"

Felix tried to speak, but the words wouldn't come. His eyes were beading up with tears. The wave of emotion hit him square in the gut.

Brady saw his brother struggling and jumped in. "The wing broke. I—I needed to glue it back on."

Felix wiped his eyes with his sleeve and tried to pull himself together. It was useless. He ran up and hugged his father tight. Brady waited a second before joining in.

"Um..." his father said awkwardly. "Thanks—but are you sure everything's okay?"

"It's fine, Dad, we're just happy to see you," Felix said. At last they pulled away.

Confused, their father patted them on the backs. "Okay, well if you guys have some time, would you mind giving me a hand with something?"

"Sure," Brady replied.

Felix nodded.

"Come on then—the engine's in the garage." He was heading around the side of the house when he stopped suddenly. "That's weird," he said. "Weren't you all wearing different clothes just a few minutes ago?"

"We got dirty riding our bikes around so we decided to change," Brady called back as they hurried to catch up with their father.

In the garage, they found a stripped-down boat attached to a pickup truck parked in the driveway.

"Since when did we get that?" Felix asked.

"What do you mean? Oliver Willoughby gave it to us." Their father looked at Felix curiously. "You seem like you're not yourself today."

They walked into the open garage where the engine was sitting in pieces on the workbench.

"Do you mind staying here for a second?" their dad asked. "I need to go grab the rest of my tools."

"No problem," Felix responded.

Their father opened the door to the laundry room and walked inside. They could hear their mom's voice coming from down the hall.

Brady pulled his brother outside the garage where they could talk. "This isn't right," he said quickly once he was sure his father wasn't in earshot. "We're not supposed to be here—this isn't our world."

"Who says? Why can't we stay here?" Felix argued.

"I understand why you want to stay. Dad is still alive here. Believe me, I want to stay too. But we can't."

"Why?"

"Because our twins from this world are going to be back here soon, and then there's going to be real trouble."

"Why can't we just send them back through and we stay here? We can trade places."

"You know why. Because it wouldn't be fair to them, to lose Dad so suddenly. We've had our whole lives to get used to it."

"I get that Brady, it's just that… I was a baby when Dad died. I never really got a chance to know him. You wouldn't understand."

Brady reached out and hugged his brother.

"It's okay, Felix. I do understand. Doesn't it make you feel better knowing that there's a place where he still exists? A place where we grew up with a father?"

They were interrupted by a voice calling out from the garage. "Hey guys, I'll be right out—can I grab you a snack or something?"

They looked back at the open laundry room door, where light spilled out onto the steps leading down into the garage. Their father was still somewhere inside, just beyond the door.

"Come on, Felix. We need to go back to our home—to our real mom."

"Brady? Felix? You guys still there?" their father's voice came again.

"Just a bit longer. Please," Felix pleaded.

"We have to go now!" Brady insisted. He grabbed his brother by the arm and pulled him away. It was by far the hardest thing he had ever had to do.

Tears ran down Felix's face as they left. Brady did his best to keep it together for his brother, but soon he was crying as well.

On their way around the corner of the house they heard the sound of their other selves coming from somewhere in the forest. Careful not to be seen, they waited for their twins to clear the woods before sneaking around the edge of the back yard. Then they crouched down under the cover of the trees and looked back toward the house. They could see the outline of their father standing by the side of the house, probably looking for them.

"Brady, Felix?" he called out.

"Yeah, Dad?" the other Felix responded.

"Okay, we're safe now," the real Brady said. "Give me your phone."

"Why?"

"Just do it." Felix unlocked his phone and passed it over to Brady. "What are you going to do with it?"

Brady zoomed in and took the shot.

"Got it. Now we'll never forget…"

Felix looked down at his phone's screen and smiled.

They heard something approaching behind them. When they turned, they saw familiar eyes glowing at them from the edge of the woods.

Achilles was waiting for them.

It was time to go.

10100110

Nova and Achilles had been waiting for them under the tall trees that looked down on the yard. The steel canine leapt at Felix and almost knocked him down in his excitement. Brady was happy to see his brother smile again. Together they made their way back to the portal Nova had opened for them earlier.

Brady eyed the Glia Box strapped to Achilles' back. "What happened?" he asked.

"The Elder Minds…" She paused. "Everything we had there was destroyed. Our home is gone, and my father—he barely survived."

Brady and Felix were alarmed and saddened at the same time. "Our mom?" Brady asked reluctantly, fearing the worst.

"I don't think the golems went anywhere near your house. They were there for my father. She should be fine—except for worrying about you guys. Everything okay here?"

"Sure, everything's okay," Felix said, locking eyes with his brother.

"Okay then, the portal is right up ahead."

To their surprise, they heard a boom and saw a different door open. A dash of white erupted from the flame and streaked across the forest.

AJ stopped abruptly in front of them.

"Something terrible has happened," the bot said breathlessly.

"What, AJ?" Nova asked. "Did you find more Evercells?"

"I didn't have a chance to look," AJ explained. "When I went back, I found an army of golems preparing to pass through a different portal. So I followed them."

"And...?" Felix prompted.

"They went back to your world," the bot replied, looking at Brady. "They were marching toward a house farther down the mountainside. I left and came here as quickly as I could. We have to get back there!"

And with that, the bot turned and ran off.

"AJ! Wait!" Brady called, but the bot sped through the portal.

Suddenly it hit Brady like a ton of bricks. "Our house... Mom!"

Brady took off toward the door and didn't stop even though he heard Felix and Nova calling his name. AJ's portal glowed ominously in front of him, waiting.

He stepped through—and realized at once he had made a terrible mistake.

> Chapter 32: AJ's Bargain

IT WAS ALREADY THERE, waiting for him on the other side, as though it knew the boy was coming. Brady's eyes went wide with fear; he tried desperately to reverse his forward momentum. As he slid to a stop on the slick surface, his heart pounding in his ears, he tried to turn around—but he never had a chance. A large arm grabbed him by the waist and pinned him against the wall with ease.

This wasn't home.

The creature leaned in toward Brady, their faces only inches apart. Brady could see his own frightened face reflected back in the monster's metallic skin, his image broken by the empty sockets and the mouth that hung open in a perpetual scream.

But the monster looked different now. The Elders, no longer forced to control the golems across the incalculable separation of quantum realities, could sculpt their puppets with ease. This golem's body was well-defined; its exterior was rock solid and cold to the touch.

Brady turned his head sideways and looked back at the portal. It was within reach, he thought, if only he could free himself. But before he could even attempt to move, Achilles, Nova, and Felix bounded through the flame.

"Go back!" he screamed, but he knew it was already too late.

He saw the grim recognition spread quickly across their faces;

their curiosity was displaced by dread. They knew they had walked straight into a trap.

Achilles scrambled around, but the portal collapsed, locking them together in the nightmare.

With the arrival of the others, the golem released its grip on Brady, who slid down the wall and collapsed in a pile on the floor. Nova and Felix raced over and helped Brady to his feet.

Together, the three friends looked around the massive drum-shaped room. A brilliant ball of white light burned between two delicate needles. The first was attached to a massive drill that extended down from the ceiling. The other rose up from an opening in the floor, where bundles of wires and cables intertwined together like a pit of snakes.

Brady recalled the fusion reactor chamber Nova had spoken about when they were at the power station. Somehow he knew that's where they were. Megawatts of energy must be flowing from the controlled explosion; the bright ball cast out branching arcs of light, which played across the walls and electrified the room.

A circle of golems had formed a ring around the fusion core. Tangles of lifeless tentacles scraped across the floor with a wretched sound as the Elder Golems hoisted Neurogeist bodies up into the air and fastened them to large steel hooks that hung from the ceiling. They were hard at work, readying the room for the mind transfers. Two more golems stood guard by the room's only exit.

The brightness of the fusion core made it difficult to see much of anything beyond it. It was like staring into the surface of the sun. Nevertheless, Brady saw motion on the other side of the room. More golems, he thought, an audience waiting for the main attraction to begin.

Slowly, his eyes adjusted to the light and he was able to make out more details. They weren't people at all. Dozens of Artifex were lined up against the wall, still as statues. At first he didn't understand why they weren't moving, but then he realized: they must be trapped inside Time Huggers, just like Nova had been when they first rescued her.

Thick cables ran from the bots' heads and attached to the Neurogeists that hung from the ceiling. AJ's father was among them, frozen like the others. His expressionless face stared out at them behind green eyes that had been dulled by time suspension.

And then, in an instant, it all became clear.

AJ stepped out from behind the sun and joined the circle of golems. Brady immediately felt foolish for having ever trusted him.

"Why, AJ?" Nova asked.

The child did not respond; he just stared at the fusion core.

Achilles must also have been aware of the child bot's betrayal, because he let out a thundering growl, and the room quaked from his might. Brady watched in horror as one of the golems turned away from the Neurogeists and began to walk toward the canine. Achilles dug his nails deep into the steel floor and prepared for war.

The canine let the monster get close, then leaped through the air in a graceful arc and latched on to one of the golem's arms with his razor teeth. But the monster simply reached over and tore the dog off with ease. The golem flung him to the floor and pinned him beneath its massive foot.

Nova tried to run to him, but Brady grabbed her arm and pulled her back. He knew there was nothing she could do.

As Achilles yelped frantically beneath the foot, the golem reached down and ripped the Glia Box from his back and slid it across the floor. Then he dragged two cables from the ceiling and attached one to the box and the other to the canine's head.

At the same time, three other golems broke away from the circle and headed toward Brady, Felix, and Nova. The Elder puppets ushered them into a set of iron chairs. A fourth chair sat empty.

"Okay! I did what you wanted," AJ said, stepping forward. "I gave you Orion. You promised you would let my father go."

The fusion core hummed softly. There was no reply.

"Give me my father!" AJ demanded, slamming his foot repeatedly on the ground.

A golem left the circle and started walking toward Sudo.

"Good…" the child muttered. "Free him so we can leave this wretched place."

But then, to the child's surprise, the monster turned away from Sudo and, with one large hand, grabbed AJ by the neck and carried him, screaming, over to the empty chair.

The golems then attached cables to their four captives' heads. The prisoners resisted, tried to escape, but couldn't. Some sort of mental block from the cable was holding them in place.

The golems then returned to the circle, where they began to jerk back and forth. They moved slowly at first, but then sped up until they vibrated in place with a fervent intensity, mere blurs of motion. Drops of liquid metal beaded up on the creatures' skin, then lifted off and joined the nano-clouds that formed around the room.

Molecule by molecule, the golems came apart—and soon there was nothing left. Only the swarming nano-clouds of the Elders remained, buzzing together as a collective.

"We have learned of your secret, Orion," came an androgynous voice from somewhere in the cloud. The cloud expanded and contracted when the Elder spoke, the particles riding the wave of sound.

"You have disobeyed us for the last time," came another voice from the circle. "Now you will witness the cost of your defiance as the Neurogeists are reborn."

"And this time…" said yet another voice.

The cloud ring rose and fell together as the many voices spoke in unison.

"We have corrected it for humans."

Brady looked up at the Neurogeists and shook with fear. He felt a stinging sensation in his head again and the dizziness began to set in. He looked around the room, helplessly, and his eyes began to blur.

Just when he had lost all hope, a message appeared—blurry, but readable.

Connect the cable to Orion!

Brady remembered that he was still wearing the contacts. He looked around the room, wondering who had sent the message. Everything was out of focus.

Another message.

At my feet—AJ.

Brady looked over at the child and saw bright eyes staring back at him—and then the bot's head slumped forward in his chair.

They were beginning the transfer process.

Brady looked down at the foot of AJ's chair. And there it was: a thick cable running out from the fusion core.

A power source.

He could get to the cable, but where was Orion's Glia Box? He struggled, trying to pinpoint its location. His vision was spinning now.

There!

Just out of reach.

He realized what he had to do.

The world he knew was beginning to fade. The transfer algorithm drilled deeper into his mind, and it was a struggle to remain conscious. He tried to move forward but couldn't.

He concentrated and cleared his mind. Slowly he fell from the chair and started to crawl forward, the cable still attached to his head. Inch by inch he made his way toward the box. He could see the swarm behind him.

He grabbed one end of the cable and tugged it toward Orion's Glia Box. With all his energy, he united them.

The ball of light flickered for a second and then went out, casting the room into darkness. Seconds later, it exploded back to life, this time brighter than before. The box that stored Nova's father glowed in increasing intensity.

The Elder cloud must have realized the threat, because all at once they began to swarm around the box. But the light in the core dimmed as Orion's light grew; Orion was consuming the core's energy like a vacuum.

The earth shook. Chunks of the floor and walls broke off and came together into a new form. As more pieces joined the growing shape, it expanded, until the room could barely contain it. The mass assembled itself into a new golem—one that was so large it propped the ceiling up on its massive shoulders.

The Elder cloud twisted up and around the creature just as its arms began to take shape. The giant golem roared as its hands materialized, then grabbed onto the needles and snapped them apart. It swung the lances at the cloud that tried to burrow into its rocky flesh.

Brady saw the giant foot of Orion's golem descending toward him. He rolled out of the way as it came crashing to the floor.

Nova was already on her feet and called out to AJ, who was standing next to his father. "You need to get the Artifex out of here, now, while we still have a chance!" She grabbed a Field Wrecker canister from Achilles and tossed it across the room to the young bot.

"What do I do with this?" AJ asked as he looked around at the crowd of trapped bots.

"Just spray it around them—quickly, though! It'll do the rest for you."

While Orion distracted the Elders, AJ began spraying the nano particles. One by one the fields broke apart, freeing the captive Artifex from their invisible prisons.

Still fighting off the cloud, Orion's golem swung an enormous fist that punched through the wall like it was paper. The Artifex escaped through the resulting hole. Only two stayed behind.

Sudo and his son.

"We must go, AJ!" Sudo shouted.

AJ ran to his father's side, and together they made their way to the opening. AJ looked back once and waved at Brady, Nova, and Felix, and then the two Artifex disappeared through the hole.

Orion's golem continued to grow until its back was pressed against the ceiling. It opened its large mouth wide and cast its bulging arms to its sides. It took a giant breath and began to pull the air up into it. The Elder cloud was unable to escape—it was sucked up by the force of the vacuum.

Felix, Brady, Nova, and Achilles braced themselves by grabbing on to the cables that ran along the floor.

"Hold on!" Nova screamed.

When the last of the particles had been inhaled, the golem closed its mouth, and the air in the room returned to normal. It stood there, motionless, as if in a trance—and then it took an unsteady step backward and crashed into the wall. Debris rained down from the ceiling, forming large piles of rock around the creature.

The surface of the golem's mouth began to expand as the froth of nano particles tried to escape, but Orion reached up with the puppet's enormous hand and pushed the swarm back down. As it battled the cloud from the inside, its skin began to glow red hot and its body began to lose shape and break apart, forming a new cloud. Soon the two clouds were twisting together, flying around the large room like warring helixes. The clouds grew brighter and brighter until at last they fused together and dropped to the floor in a pile of dust.

The Elder cloud had been destroyed.

Nova turned toward the Glia Box.

Its light was dim.

"Father?"

"I don't have much time, Nova."

"We can get more cells, Father. There is plenty of power here."

"No, daughter. It's too late. The Elders altered my nets with a virus during the fight. I have been reprogrammed to decay."

"There must be a way," she pleaded.

"Nova—please, there is something I need to show you before I go. Please…"

10010110

A series of lights erupted from the circle on Orion's container, filling the room with lifelike holographic projections that settled in among the rubble. Particles of dust filtered through the spectral images, lending them substance and dimension.

The projections showed a woman with dark, straight hair, sitting alone behind a long lab bench overflowing with scopes, meters, probes, and other digital equipment. The light from a computer screen caught the side of her face, and she focused intently on her work, completely unaware she was being watched.

Nova, Brady, and Felix circled the scene. A glowing hot soldering iron rested on a table next to a translucent dome that was about the size and shape of a brain. Hair-thin traces ran across the dome and ended with dozens of probes that poked into the brain like pins in a pincushion. Wires ran from the probes to the woman's computer.

The woman gnawed on a pen as she pecked away on the keyboard. "Okay, last time wasn't so great. Let's give this another shot and hope it works," she said. She hammered the return key with finality and spun in her chair to face the dome-shaped object.

"Boot O51DR," she directed.

"Booting O51DR…" came a voice.

"Okay, O5. Ready for your test?" She glanced down at the brain.

"I am ready." The voice was stiff and robotic.

"Let's get the easy stuff out of the way first. What is my name?"

"Your name is Navaeh Origo."

"Good." She drummed the pen nervously on her fingers. "Okay,

O5. How do you *feel* today?"

The lights on the cable connecting computer to machine flashed rapidly; millions of bits from the neural simulation were flowing back and forth across the line.

"I feel okay today."

"Why just okay?" the woman asked.

"Because today is just like yesterday, and yesterday was okay too."

The woman frowned.

"Navaeh," the voice added, "I was thinking about my name, O51DR. It seems strange to me."

Navaeh laughed, then quickly caught herself and covered her mouth with her hand. She hoped the O51DR hadn't noticed.

"It is funny that I am unhappy?" the machine asked.

"No," the woman responded, shaking her head. "Not at all. I laughed because, well, your question. It's so… unexpected, I guess." She scrunched her mouth up. Perhaps there *was* something interesting here after all. "Anyway, you have a point. Your name *is* kind of weird. What would you like to be called?"

The voice paused.

"It is inappropriate to choose a name for oneself," it said at last. "Someone else should choose your name. I would feel better if you chose it for me."

Navaeh glanced back at her screen. The neural feedback paths were spiking higher than she had ever seen before. There was conscious activity.

"Okay then," she said. "How about Orion, after the great hunter?"

Their conversation was interrupted by the sound of a baby crying. Brady hadn't noticed it before; it lay in a carrier at the side of the room.

"I'm sorry," Navaeh said. "Do you mind holding on a second?"

She got up from her chair and scooped the child out of the carrier and up into her arms. The ghost-like hologram passed right through Felix as she walked back to her chair.

"It's okay, sweetie," she said, cradling the infant closely to her.

The crying stopped.

"What is that?" asked Orion.

"This, Orion? This is my daughter."

"What is her name?" he asked.

"Her name is Nova."

"She is... important to you?" the voice asked.

"She is—the most important thing in the world to me," Navaeh responded. She continued to rock the child in her arms. "You have an important test today, Orion. It's a difficult test, but I think you are finally ready." She coughed into her shoulder.

"You are sick?"

"Everyone is sick now," she said sadly.

"Please tell me about the test."

"I want you to try to create something."

"What kind of something?"

"Pay attention—this is something very important. Something no algorithm has ever been able to do before. I want you to create another being like you. A friend."

"I'm not sure I can do that," Orion responded.

"Well, that's what we need to find out," Navaeh said. "That's the test. Can you create another consciousness like yourself?"

She coughed again, this time harder than before.

"I will try."

"You'll do more than try." She laughed again. "I've poured way too much of life into designing you."

Navaeh looked down at her child. The baby reached up and curled its tiny hand tightly around her outstretched finger and giggled.

"Since names are important to you," Navaeh said, "what name

will you give your friend?"

"I will call her... Alethea," Orion said.

11000110

The holograms dissolved into the darkness of the room. Brady and Felix glanced over at Nova, who stood frozen, her watery eyes fixed on the spot where her mother's apparitions had been.

"That is my first memory, Nova. That was the day I became aware."

Orion's voice was slower and fainter now.

"Always remember. No matter where you are, you will never be alone. We are all bonded together unconditionally. I love you."

The light on the box extinguished.

Nova's father was gone.

Achilles walked to her side and lowered his head.

Brady and Felix walked over and took her hands. The four of them stood together in the dim glow of the room.

"What will you do now?" Brady asked Nova.

"I don't know," she said. "But there are more Elders, so... I'll go and finish what my father started." She looked at Achilles. "I've got help too—right, Achilles?"

The canine barked loudly and pushed his muzzle into Nova's arm.

"Also, Alethea is still at the Heap," Nova said. "I can't leave her there."

"Why don't you come back with us?" asked Felix.

Nova gave Felix a warm smile. "It's kind of you to say that. But... not until this is over. Then... maybe."

Nova tapped something on her watch, and the portal opened.

"No sense saying goodbye again," she said. "We've seen how well that works out."

They hugged one final time before the brothers left her world behind and returned to their own.

> Chapter 33: From the Ashes

BRADY AND FELIX stepped through the portal and back into the forest of their home. Thick, smoky air singed their lungs. The flames had died down while they were away, but the yellow-orange embers still glowed radiantly against the pallid, scorched wilderness. Tiny flakes of ash rained down on them like a joyless gray snow.

They were finally home—what was left of it. The Elder Golems had spared nothing.

Brady and Felix turned back to the quantum door. The cold, blue flame flickered quietly in the hazy gloom of night. They stood in somber silence watching as the door folded in on itself with a final thunderclap and disappeared, taking their friends, and the strange other world, with it. For a second, Brady imagined that Nova and Achilles were still there, standing right next to him, in the rubble of the fallen power station superimposed on their world. How could it be, he wondered, that they were separated by immeasurable distance, yet they were only a few feet away?

Brady looked over to where Nova's house once stood and gasped. The home was nowhere to be seen. In its place was a wide crater burrowed deep into the mountainside. There was no trace of what had been.

With their arms supporting each other, the boys moved forward, unsure which direction they were heading. They were coughing in fits now, the smoke strangling out the air around them. Felix slipped in the mud, but Brady picked him up and forced him to keep going.

Just when they thought they would collapse from exhaustion, they heard the familiar screech of the great eagle flying above them. Twin beams shone from her diamond eyes, providing a guiding light amid the smoke. She led the boys away from the carnage toward home.

The smoke gradually dissipated as they stumbled forward. Soon the air was breathable again, and the boys eagerly inhaled the fresh air with great relief. Their eyes still watered from the smoke, but they were okay.

They moved down the mountainside to the rushing stream where they had found AJ earlier in the day. With a sigh of relief, they realized they were getting closer now. They pressed on toward home, Nyx lighting the way.

As they neared the fence, they saw a squad of police cars arrayed in a line down their driveway. The vehicle emergency lights flashed, and a group of officers were huddled together at the side of the house. Nyx arced upward and took off into the sky. She cried out in a final goodbye and disappeared.

The boys climbed over the fence and dropped to the other side. They found their mom standing out front, talking to a man dressed in a sheriff's uniform. The sheriff was leaning casually against his car door, taking notes as Ms. Banks provided an impassioned description of her children. Her hair was frazzled and she looked like she hadn't slept in days.

The brothers thought she had never looked better.

"Mom!" they both cried out and ran toward her.

Ms. Banks stopped what she was saying in midsentence and looked in their direction. "Brady... Felix?" Her voice rose in excitement as she strained to get a better look. "Is that you?" Life was returning to her face.

The boys collapsed into their mom's arms. She pulled them near and hugged them dearly.

"Are you okay? Where in the world have you been?" she asked, wiping tears from her eyes.

"We're fine, Mom. At least, we are now," Felix replied.

The sheriff studied the brothers. "I'm happy you boys are okay. You gave your mom quite a scare."

The boys looked back but remained quiet.

"We were able to get the forest fire next door under control." The sheriff eyed the layers of soot and ash that had collected in the boys' hair. "It's strange that we would have a fire after so much rain..." He raised an eyebrow. "Would either of you happen to know anything about it?"

Brady opened his mouth to speak, but Ms. Banks interrupted before he had a chance. "Maynard, can this wait until morning? I'd like to get my boys inside."

The sheriff tucked his pen into his notepad and closed it. "Sure, Sarah, I'll tell you what. Why don't you get them inside where they can get some food and rest, and I'll swing by first thing tomorrow?"

"Thank you, that works great," Ms. Banks said, leading her boys inside their home.

11001110

Brady stretched out and rolled over on the rug that lay at the foot of his mom's bed. He had been awoken by a rapping on the window, like a nail striking glass. The wooden blinds were turned open and the sunlight streamed in, coaxing him into finally starting the day.

With a wide yawn, he looked around and realized he was the only one here. Last night, he and Felix had brought their pillows and blankets into their mom's room and set up beds on the floor— something they hadn't done since they were kids. Felix must have already gotten up and left.

Brady put his head back down on the pillow and just stared up at the ceiling, pondering everything that had happened.

His thoughts were interrupted by the sound of a car pulling up in the driveway. He heard the click of the car door, and shortly thereafter, the ring of the doorbell.

A minute later, Felix slipped into the room and closed the door softly behind him. Brady ignored him, rolled over, and stuffed his face into his pillow.

"Wake up, Brady," Felix said, shaking his brother.

"I'm already up, Felix! Give me a break," Brady groaned.

"C'mon, Brady," Felix said. "You've gotten enough rest. The sheriff's downstairs, and he wants to talk to us about what happened. Have you looked outside?"

Brady ignored the question. "You call last night rest?" he said groggily. "I would sleep all day if you'd just leave me alone."

Felix sighed. "Okay, Brady. I'll try to buy you some time. Just don't leave me down there by myself forever, all right?"

"Deal. I owe you one. Thanks, Felix. What are you going to tell him, anyway?"

"I don't know. Maybe the truth, I guess," he said.

"Right, like anyone would believe us."

"That's their problem, isn't it?"

"I guess, as long as we don't end up in jail. You remember Nova's house. It looks like an asteroid struck."

"Do you think we'll ever see them again?" Felix asked.

"Your guess is as good as mine. I hope so though."

"Me too."

"Hey, Felix, what happened yesterday... I sort of think it was a gift to us from Nova."

Felix looked confused. "What do you mean?"

"Where's your phone?" Brady asked.

Felix pulled it from his pocket and handed it over.

Brady turned on the device and scrolled through the photos until he arrived at the picture he took of their dad.

"*This* is the gift," he said, handing the phone back.

Felix studied the picture for a second, then powered down his phone. "I think you're right, Brady."

Ms. Banks called up from below. "Felix, Brady? I need you guys down here now!"

"See you downstairs in a minute," Felix said, shutting the door behind him.

Brady sat up and ran his hands over his face.

There was a knocking outside the window again—the same sound that had awoken him. It took him three tries to stand up; he had never been so sore in his life.

Bam, bam.

Brady walked over to the window to investigate. There was nothing there. He looked out beyond the fence and immediately saw the gray plumes of smoke rising from the trees in the distance. The green of the canopy faded into charcoal cinders as his eyes followed the hill upward.

Then he looked down and saw the sheriff's brown sedan parked in the driveway. Its side was emblazoned with a yellow stripe and star. *Ugh*, he thought. *Let's get this over with.*

When he looked up again, he found himself staring into a pair of tiny sapphire eyes. He jumped back, startled.

It was Thorn.

Brady quickly pushed the window open. The bird flew in and settled on his mom's dresser. The blur of the wings slowed gradually until they came to a rest by the bird's sides. Then the blue eyes dimmed, and the bird drifted off to sleep.

"Get some rest, Thorn," Brady said, picking the bird up and leaving his mom's room behind. He could hear Felix's voice from downstairs. He walked into his room, set the bird gently down on his own dresser, and headed downstairs. As he went, Brady smiled at nothing in particular. For the first time in years, he wasn't worried about a thing.

www.ingramcontent.com/pod-product-compliance
Lightning Source LLC
Chambersburg PA
CBHW061945170626
46813CB00006B/2532